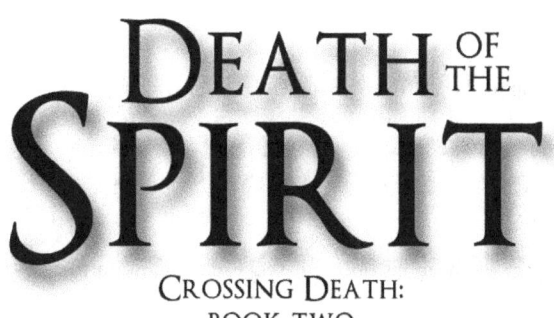

DEATH OF THE SPIRIT

CROSSING DEATH:
BOOK TWO

Rick Chiantaretto

ISBN-10: 1940748054
ISBN-13: 978-1-940748-05-4

Published by Orenda Press
Copyediting by Bev Sninchak and Kathryn Star Heart Huggins
Cover Design by Eden Crane Design
Production Management by Orenda Press

To know your enemy
you must become your enemy.

~The Art of War by Sun Tzu –misattributed

To all the religious and spiritual leaders who influenced my life,
except that Sunday School teacher I had when I was sixteen.

You, sir, are a dick.

Printed in the USA
This Edition, March 2015

PROLOGUE

I watched in disbelief as blood seeped through my fingers and dripped, thick as syrup, to the ground. I heard each drop thud against the ground beneath me. The echo in my ears beat louder than any drum.

This time, it was different.

This time, it was someone else's blood.

The descent into insanity was like plunging into a frigid lake. The hair on my arms stood on end as blood turned to ice in my veins. Waves of goose bumps danced over my skin, scurrying up and down my arms like bugs—thousands of tiny feet skipping along my flesh, crawling through the hair of my arms, legs, and head.

I scratched at the thought, which did nothing but smear the now-tacky blood all over. As soon as I felt its hot fire on my skin, the itching changed to frantic and futile attempts to wipe it off. I whimpered. My vision clouded over in foggy red. I knew no matter how much I washed, I would never feel clean again.

Then the ringing started. It wasn't just the annoying soft under-ring you sometimes hear when you're smothered in silence while your mind tries to compensate by making up an imaginary noise. This was an alarm blaring impossibly loud, waking me out of a nightmare. I clasped my ears and screamed at the top of my lungs, but I couldn't hear my own voice over the ringing. I was barely conscious enough to realize that the *buzz buzz buzz* in my ears matched the beating of my own heart.

My muscles convulsed, the bugs crawled, and the ringing consumed all five of my senses. I could feel nothing else, hear nothing else, and all I could see, taste, and smell was blood.

A jolt of adrenaline hit my system as my brain registered that I had just committed murder, but instead of that adrenaline triggering a flight response, it made me aggressive. Rage boiled from a dark pit in my stomach like lava boiled out of a volcano… hot… thick… destructive. I had to put that rage into something, anything! The black veins in my forearms were about to pop under the pressure. I grabbed the knife and struck the woman over and over and over again. I heard the blade sink into her body, slicing through flesh, muscle, and bone. The slurping sound it made as it retracted was like therapy for my diseased mind.

I laughed as I stabbed. I grunted as I cut. I felt charged and powerful as I slashed the tip of the knife deeper and deeper, harder and harder into the sticky flesh.

Venting my rage with the blade was arousing… until the world started spinning.

My body felt strong, but my knees buckled as the cavern spun around me with dizzying velocity. I crashed, tears flooding my eyes. I hyperventilated until my vision cleared and I woke to the horror of the scene around me.

My spirit was weak.

A bleeding spirit is much like a bleeding body. I'd heard of people on Earth who were spiritually dead—murderers who had no remorse for what they'd done, who walked around with cold hearts and hollow eyes. I could never understand just how sick they were.

Until now.

I dropped the dagger, letting myself fall the rest of the way to the ground, not bothering to catch myself. The rocky earth was hard, but I couldn't feel it anyway; all I felt was the crawling of my skin and the stickiness of someone else's blood.

My vision blurred again, but the vertigo remained. I convulsed and shivered. I saw flashes of red lightning as my mind lost perception of reality, red lighting that illuminated the face of my victim. Her eyes were still staring at me.

Those eyes had pleaded before. There had been a brightness and quickness behind them that echoed the sharpness of her soul. Now they were vacant and empty, her true self gone, her carcass so mutilated she was hardly recognizable.

I knew where she would go. I knew she would be born again on Earth to live a normal human life. I guessed she would probably be a talented witch there.

Is it truly murder if you know that death is only a door to another place?

Why did death on the Level of the Body, Earth, seem so definitive and final?

The only thing that truly ended was her memory. She would never remember. She would never know who she had been or the full potential of her power. I stole that from her, and the thought made me laugh maniacally. I couldn't *control* my laughter. The power! How easy it was to simply take. It was just one itty-bitty life. And what was memory but a fragile, useless, pointless, selfish, defective, pile of shit?

Joshua had already stolen that part of her anyway. He was the one who'd enslaved her, who'd made her forget her family, her life, and her strength. All I did was ensure that she'd be born again into a life of freedom and free will, a life where she could choose to be whomever she wanted to be. A life where she was free from the burden of knowing she was my mother.

PART ONE—THE FIRST HEAVEN

ONE

An image of Xia's chocolate eyes lingered on the back of my closed eyelids for a brief moment before I opened them wide in horror. I'd been wrapped in her embrace, feeling the heat of her body on my own. The connection of our skin had been so charged it felt electric—a sensation that never left my body. It was a connection I couldn't deny, couldn't understand, and couldn't escape.

I was consumed, ever-present in this moment. My thoughts and emotions were tied to her. She had enveloped me so entirely that I spent days doing nothing but lying in bed, unable to recover, unable to move, unable to think of anything else but those eyes and electric skin. The feeling was always erotic. My entire body crawled with desire for her with a lust I couldn't slake, a love I couldn't shake. It was Hell.

The dreams were always warm—we were always

warm—although I could feel cool pulses in the air around us, a sensation that echoed the cool pulses I used to feel wearing my father's ring. They were a reminder that the dream world wasn't real.

Maybe that's why the dreams never ended well. The last images were always of Xia's bright eyes pleading with me as I pulled her body tight against my own, a shiver of pleasure overwhelming me before I plunged a cold knife into her back. Her eyes would then widen with alarm, the scent of her rusted blood flaring my nostrils so strongly I could taste it.

That was the image that always remained, a horrifying mixture of brown eyes dimming in death, an erotic current, and a taste of rust that I had to rinse out of my mouth every morning.

"You were thrashing again."

The voice and the phrase had become so routine that I used them to confirm I was really awake. My mother (I use the term loosely, however, because she still hadn't remembered me) stood in the doorway with the same irritated look on her face she always had, and a fresh bundle of sheets in her arms.

My body was covered in a heavy sheen of sweat that smelled of sex and fear. I was definitely awake, even if it still looked like Xia was cowering in the corner being attacked by the shadows.

I did what I always did; I peeled my sticky body from the mangled sheets and stumbled into the bathroom to start my morning.

As the shower's hot water ran over my face, the illusions of Xia were erased, although the water only amplified the humming electricity I could feel coursing through my body. I felt the magic within me shift in response, like the electricity was an invader and my magic was an immune system trying to fight it away. I used to be able to succeed at calming the tingle by sitting naked for hours in a cool breeze, but it always returned; the next night's dream always brought it back.

I quit fighting it weeks ago. Surrendering made it part of me. It seemed less real, less jarring, less exhausting when it was ever-present. I was already so tired all the time; I couldn't spare the energy to fight anymore.

My head slumped back against the shower wall. I closed my eyes, testing to see if she was still there. There were no more images of Xia, just the usual red, bloody glow of my inner eyelids.

The shower had a second benefit: the white noise of the water drowned out the trees. There was almost nothing about Orenda that I recognized anymore, nothing left of the old world. The men that inhabited the city changed everything. The old cobblestone streets were worn and unmaintained. Instead of the stones being cared for and replaced as they were when the mages inhabited the city, the men simply filled the holes and cracks with asphalt and tar, turning my warm, gentle, inviting city into a smaller version of the cities I had known in my human life.

I couldn't blame them. They were stuck in their habits. Habit was all anyone knew.

The trees were different too. I remembered straining to hear their voices as a child, feeling an immense pride when I was finally able to differentiate them from the sound of the wind. Every tree had been soft and gentle, calm and stalwart, grand and regal, just like my city. Now the trees that still bothered to talk did nothing but shout, engaged in a war with each other that they were too busy to explain to me. The rest were silent. All had stopped listening for my kind.

I shut the shower off and stepped out into my small apartment. I had been assigned a 200-square-foot space in a new high-rise that hadn't existed when I was a child. It was a 'charming' studio (for lack of a better way to say 'shit-hole'). There were no interior walls, just one large room with a row-style kitchen taking up one side of the unit. A bed was my only piece of furniture. The bathroom felt spacious because it wasn't enclosed; it sat in the corner of the room like a pile of tile and glass, an awkward focal point that would make any interior designer cringe.

Not that it mattered much. I wasn't one for modesty, and my mother (my domestic, as she was called now in this reality) would put out my clothes and leave, taking the sheets when I got up to shower. Often, I wouldn't see her again until dinner.

She had the whole floor to care for, all filled with single people who either had no family or couldn't remember who they were before their life in Orenda. Technically, if you couldn't remember, I supposed you wouldn't be waiting for family to die and meet you here anyway.

The only people who remembered their family were humans coming from the Level of the Body. Since most of those souls were stolen at the crossroads by energumen, a human crossing over had become a rare event. Technically, *any* crossing over had become a rare event.

Living with Nicholas in college had at least taught me how to accessorize. I made a comfortable space with my limited belongings, but my room was at least stylish. My toes squished into a warm sheepskin rug as I brushed my teeth. A modern mirror with a beveled edge reflected my tired, honey-colored eyes.

I went to the bed to see what clothes were laid out for me. I didn't need a closet. My mother would put out the day's clothes every morning. This place didn't have room for a closet anyway. I couldn't help but smile every time I slipped on my pants, realizing my mother was dressing me. It was funny, even if I couldn't tell anyone else.

The clothes today were different. Instead of my usual shorts, t-shirt, and flip-flops I found a button-down shirt, black slacks, a tie, and dress shoes on the bed.

Today was my first Planning.

I was still a California guy at heart. I admitted it was odd, really, that in California I spent my entire life trying to incorporate Orenda. Now that I was here, I couldn't help but miss California.

I pulled open my front door, still naked except for my underwear. My mom hadn't knocked, but I knew she'd be there with a tray that had a glass of freshly squeezed orange juice, a toasted bagel, and a version of coffee that was the closest I could get here in Orenda. It wasn't bad, but it made me miss real thing. Orenda used to have a hot tea my mom would make from a root that grew on the high mountains. That drink seemed to have disappeared too, and I had no idea why.

"There is no way I'm going to huff around in this getup all day," I chided, my neck already itching from the thought of the shirt collar rubbing against my humming skin.

She handed me the tray, then slumped her body in a kind of bow. It wasn't really a bow, even. It was a way to make her look smaller, subservient. It was a bow the men taught her to do when she was being directly addressed, a way for the domestics to show submission like a dog taught to shrink in front of its angry master. It made me sick to my stomach.

"I'll set out a second set of clothing for you to change into when you return, Master Alexander," she replied timidly.

I tucked a loose strand of hair behind her ear, feeling apologetic for my tone. But I knew any sort of apology would elicit more groveling. She shied away from my touch as it was.

"Thank you."

I closed the door, a physical gesture of the feelings I kept behind the closed doors of my mind. I could only deal with so many emotions at once and, thankfully, I was pretty good at doing something most men were good at: compartmentalizing. I shoved all of the emotions I had for my mother into a little box in my mind, shut the door on them, and promised to deal with them... eventually.

I sat on the end of my bed with my tray and took a bite of the bagel. The morning's pink light spilled through my one and only window. The sun wasn't up yet, but the northern sky was always so brightly ablaze that we only got to see the stars each night for an hour or two. That was another change from when I was a child, but there wasn't a human here I had talked to who would admit that they remembered a time when the sky wasn't that color. No one seemed to know why it had changed, either.

After I ate, I laid back on the bed, allowing the cool air from the vent above me to wash over my bare skin. I didn't lie there long enough to erase the prickling feeling of my dreams. I wasn't going to expend the energy to get rid of it entirely; I only needed to calm it enough to make the day bearable.

Finally, I finished getting dressed, cursing the shirt with the collar. I purposely left the tie on the bed and headed out the door. I took the elevator that descended to the building's lobby so slowly that I could barely feel it moving at all, before making my way toward the parliament building.

The morning air was cool as the sun peeked over the western hills. The smell of wheat and dew from the nearby fields carried on the same wind that buoyed the angry chatter of the trees; it would have been nice, except for that one undesirable component. I wished I could understand the smiles of the people I passed on the street. I must always look like the unhappy kid in town.

I breathed a small sigh of relief when the doors of the building were finally behind me. Parliament was the only thing in Orenda that hadn't changed. The hallways of pristine marble were still lined with small trees in gold pots, and the air still smelled of cinnamon, vanilla, and pencil lead. The thing I cherished over the familiar sights and smells of home was the familiar sound: the halls were silent—a quality I appreciated more than ever. Anywhere the wind couldn't blow hushed the sound of the trees outside, but this building had a particular way of insulating itself from the outside world. It was the one piece of memory that still fit entirely save for one small exception: everything looked smaller now that I was grown.

On one hand, I appreciated that the building was a reminder that I was really home; on the other, it was a bleak symbol that *this* Orenda was my new reality. My home was not the same as it once was.

I took a few deep breaths, exhaling slowly, listening as the air escaped my lungs. I filled them a few times with the cinnamon-scented air. I tried to convince myself that I wasn't nervous, but the more I lied, the more nervous I became. Each person had to endure three Plannings. I had no idea that the first one happened so soon after… well… dying.

The large room was open to the public and reminded me of a courtroom. There was a small table where the subject of the Planning would sit, followed by a railing and seating for spectators. I sat in that section for now, in the last row in the far corner. There, I could see all of the entrances and exits to the room. I liked to be early; I liked to watch people come in; I liked having an escape plan.

I didn't have to wait long. The first Planning usually started right after sunrise. The human came in first, dressed almost like me except I didn't put on the tie or do my hair. He brought two women with him, one who was a bit older and looked like his mother, and a second who was younger. I couldn't tell if she was his sister or his significant other.

At the front of the room was a tall podium in the same fashion as a judge's bench, only more ornate. The wood was intricately hand carved and reminded me a bit of something I would see in a Catholic church back on Earth. The only difference was the black finish, which hid most of the details from where I was sitting in the back of the room. The scent of wood still permeated the air, mixed with polish and stale perfume.

The person at the bench would be someone I'd only

glimpsed a few times in the three months since my death—the only other living Elder I knew besides Joshua, and perhaps the only other living mage with free will, Samuel.

When he entered the room, everyone stood. Oddly enough, this wasn't just a formality; when Samuel entered in his Elder's robes (quite likely the same robes he wore when he taught me as a child) the air around us came alive with his power. The change was so evident that my leg muscles tensed, propelling me to my feet.

Samuel didn't waste any time storming into the room, or taking his place at the bench. He spoke before he even had a chance to organize the stack of papers in front of him.

"Mr. Haynes, is it? Please step forward. It's great to see you again. Let's get started… or should I say finished? Today is your third and final Planning, correct?"

Samuel continued to shuffle papers, but didn't look down at them. He moved to the edge of his seat in one swift movement so he could peer at the man over the wooden bench. Mr. Haynes hugged the members of his family while Samuel's expression shifted from expectation to impatience. Samuel had never been one for delays.

My mind flashed back to when I was a child. Samuel was teaching us about physics. While the rules remained the same as I had learned on Earth, Samuel's teachings were more spiritual. I could almost recall a formula for calculating the density of spirit, but I hadn't been paying attention. My lack of focus had earned me the same impatient look that the Elder now turned on poor Mr. Haynes. The only thing missing was the finger. Oh, there it went... *tap tap tapping*.

I couldn't help the grin that spread across my face. It felt good to smile. It had been too long. I hadn't realized how tightly I kept my jaw clenched in an effort to control my buzzing skin. The smile not only gave my jaw a much-needed break, but also released a sense of euphoria that calmed my nerves a bit.

"We have a long day of Plannings. Please approach."

Mr. Haynes gave his wife one last hug. I still didn't know if they were actually married, but the way he lingered with his hands wrapped around her spoke of a romantic connection. They say blood is thicker than water, that family ties run deeper than all others, but I think love transcends both body and spirit. I believed, or hoped perhaps, that love was the life force of the soul.

Samuel showed his irritation, not by calling out for Mr. Haynes again, but by beginning as if the man had been seated at the correct spot in front of the bench.

"So, Mr. Haynes, we talked a bit last time about your gambling problem, and your inability to manage money in your previous life. How long have you been here in Orenda?"

"It's been about twenty-four years, give or take," Mr. Haynes responded, taking his seat at the table.

"And you spent your time here running a casino."

It wasn't a question. It sounded more like an accusation. Samuel had lost his tact as the years advanced.

Almost as if he could sense my thoughts, Samuel's gaze flickered toward me and his finger started drumming on the desk again. Images of that day in school flashed through my mind again. Somehow, I knew that drumming finger was meant for me.

As soon as that thought centered in my conscious mind, Samuel crossed his fingers beneath his chin and rested his head on them, turning his eyes back to the man in front of him. "And you thought that would be a *good* idea?"

"I figured I should do something I loved. This is heaven, after all."

Samuel raised an eyebrow at the response. "Have you decided how you want to handle this issue in your next life? Is it something you'd specifically like to address?"

"Definitely. I have a simple solution. I want to be rich."

Samuel was now writing something on his stack of papers. He wrote with a large feathered pen that looked outdated even by Orenda's standards. Technology wasn't of utmost importance here, not when you had magical servants to do all your dirty work. But no one wrote with feathered pens. The ink at the end of the quill was unusual as well—red. It made it look as if the feather was recently plucked from some living bird, the blood still dripping from the tip as Samuel scratched it along the pages. I had a strange desire to watch what the pen was writing—to feel what it was like to hold it as it made that textured scratching noise against the paper.

Samuel's gaze flickered toward me again.

"I see," he said, surprisingly calmer than expected.

"And what of Mindy there? Is she going to go back with you this time?"

"Well, we've discussed that. I think this time she would like to take on the role of one of my spirit guides."

Samuel raised an eyebrow again; this time it wasn't in disgust, but curiosity. "Oh? Well, Mindy, let me take note of that and we can discuss it at your next Planning. I'll want to make sure you're up to the responsibility of playing such an important roll. Now Mr. Haynes, what about children?"

"Well if I'm wealthy I plan on having a helluva lotta sex, ya know?"

"Ah, I see. Well, your mother is scheduled to go back a few years after you. Let's plan on having her as your daughter this time around, shall we? With her nurturing spirit she shouldn't be too hard to raise during your... philandering."

The mother chuckled at this, "A little payback may be in order."

Samuel's lips pursed into a slight smile before he continued, "I'll tell you what, Mr. Haynes. It seems you need to learn a bit of charity this time around. I'll promise you more money than you know what to do with, but only if you're willing to give it away to charitable causes. The more you give, the richer you'll become."

"That isn't what I want."

"It may not be what you want, but it's certainly what you need. Your body, spirit, and soul need progression. Life is about education. We've had this conversation before."

"You mean *you've* had this conversation before. I've done nothing but listen. I want to learn what it's like to be privileged. No strings attached."

"No, you simply don't want to earn what is yours."

This angered Mr. Haynes. He balled his fists and beat them once on the table, hard. "I'm supposed to choose what I want to learn."

"That doesn't mean you get to be lazy. You've learned laziness quite well enough already."

Mr. Haynes was too angry to respond. His exasperated expression was amusing. I found myself wishing I had been at his other Plannings to see why he was getting flustered so easily.

"If you're unable to hear, yet again, that life is meant to be hard, I can finish your Planning without your input. I'd prefer you to have no surprises. I prefer all people to have input on *how* they go about learning the lessons they need to learn, but maybe you need to trust this process."

"How can I learn to trust when we can't even remember what we've learned in our past lives? All the memories we get to keep are from the most recent incarnation. Then we get sent back with no memories of anything at all?"

"Your spirit progresses and learns. Your personality is shaped until you're ready to progress *forward*. Just because you don't remember doesn't mean you aren't changing. This is the way of things."

"It's stupid."

Samuel glared, but his expression remained under his control. "You are a young soul," he responded carefully (although I was sure it was meant to be an underhanded insult). "You have much to learn. This concludes this Planning. Please share the remainder of today with your family. Tomorrow you will be reborn."

"That's it?"

"I have everything I need."

Those words were more than just words. The finality of the pronouncement dropped the whole room into silence. The words were a spell; something had been bound. I didn't know exactly what that meant, or how the spell was cast, but even Mr. Haynes recognized the shift of the feeling in the room. He sat stupidly, his mouth hanging half open, like he was about to protest but couldn't. His Planning was over and he knew it. His course was fixed, his next life set.

He was still angry. The frustration was evident by the protruding vein on his forehead, but there was no argument in his expression. Samuel declared himself finished. The pen that had scratched notes onto the stacks of papers in front of him was dormant atop the bench. The pen itself was filled with an emotion—and if I was reading it correctly, it was exhausted.

Samuel stood slowly before making his way down the few steps and into the center of the room. I wasn't sure how smart it was for Samuel to approach Mr. Haynes while he still looked like he could explode.

To my surprise, Mr. Haynes stood and gave Samuel a brotherly hug. In fact, everyone gave him a hug before Samuel escorted them out of the room.

After they left, Samuel closed the heavy wooden door, his hand lingering on the knob. He turned and looked at me.

"You're next, my boy."

My boy? I still considered myself to be twenty-one, which was an adult by anyone's normal definition. Perhaps in comparison to however old Samuel was, I was still a boy. I decided to take the label as a compliment.

"Do you expect anyone to come support you?" His eyes peered deeply into my own as images of my mother and father, of Ralph and Hailey, of Nicholas and Xia, and even of my foster-sister Jane flashed through my mind. No. Obviously none of them were coming.

"No…" I had to stop myself from addressing him as 'Elder.' I swallowed the word. Old habits die hard. "No one is coming."

My heart thudded as I watched him turn a lock on the door.

"Go ahead and take your seat, please. Tell me your name, my boy. I don't have it on the official record." Samuel's gaze slid toward me as he walked toward the bench.

I followed behind him to the table. It felt like he was watching me even though I was behind him. The feeling reminded me of the nuns at Saint Vincent's orphanage. They always seemed to have eyes in the backs of their heads too.

"Alexander," I responded as I sat. "Alexander Michaels."

After speaking with my father at the crossroads, I quickly decided it would be best to let people think that I had not come from Earth. It was easier to convince them that I had come from an upper level and had forgotten everything. Strangely enough, this was the most common occurrence in Orenda lately, even if people crossing over was rare. It gave me an airtight alibi—no one bothered to ask me about my life prior to arriving in Orenda.

I had also decided against using my real name. I didn't know if Joshua was still looking for me but if he had been, he would start in the Level of the Spirit among the energumen. I didn't think it would take long for him to discover that I wasn't there and that my father was—he would put two and two together and come looking for me here, eventually. My best plan, for the moment, was to fit in and not let anyone know my real name.

It wasn't a good plan but it was the only one I had,

and it had worked until now.

Taking Father Michaels's surname was by accident, but it worked.

Samuel nodded, picked up his pen, and started scratching. When he looked up at me again, he was smiling with the same intensity as if I had told a good joke. I didn't understand why.

"Okay, Alexander Michaels. Tell me about your life on Earth?"

"I'm sorry…" Why was it so hard to not call him *Elder*? "Sir," I substituted. "I don't remember anything from my life prior to here."

The toothy grin fell from Samuel's face, replaced by an expression of confusion (or was that anger?). "I see. And what do you think that means?"

"I'm told, by others in my apartment, that I came from somewhere *above*," I gestured the final word with a motion I had practiced in the mirror long enough to know it conveyed 'up' while maintaining the perfect amount of 'doubt.'

Samuel didn't write anything down. In fact, he put the pen down. His eyes shifted toward the locked door before returning to meet mine with a stern glare.

"That's clever, my boy."

Visions of my previous life in Orenda flashed through my mind again. I was back in a classroom, learning a lesson Samuel had been teaching. He had smiled warmly at me as I'd answered one of his questions:

"If intelligence is glory, and intelligence is light and truth," he asked, *"then truth is?"*

"An elemental energy, just like light" I answered, *muttering under my breath.*

"That's clever, my boy."

My heart thudded so loudly that I swallowed and pushed my budding anxiety down to my feet and into the planet before I even thought about what I was doing. Samuel knew something. My nervousness intensified as his gaze slid to where my feet connected with the floor.

"So, Edmund, I see your father has managed to pass on his cloak and scythe."

TWO

The sensation I felt at the mention of my real name was a mixture of terror, excitement, and anxiety. The combination made my already humming skin prickle and burn. Samuel hadn't even finished his sentence, his comment about the cloak and scythe unprocessed, before I was standing. It felt like my seat was on fire. Even after I was standing, the burning sensation didn't leave.

I watched in horror as the normally blue veins in my arm pulsed black in time with the thudding of my heart. Wafts of smoke spilled from my pores. Heat and pain centered between my shoulder blades.

The smoke didn't behave like normal smoke. It didn't ascend upward, but instead curled around itself and around me.

The pain in my back exploded with such fury that I buckled over. It subsided only after my giant black wings sprouted, flexed, and stretched.

The scythe was in my hand, at Samuel's throat, before I had noticed I was standing again, the black smoke now forming Death's flowing cloak.

Samuel gasped as the sharp blade pressed against the drooping skin under his chin. "Edmund, it's okay. Of course I recognize you, but it's okay," he repeated.

It wasn't okay. Not to me. This was an Elder—an Elder who somehow survived. He had to be in cahoots with Joshua. And, he knew who I was.

Samuel must have read my expression and deduced my thoughts, because his arms reached out toward me in a pleading manner. "I knew your father. We were friends…" he started.

"My father's dead," I growled through clenched teeth.

"I know. I'm not with Joshua. I don't agree with him. Your father—I side with your father."

"Then how are you still alive?"

"Joshua needs someone to send the humans back. That's the only reason. He needs me."

At first my stance relaxed, but instead of dropping the scythe, I surprised myself by pushing it into Samuel's throat, breaking the skin. A single drop of blood escaped from the wound.

"Edmund. Please. I want to help you."

I felt the intensity behind my honey-colored eyes now inflamed to the color of hot white glass. They burned into Samuel's. My power rushed through them, like it did when I convinced Nicholas to give me the desk I wanted. But the magic was different here—more refined. I could see Samuel's control of his own mind slip. I felt him turning his will over to me. For one small moment, I debated seeing how far I could push it. How much control could I gain over him?

I blinked and dropped the scythe. What was the difference between mind control and possession? I wouldn't become an energumen.

Samuel let out a labored breath and reached for his throat. "Good God, my boy, you are one scary angel." His gaze darted around the room before he continued, "Put that away before someone else sees you."

"I thought you locked the door?"

"Locks are only designed to keep honest people honest."

I swallowed and pushed my anger down through my feet into the earth. As I regained control, the smoky cloak dissipated. The wings and scythe fell into another place. It was a place that was always accessible to me. It felt more like a place inside me, like the cloak and wings belonged to my spirit or my soul, not my body. It felt like they belonged to a level within myself.

"That's better. You're going to have to work on your emotional control if you want to continue the pretense of humanity. Do you remember when you were younger? When you were here before, in Orenda? We taught you control because bad things happen when an angel's emotions are allowed to run wild.

"What were you—twelve? —when you fell to the Level of the Body?"

"Ten."

"I bet you had more control then than you have now. Humanity doesn't treat our kind well."

"Angels? Our kind?"

I'd learned that my father was the Angel of Death, but it hadn't crossed my mind until now that all of the mages were angels.

Samuel responded. "We call ourselves mages—we always have—but the humans call us angels."

The nuns talked about different kinds of angels: destroying angels like those who took out Sodom and Gomorrah, avenging angels like those who fought in God's army, and guardian angels who would help us if we prayed to them. Connecting these types of angels to the roles each person played in Orenda was like opening a new doorway, a new understanding. I wondered if my mother was a guardian angel before her freedom was stolen from her.

"Then," I paused. This was going to sound stupid. "Is there a…" I swallowed hard. "…God?"

There was a glimmer in Samuel's eye. He smirked. "Maybe."

I wasn't satisfied. The expression on my face no doubt reflected that dissatisfaction.

"That's a question a lot of humans ask. No one really knows, but there are many levels of existence, Edmund.

29

Discovering and *becoming* God is Joshua's current obsession. Maybe you should ask him?"

My temper flared with how causally Samuel rambled off the last question. The conversation about emotional control was still fresh on my mind, so I reached into my childhood memories to calm myself, searching for the lessons on emotional control that Samuel had been talking about.

"Walk with me?" Samuel motioned with his head toward a door behind the bench.

"Where?"

"Away from here."

Samuel backed up slowly before turning away. I found the motion cautious, but trusting. After all, now it wouldn't take much for me to plunge my scythe into his back. I wouldn't even have to swing first. I could probably make it appear lodged between his ribs.

As we passed through the doorway that led into the expansive marble hallways, I hesitated. Samuel walked straight, eyes forward, purpose in his stride.

I was worried. What would someone think if they saw us walking together? What would our walk down the hall hint at? What if the wrong person saw us? Were there still 'wrong people' I had to worry about?

"Do try to keep up, my boy. I don't have all day," Samuel chided. While his feet sounded soft and light on the solid marble floors, they moved quickly.

I had never been to this part of the parliament

building before, but after a few twists and turns through corridors that all looked the same, we entered one that was longer and wider than the rest. Here, manicured trees planted in ornate golden pots lined the hallway, alternating with floor-to-ceiling mirrors.

I had stared into these mirrors before. Even now, I remembered the disheveled ten-year-old boy gazing back at me.

It was real. It was *all* real. Everything that had happened to me. I was standing in the exact same place I had been all those years ago when I'd found my father.

We were going to my father's office. I had no doubt about that.

"Do you still hear the trees, Edmund?" Samuel asked, breaking into my thoughts.

I turned away from the mirror to find him standing in the middle of the hall, facing me. His black robes against the white marble backdrop made him look domineering and out of place, like a giant black smudge on a perfectly waxed tile floor—the kind of black smudges I used to make with my sneakers on purpose as a kid to piss off the school janitor.

"Define *hear*," I responded, not trying to be difficult. I wasn't sure if he wanted to know if I could *hear* the trees, or *understand* their conversations, which, due to their noisy arguing, I couldn't.

Samuel smiled, turned, and talked while walking away from me. "Ah, yes, they are quite difficult these days,

31

aren't they? I suppose a simple 'yes' wouldn't have been honest."

I followed. "I suppose not. Why do you ask?"

Samuel stopped, turned toward me again, and motioned behind him. "Because you'll want to listen to this one."

He stepped to the side, revealing the entrance to my father's office. The mirror had been broken, but a large topiary, just like the ones planted in the ornate golden pots, filled the doorway.

"This tree, Edmund, has a determined spirit. Days after Joshua discovered this entrance and took down the mirror, this tree grew to cover the entrance."

I stepped forward to examine it better. The twisted vines formed a tightly woven net that perfectly filled the rectangle of the doorway.

"Joshua has cut it down multiple times. He even threw out the entire pot once, but the tree always came back."

I searched for the trunk. Couldn't Joshua just have moved the tree's pot out of the way?

But the tree had fastened itself down, through marble, into the ground beneath the building.

"It broke through the marble," Samuel echoed my thoughts.

I was in awe. This tree's energy oozed protection and duty. Just being close to it made my body feel centered and alive. For the first time since coming back to Orenda, the electric current in my skin gathered to the place just above my heart.

I remembered.

If every natural creature and element were connected to the ocean, and if I could see the beauty of the sea as it heaved and rolled, the resulting feeling that rose in me was as if someone was reaching inside my chest and holding my breastbone. That pressure, just above my heart, was where the feeling settled. That is what it felt like to be connected to the world as I was.

The tree was there for me. It was the same tree that helped me get through the glass the last time I stood in this exact spot.

While not as strong, or as kind, or as old as Mother Tree, I had a friend in Orenda.

At this thought, the woven branches rustled. They pulled apart in the center, gathering tightly around the edges. Eventually it formed an arched entryway, revealing the winding staircase beyond.

"Your way is much cleaner than Joshua's," Samuel smirked.

"Let me guess," I said with a hint of contempt in my voice. "Joshua's way included fire."

"Let's just say this tree has endured more than its fair share."

"In that, we are the same, this tree and I."

Samuel's smirk turned into a smile. "I do believe you are right. After you?" he asked, motioning toward the staircase.

I turned and descended into the dark.

THREE

The descent to my father's office had not changed. If I closed my eyes and inhaled the damp-tasting air, I could almost imagine myself as a child again. With my eyes closed, the whole world became a stage of orange and black that played on the inside of my eyelids. The light of the flames burping from the copper pipes cast shadows that danced like shadow people from another world. If I looked closely enough, I could almost see their yellow eyes.

With my eyes open, I saw only empty shadows of the past. The shelves and tables that had been covered with books and scrolls were empty—all of my family's secrets and knowledge, gone.

Rooms always felt bigger when empty, but these rooms were deceiving. With my eyes closed I could still smell the paper, the tanned leather that bound most of the books, and the ink. Even the twine used to tie the scrolls had a smell that lingered in the air.

But with my eyes open, there was nothing.

I didn't feel sad. I wasn't angry even though I knew Joshua was responsible for taking my father's belongings.

I felt empty, just like the room.

"Why did you bring me here?" I finally asked. My voice sounded tired and misplaced in the unnatural stillness of the office.

"There are many reasons," Samuel responded.

I waited for him to collect his thoughts and continue, but he never did. Instead, his eyes simply met mine.

I held his gaze until I began to get uncomfortable. What was he searching for with those probing eyes? What was he seeing? What was he looking at?

"Many reasons such as?" I drew out the last word.

"To talk about your father, for one. I told you that I was on his side, and not in league with Joshua. You need to understand that the two are not mutually exclusive. Your father…" Samuel didn't even blink, "…was on board with Joshua's plan—his plan to trade the humans to the energumen."

He continued to watch me carefully, probably for some outburst of anger. I realized he was afraid of me.

But I didn't feel angry. I remained stoic, void of emotion. Something about being in this vacant place stripped me of feeling.

"The plan was simple, really. Your father would stop collecting souls as they died on Earth, allowing the energumen to take them. In exchange the energumen would leave our people and our children in peace: no wandering in our level, no appearances, no possession, no fear."

My father was a flawed man; I had no doubt about that. All of my memories of him were from a child's point of view, but I was no longer a child, and I knew better than to believe my father had been perfect.

But I had just spoken to him a few months ago. He sacrificed his spirit to the energumen so that I could take his role as the Angel of Death and *save* the humans from being taken.

"Many of the Elders felt that by changing the human existence, by not bringing them back to Orenda, the jobs we've been required to perform for centuries could be modified," Samuel said, a hint of ice in his voice. "Many didn't want their children to continue to carry the responsibility and burden of serving humanity."

"My father made it quite clear that the human cycle and our cycle are interconnected—even more so now that *our* people have started to die here and go to Earth."

Samuel shifted, and started walking up the wrought iron spiral staircase that led to the loft. "Yes," he said. "Joshua surprised many of those who were on board for his original plan when he sold us *all* out."

I still didn't know if I could trust Samuel. Actually, I was pretty sure I couldn't but the way he talked made the wheels in my head spin. "So, how many of the other

Elders knew of Joshua's end game? How many weren't 'sold out'?"

Samuel turned and grinned at me from the balcony. The red sky reflecting off my father's mirrored ceiling and the whites of Samuel's eyes and teeth made him look wild and cunning.

"Joshua had planned on three surviving. Him, your father, and me. One Elder with knowledge of each death."

He said the last part so quietly that I had to start climbing the staircase myself to hear him. Now I was even surer I couldn't trust him, but if my father had been meant to survive, what did that mean? Why didn't he?

I wasn't sure what was happening, but the reddish tint of the sky had started to deepen to the point where the resulting light in the office wasn't enough to see by. It couldn't have even been lunchtime yet; I had no idea why the sky was turning the same color it would at dusk. Maybe it was my perception because my thoughts toward Samuel were darkening.

"Your father's ceiling is quite magnificent, isn't it? We discovered a spire with a small glass orb so carefully constructed that it has the ability to reflect light down a thin tunnel, condensing a large image much like an extraordinary camera lens. The illusion is completed by a series of mirrors that give a complete 360 degree view of the sky outside." He sounded like he was stalling. "Except everything you see is inverted and backward. Did you know that some mystics believe that life is that way?

Inverted and backward? If that's true, what you are seeing in the reflection is *actually* real life. I'd bet your father used it as a way to maintain his perspective."

Samuel didn't meet my eyes as I climbed the staircase. He looked up at the ceiling, getting some perspective, perhaps.

"Joshua left you something here, something he said belonged to you," Samuel continued as I reached the top of the staircase.

He stepped aside, motioning toward my father's desk.

As I'd already noticed, there was nothing left on the shelves. The books and scrolls had all been removed. The desk had never been cluttered, but was just as empty as the room, stripped of almost everything. Almost. Sitting squarely in the middle of the desk was one single book.

I didn't move. I didn't have to. I didn't need to take one step to know exactly what book Joshua left me. It was my father's book, *Crossing Death*.

When I didn't move, Samuel eyed me warily. "You don't trust me, do you Edmund?"

"You're just figuring that out?"

"Actually, I think you're just figuring that out."

His response was confusing.

"One ability that helps me do my job well is the power to read other people's minds. It isn't constant, and I can't see everything. It's more like flashes. It helps me in the Plannings to really gauge what someone is thinking, to know what they need. Like the two times you considered killing me." Samuel reached for his throat. "The one time you almost did. And the childhood memories? I knew who you were the moment I saw myself echoed through your childhood eyes. Take the book, Edmund. I can see you thinking about it."

The funny thing about Samuel explaining his mind-reading gift to me was that I was finding his thoughts easier and easier to read myself. "Joshua never figured out how to read it, did he," I stated.

"Joshua is convinced there is nothing to read."

I moved for the book, snatching it without taking my eyes off Samuel.

It was smaller and lighter than I remembered, but even in the red light, the gold letters on the cover reflected with a cascading golden light as if they were backlit.

I thumbed through the pages, not entirely surprised to find that the front of the book had words on the pages. I stopped when I came across a word that made me almost drop the book, and sent the buzzing sensation flowing over my skin into overdrive: Xia.

I could go on and on about her amazingly shiny black hair that fell in carefully constructed ringlets around her soft skin, or how her long legs and netted stockings made her look almost as tall as her cousin Quon, or how she dressed just provocatively enough in a short skirt and baby doll tee to pique a man's imagination without giving too much away, but it was her aura that really screamed beauty. She was literally on fire with radiant orange colors radiating from her. It was a wonder that no one else in the room could see it.

I turned the page frantically, reading another familiar scene, my eyes widening in horror.

"What is it, Edmund?"

"It's me!" I couldn't contain the shock and surprise spilling out of me, whether I trusted Samuel or not. "It's my story!"

I turned to the first printed page, which had four words printed in bold letters:

Death of the Body.

FOUR

I was still clutching the book when the thunder started. There was a loud boom, followed by a sound that resembled the sound effect they put into movies when icebergs crack. *Boom, crack, crack, boom!*

The thunder shook the room. I wondered if it wasn't thunder at all. It could have been an earthquake. My vapid emotional state registered that something bad was happening, and I should have been terrified, or at least nervous, but I was paralyzed by apathy.

Samuel's eyes flashed toward the ceiling as a large crack ripped through the mirrors that made up my father's carefully constructed ceiling.

My body felt sluggish, but I lunged toward him, knocking him to the ground, shielding him with my body, preparing to be showered with pieces of broken glass at any moment.

Then Samuel started laughing. "He actually did it.

That son-of-a-bitch did it."

I looked into his face, but he was still staring at the ceiling, completely oblivious that I had knocked him over and was on top of him. He wore the same diabolical grin that he'd plastered to his face earlier.

I looked up, half expecting to have my eyes gouged out, but it wasn't glass that I saw falling.

It wasn't the glass that had cracked at all... it was what the glass was reflecting—the sky.

"The sky is falling. The sky is falling," Samuel laughed manically. I had been recalling the nursery rhyme and had thought the same words.

I rolled off Samuel, onto my back, so that I could see the full view of the sky without having to twist my neck.

I was in awe and horrified all at the same time because I had no idea what I was watching. The sky was splitting, cracking like ice when it was too thin. When a piece of the sky cracked all the way around like a piece of spidered glass, it fell in a blaze until it burned up. Sometimes, *things* that looked like small specks of black dust would fall from the space where the sky had been. The hole left behind was the color of a raw steak and reminded me of what it looked like to cut away a piece of flesh from a body, leaving the underlying muscle exposed.

I watched a number of specks tumble out of one of the holes in the sky. As they caught fire, it reminded me of watching a comet or space shuttles entering the atmosphere on a science TV show, with a large smoking trail stretched behind them.

But as they fell closer, they didn't burn out, and started to take shape. Now they looked more like birds, complete with wings. I stared in amazement as the creatures' details started to fill in: large wings with jet-black feathers, much more mass than I originally thought. They had strong defined muscles and a curving back that… wait… were those hooves?

There was a word for these half-human, half-horse creatures… centaurs. These were centaurs with wings.

"What?" I turned to Samuel, to discover that he was on his side, his head supported by his arm as he studied my face. Catching him staring at me was startling.

"Angels, my boy."

"I thought we were angels."

"Those are *our* angels, from the place our people go when we die, when the cycle was different. Before…"

"Before Joshua," I finished.

Samuel nodded. "They are from a level where instinct rules; they are instinctual creatures."

"The level above us?

"Above us is the Level of the Mind," Samuel nodded before I looked back into the mirrored ceiling. The sky had almost completely fallen away, and I was starting to hear the sounds of panic filter through the walls of the parliament building as hundreds of creatures fell.

I didn't feel panic, but I was starting to feel nervous. Whatever emotional void I was in had started breaking down.

"Joshua wants more souls, doesn't he?" I asked. "He broke the boundaries between levels so that he can send these creatures to their death here."

"Not many will survive that fall, even with their wings. Those that die will be reborn on Earth as a human, as you were. But he won't stop there. He will bring them down further still. He'll give them all to the energumen."

Samuel pushed himself up and got to his feet. I followed.

"Now that Joshua has completed his work on the Level of the Mind, he will come back for you. You cannot stay here."

Samuel reached out toward me, the gesture making me react by drawing in a quick breath. I wasn't afraid of his touch; I just didn't understand it… until it fell on the book.

"He will not be happy until he owns all of the souls in the Level of the Spirit. The soul gives the spirit power, Edmund. Do you understand?"

"Honestly, no."

"Do you see?"

He was rambling now, nervously.

"See what?"

"You can't stay. There is a group of mages that escaped. They congregated at the ancestral ruins on the other side of the mountains."

My heart leapt. Hailey and Ralph! Could they have

escaped?

"Getting through the mountains is tricky. They're protected."

Samuel was talking too fast and walking back down the winding staircase, toward the office door. He mumbled something I didn't hear.

"I won't leave without my mother," I said, just as Samuel's hand landed on the doorknob.

He turned to me slowly. "The spell that was used to enslave her cannot be undone, Edmund. She is lost to you."

"I don't believe you."

"Then take her with you. A domestic must do all they are asked if it's in service to a human," he responded.

Images of some of the things a human might have asked her to do filled my head—especially a human like the one I had just witnessed Samuel chastise at his Planning. I felt nauseated.

Samuel flinched.

My brain synapses registered the tic in his eye as he studied my face. He had always seemed to be able to sense my thoughts. My synapses fired, and I connected the dots.

"You are an Elder of the Level of the Mind! *You* taught Joshua how to bring that level down!"

"Took you long enough," Samuel said, pushing the door open and holding it for me. As I moved forward, he grabbed me and shoved me through the door in front of him. "Now get out of here before Joshua gets back, if you know what's good for you."

FIVE

Outside was chaos. It wasn't just the hundreds of mangled, bloody, and broken bodies in the streets. Nor was it just the cries of the humans as broken animal bits shattered windows and their carcasses shook buildings. It wasn't just the air that thundered of invasion or the sky that rained blood. It wasn't just the plants that now joined the trees in anger and hatred, speaking so loudly that they no longer sounded like the wind but like a tornado. It wasn't even that the whole earth quivered in pain, or that its pain caused my skin to hum so frantically that I wasn't sure if my feet were even hitting the ground as I ran, or that the vibration was so strong I could've sworn it had lifted me into the air.

It was that above all the chaos, I could hear laughter—deep, guttural, maniacal laughter.

And I realized that the thing inside that shook me, that vibrated my whole body in time with that laugh, was fear—a new kind of fear—fear of the unknown. I had no idea what was happening, how it was possible, or what it meant.

I ran through the cobbled streets that had been transformed into rivers of red. I ran past buildings with spires that impaled falling bodies, and buildings that dripped with blood.

I ran until I ran right into one of *them*.

I don't know how I didn't see him, but I rebounded off his powerful ribcage and found myself promptly on my back, instinctively crab walking away from the beast as he reared onto his hind legs and kicked his powerful front hooves in my direction. Somehow this one had survived the fall, but his eyes were wild with confusion and anger, his survival instinct completely taking over.

His fur was caked and matted. As he sprang up again on his hind legs, this time close enough to trample me on the way back down, he somehow lost his balance, and fell backward over himself.

He didn't get back up. He clenched his sharp teeth with his coal colored eyes locked onto mine. He breathed heavily, exhaling with a hissing each time. Now that he wasn't towering above me, I noticed a large head wound.

His eyes shifted from fear to panic before widening in death. After one final breath, they emptied.

The noise was too much, too loud. I couldn't hear myself think. Among the screaming humans, the roaring wind, the booming thunder, and the laughter that echoed from everywhere, I found myself curled in the fetal position lying in a pool in the middle of the road. I felt like I was being attacked from all sides in a sensory overload that was bound to cause me to implode. The pressure I felt was becoming physical as the weight of the world bore down on me and the sky rained blood. I cursed my connection to the world. It felt like it would be my destruction.

I didn't even realize that the creatures were surrounding me until it was too late. If these creatures were in the angelic life cycle, where I would have gone at death had Joshua not doomed us all to be cast down to the Level of the Body, then I understood why I could speak to animals when I was a child.

They spoke by expressions and instinct. The look on their faces could not be misread. They didn't know what I was or what was happening either, but they thought I had something to do with the death of the fallen centaur whose empty eyes were just inches from my own.

They were going to kill me.

The world went perfectly still as they charged, a high-pitched ringing in my ears replacing all other noise. I knew their war cries were ferocious, because I could see their open mouths and the tension in their jaws as rows of sharp teeth snapped at me.

A single thought entered my mind—I would die without my father's ring, and forget who I was… reborn on the Level of the Body… again.

I closed my eyes and prepared for the pain. It always followed the ringing in my ears, like when Joshua killed me as a child, like when he killed me as an adult.

I didn't want to feel the pain of death again. It was too familiar already. I looked deep inside of myself and tried to focus on anything but what was about to happen to me. There were my wings, long and angelic, black as night and light as smoke. I folded them over me, into me, anything I could do to possibly add one extra layer of protection—but I knew a layer of smoke wouldn't do much against an army of hooved, powerful, majestic, and terrified animals.

I knew what came after the pain anyway. It was that sensation of floating before complete evaporation. Was that the explanation for the floating feeling I was experiencing now? Was it possible I was already dead, past the pain and anger, drifting in the endless cycle, ready to be reborn a mere babe on Earth?

* * *

When I opened my eyes, they were flooded with white smoke, heavy and fog-like. My mind immediately returned to the day in the graveyard. The fear I felt in the morning mist when the ghosts of Mary Chantale and Mary Elizabeth taunted me returned. It raced up the back of my spine as my smoky cloak burst out of my skin in stark contrast to the white swirling around me. I held my scythe at the ready, waiting for something to emerge from the murky haze. Would I hear my name again? Would a centaur be calling it this time? A ghostly nun? An energumen?

At the thought, the entire scene burst into a stain of yellow, the color of an energumen's eyes.

"Who's there?"

The voice wasn't my own. It was soft and timid, but enough to cause stomach bile to rise into my chest and my heartbeat to race through my skull and pound out through my ears. I spun around, but couldn't make out anything through the haze.

My heartbeat quickened as the fog danced playfully with the dark smoke emanating from my body. The fear was too real, too alive, for me to be dead.

But if I wasn't dead, where was I?

I took one step forward, turning again as my other senses asserted themselves, trying to make up for my inability to see clearly.

Beside the sound of my heart I could hear static, not as roaring or as deafening as the sound of a large waterfall, and not as electronic or piercing as the static on a television. This sounded more like a hundred hushed voices of a hundred disembodied spirits each quietly whispering, "Shhhhh."

The chill pulsing through the air was not something that emanated from within me. It wasn't an emotion or an extension of my fear. It was real. I could see it ripple through the air as the tiny particles of fog turned to ice and crystallized with the pulse. Each tiny particle vibrated in the cold and then hung, suspended in the air, like snowflakes that refused to fall.

I pushed a handful aside, and watched my breath as I exhaled. This was a cold I knew. This was the same cold pulse I had felt from my father's ring. This was the same pulse I felt in the dreams with Xia.

Something about where I was didn't make sense.

The sound of the static became perfectly clear once it mingled with the smell. There was a musky odor in the air, wet and masculine. It smelled like a gym bag or a locker room, or...

A sauna.

"Nicholas?" I questioned without even thinking his name. When I did, all of the iced particles fell away, coating the tiled sauna floor in a thin layer of powder-fine snow.

Nicholas was huddled in the corner, his back pressed firmly against the wall.

"Stay away!" he cried, not timid or quietly, but with a tremor in his voice I'd never heard from him before. He was afraid.

The air pulsed cold again.

"Nicholas it's me!" I took a step toward him.

"No! You're not *him*. You're one of *them*."

"What? No! It's me. *I'm* me."

Nicholas looked at me, his grey eyes locking onto my

own with intensity I had never felt before. "No," he said. "Stop using his voice. Edmund doesn't have yellow eyes."

The whole scene shifted. I was now standing in a hall of mirrors. My dark cloak was pulled high around my face. It looked so deep and black that I couldn't make out any of my features in the mirrors except two piercing yellow eyes.

I tried to put the cloak away as movement caught my eye. Nicholas, now in full running gear, was galloping down the mirrored pathway, away from me.

"Nicholas, wait!"

"Not in this life, demon. This is *my* dream!"

Dream? The air pulsed cold again as an infinite number of Nicholas's reflections ran in all directions away from me.

I picked a direction, running after him. Futile or not, this was starting to feel familiar, like it was with Xia. It was like when I dreamed of her.

If these mirrors were my own creation, it didn't matter which way I ran. The only thing missing from this dream to make it exactly like the ones with Xia was the erotic current that caused my skin to hum. And her naked, of course.

I stopped when I thought this. There *was* a definite difference here. The steam room would have been something Nicholas would have created—a perfect representation of a piece of *his* life. Of course he would be scared—he had seen shadows and was possessed once by a demon he met in the steam room. But this hall of mirrors? It felt too staunch, too perfect… too… porcelain.

I didn't know what made me think the word, but when I did a new reflection appeared in the mirrors. The reflection of a deep, ripe rose.

I spun, turning in time to catch Nicholas's grey eyes staring back at me. Only they didn't belong to Nicholas.

I choked on my words, unsure if my inflection left them as a statement or a question. "Linda Rose."

The mirrors quivered and fell away, leaving us standing in a garden flooded with the sweet scent of flowers. The scene reminded me of the royal garden at Buckingham Palace, with perfectly manicured rose bushes and lush green lawns. A small iron table with a steaming pot of tea finished the setting.

"Where's the white rabbit?" I joked half-heartedly, my soul melting into ease and comfort. Whatever this place was, wherever I was, I had no doubt this was Linda Rose. She was a woman who could not be mimicked.

"Yes, well we do have quite a few rabbit holes still left to figure out. Don't we, dear child?"

She embraced me and kissed my cheeks, even though I knew she couldn't see them through my shroud. Try as I might, I could not get the damned thing to go away.

"Oh, don't worry about that here. In this space, all things must show their true selves."

My true self? "Nicholas said I had yellow eyes," I sputtered. What a stupid thing to start out with. Not 'How are you?' or 'Where the hell am I?'

"I wouldn't worry about those, either. Shall we?" Linda Rose motioned to the table where two cups of tea were poured and waiting, a spoon automatically stirring in each.

"They aren't screaming," I joked.

Linda Rose remained composed, but the corner of her ruby lips turned up in a smile. "I have learned a thing or two since the last time we met, Edmund."

"Is this real?" I asked, finally sitting.

"Not exactly," Linda Rose explained, picking up her cup and pressing it to her lips. "You have invaded a dream, I believe."

"A dream? Whose?"

"Mine, actually. Although it hasn't always been mine."

My mind instantly flew to Xia. Each dream with her was warm, electric, and ended with me killing her. I almost flew out of my chair. "Xia? Is she…?"

Linda Rose raised a gloved hand and motioned for me to sit back down. "She's fine. Just fine. A little shaken. A little anxious. A little spastic. Much like *you* actually." She motioned with a flick of her wrist to highlight my reaction. "I know you want to talk about her, as any young man in love would, but I'm afraid we don't have all night."

Her words sounded empty and dark in the bright afternoon sun. I had to remind myself that if this was a dream, then someone must be asleep somewhere. It couldn't really be the afternoon.

I laughed. "Actually, I'm pretty sure I'm about to be stomped to death by angry centaurs, so my time may be a little limited too."

A look of confusion flashed across Linda Rose's brow before she chuckled. "Yes, I'm sure we could stay in here for hours and discuss all the oddities we've seen since our last meeting. Centaurs, you say? That is fascinating, but off topic and I must not let myself get distracted."

"What do we need to talk about then?"

Linda Rose's cheek twitched nervously as she put down her cup of tea and placed both hands on the table. She leaned forward and looked me squarely in the eyes. "I need your scythe."

I couldn't have heard her right. I'm glad she couldn't see my face flush. "Come again?"

"Your scythe. I need you to let me borrow it... temporarily."

"My scythe."

"Child, have you gone deaf? The scythe. Death's scythe. You must give it to me. Now." Her voice had risen to a pitch beyond recognizable. She was angry, frustrated. More than that, she was scared.

"No." I responded. There really was nothing else to say. She couldn't be serious. What was I going to do? FedEx it to her?

"Edmund, you don't understand—"

"It doesn't matter," I cut her off. "The answer is no."

Linda Rose pushed the tea set off the table with one

angry swoop of her arm, ripping off her glove in the time it took to put her hand back on the table.

The air pulsed cold around me. She wore my father's ring.

"You really are foolish sometimes," she yelled, before I even had a chance to react. I felt so slow and sluggish in this world, like a nightmare where you can't run because your legs are too heavy. "Do I have to explain everything to you? Xia and Nicholas stole back your father's ring. That's when Xia started having dreams of you, and you started stabbing her in the back. Now, I wear the ring, and used your connection and love for Nicholas to pull you into my dream."

I was shaking. I didn't understand, but I was angry. I felt exactly like I felt that day in the coffee shop, when Linda Rose had *mysteriously* pulled an acorn out of her clutch. Now, she was pulling out my father's ring, and intimate knowledge of the dreams Xia and I shared.

"The ring connects our world with yours. Are you really that thick? The dreams are real, and frankly, my boy, you're a bit dangerous in them. The demons are after us all now. They are hunting Xia and Nicholas. I'm trying to save them, I'm trying to keep my son alive!"

"Death isn't so bad," I finally sputtered.

"It is if there is no one to meet you. Are *you* going to collect their souls if they die?"

I balked. I didn't even know how to answer. How did she know there was no one to collect the souls of the dead? "I don't know how to find the crossroads again," I hoped I was making sense to her. She seemed to have some knowledge of what was going on.

"Edmund, it doesn't matter. Let's not get sidetracked. Listen. I promise that I will make sure the scythe is returned to you, with your ring, and I will figure out a way to help you understand what you're supposed to do. I need you to trust me, Edmund. Just for a little while. Help me save them."

"If you're telling the truth, then I don't need to make a decision now. Give me time to think about it."

"No, Edmund. There isn't time."

"This isn't negotiable."

"I just need—"

"We're done. Wake up."

The ring pulsed cold, answering to my will. Linda Rose flinched.

"Wake up!"

* * *

When I opened my eyes, I was looking into the face of my mother.

"You were thrashing again."

The voice and the phrase had become so routine that I used them to confirm I was really awake. My mother stood in the doorway with the same irritated look on her face she always had, a fresh bundle of sheets in her arms.

But there was something different about the way she said it today. Maybe I had died, stomped to death by the centaurs. Did I come back as a ghostly, thrashing apparition? The horror on my mother's face, her open mouth, her hard eyes, and her pale skin, all seemed to be the result of seeing a ghost.

The feeling of drifting came to a sudden end as the black smoke of Death's cloak consolidated around me. My wings that were curled so tightly against my body in the streets with the centaurs now felt an urgent need to stretch. I kicked them out briefly, only to watch my mother stagger back in fear.

I wasn't in the street anymore, although I was still covered in the blood that had rained on me. My face was smeared, looking wild and ferocious in the mirror on the wall.

I had somehow gotten back to my room. Confusion crossed my face as my mother turned whiter in disbelief at the horrific creature standing in front of her. I was that horrific creature. She opened her mouth and I was sure she was going to scream. Instead she gasped.

"My God," she croaked. "I knew it! You're one of us!"

SIX

"You really should let me go back. They have ways of tracking me." My mother's low voice sounded loud and harsh, like someone trying to whisper when you have a migraine and sound is screeching and amplified.

We'd had this conversation already a dozen times. She protested when I told her we were leaving, when I had her pack my bag, when I had her pack *her* bag, when we took the only horse I found in the town that would talk to me, and every time she had opened her mouth since.

"It's not safe for us there," I said, this time excluding the numerous reasons and explanations I had already gone over.

The campfire's flames against the coagulated backdrop of the midnight sky caused it to glow a dirty purple. The darkness of night didn't last long, but when it came it did so with such intensity that it swallowed the light of the campfire just beyond my mother's face. The fire crackled hot, but the air around us was cool. The front of my body, which faced the fire, was growing uncomfortably warm, while my back was too cold.

I didn't know if it was quieter out here now because we were away from the town, or if the chaos from today's earlier events drove nature into a deadly silence. The trees weren't arguing anymore. Nothing was talking.

I'd heard many people say silence is deafening, but there was something different about it in Orenda. It wasn't supposed to be silent here. I came to realize that my senses in Orenda ran together and weren't as easily defined as the five senses I was taught on Earth. In fact, the high-pitched ringing in my ears from the lack of sound, broken up only occasionally by a pop of a log in the fire, wasn't what bothered me most.

What bothered me most was the silence of my emotions. They were swallowed up in a void that took residence in the pit of my stomach, darkness I couldn't remember having before my death as a human. I could still feel, but my emotions were no longer teaching me. They were no longer speaking to me. They were there to annoy me, to feed the darkness. They had never been silent, not in Orenda, not on Earth. Now, everything was empty.

"I have other people—"

I knew this was coming too, so I cut her off. "You will stay with me." There. It wasn't a request. It was a demand. She had to obey.

I didn't realize I was looking into her eyes until the

orange glow from the fire disappeared as she blinked. She would be quiet now, at least for another hour. Then she would start the whole conversation again.

It was nice to stare into the flames. Watching them dance over the hot coals, bright and lively while surrounded by darkness everywhere else, helped me focus on what was right in front of me. I watched each flame uncurl and billow before kicking itself into oblivion. I was almost convinced that each flicker was a living creature. If they had the ability to stick around and live a bit longer, I might've even been able to feel their emotions.

"It's beautiful to watch a flame dance." My mother's voice caught me by surprise. "But, you know, if you watch only one spot, if you focus on one single flicker as it twists toward the heavens, while it may be true you see something beautiful, you also miss the flame on the other side doing a much more vibrant dance. If you focus only on that flame instead, perhaps because it is the biggest and the brightest, then you'll miss how all the flames dance together. You'll miss the bigger picture. You'll miss the orchestration."

She paused and her glowing eyes looked wet. "You're too focused."

"I feel like I'm focused on being scattered," I said, trying to sound like I was joking, but feeling the truth in my words. "I don't know what I'm doing."

"When the men came…" she stopped and took a deep breath. "I don't remember much about my life before their hex. I know I'm hexed because I wear this bag around my neck, and I know what it's for."

"I know," I said. "I'll find a way to remove it…"

"I don't need you to fix this for me. Just listen. My point is that although I don't remember the people, or the teachings, I do remember the lessons. Life is like an orchestra. You are the conductor. You can complain that the woodwinds aren't doing what they are supposed to do, but if you focus on them too much you're going to lose the strings. Sometimes you need to close your eyes and listen. That's the only way you can truly understand how the parts fit together."

I chuckled, but didn't let much noise escape my throat. I didn't want her to hear it. "You called the conductor the Grand Maestro once."

"Did I? I don't recall…"

"Never mind."

My mind was already onto other things. I had first noticed the hex bag around my mother's neck just a few weeks into my life back here in Orenda. It took me longer than that to figure out what it was, exactly. The magic it produced was dark and controlling, so dark that what it did became obvious from the first time I let myself get close enough to it to *feel* it. It took me a long time to get that close though. Thinking of getting that close, close enough to the bag to feel the magic it contained, made me instantly sick.

That's when I knew I couldn't just simply take it off.

Touching the small sachet would cause me to lose my own memory, destroy my powers, and cost me my own agency. Worse, I had no idea what touching the bag would do to my mother.

"How did you survive?" my mother asked.

I wasn't sure whether to be glad she was talking so much, or if I wanted her to shut up.

She continued despite the annoyed look on my face. Hopefully she couldn't see it. "I mean... you have magic. How did you avoid them? No—that's not quite the right question. How did you... blend in?"

I poked at a log with my mind and it shifted physically, sending a flurry of orange sparks into the air. Poking it with magic was more fun than using a stick.

"I didn't," I said, telling the truth. "They killed me."

My mother's face contorted with confusion.

"Twice." I grinned despite myself.

She smiled too. It was good to see her smile. I knew her smile was because of the laugh in my own voice, and not because she got the joke. It was a smile nonetheless.

"You really should let me go back. They have ways of tracking me," she said again.

I knew our moment together had passed. It was almost as if that satchel around her neck had a reset button it kept pushing. The smile lines around her eyes vanished as her face fell to an emotionless mask. She folded her hands in her lap.

"What would happen if you took off the satchel?" I

asked, bluntly.

"I'd die." The way she said it was cold, calculated, and dry. Her voice was emotionless, just like her face.

I considered what might happen if she took it off anyway. I allowed myself to feel the joy I felt when I saw her here in Orenda, and how hard it would be to lose her again. I also considered that with the satchel, she wasn't really my mother.

Or was she? I understood death better now. Would death be any different than what she was experiencing under this spell? She had already forgotten. Would a life on Earth, where she could escape her slavery, grow up all over again, laugh until the lines on her eyes became permanent, dance in the rain, read on the beach, meet a man she could fall in love with, be better or worse? The questions spinning in my head made me feel deeply withdrawn. I was talking to a zombie, not my mother. The mages had become the living dead.

"You really should let me go back. They have ways of tracking me."

"Stop talking, and stay right here. I need to take a leak."

It felt good to get away. The heat of the fire should have been warm and inviting, but sitting across from my mother made the air heavy and hot. The crisp air of the night crawled over my prickling skin. It made me feel alive and energetic.

I wouldn't let myself become a zombie.

After I had walked a little way into the towering pines that covered this part of the landscape, I jogged, feeling my Orendan blood course through my Orendan veins fueled by my Orendan heart.

As my heart pumped my muscles woke up and the darkness dissipated. I felt proud and strong. I could feel my pent-up energy coursing through the planet, into the ground, around my feet, through the trees, and up into the wind.

But the pride and strength were fueled by anger and frustration. As my emotions returned to me on the wind, I felt the cold and bitterness amplify within myself.

I turned to the nearest tree and unleashed. "How about you! Huh? Are you going to talk to me? Why won't you talk to me?"

I held up my middle finger on one hand while I unzipped my pants with the other, urinating on its trunk.

It helped. I felt better. As the stream of urine dwindled, so did my frustration.

The tree remained silent.

I walked back somberly, pushing away the guilt that tried to creep up on me. It wasn't like I hadn't ever peed on a tree before, but this time there was intention—I wanted to offend. I wanted to make it angry. I wanted it to yell at me.

Would something like that work with my mother? Could I offend her? Make her angry? Get her to yell? Could a strong enough emotion break through the spell of the satchel?

Maybe that's what defined life: anger. The trees were dead because they couldn't get angry, my mother was dead because she couldn't get angry, and I was only alive because I felt too much anger.

I was broken. I had just reclaimed my home and now I was on the run with my mother in tow—only she couldn't remember that I was her son and she was fighting me every step of the way.

I craved the warmth of Xia's skin on my own. I craved her touch so badly that the pain of not having it kindled the electric humming that washed over my body. I needed a deep, warm, physical connection that included her lips on mine. I craved to be near her, to sit in the same space with her, to feel the heat of our auras overlapping.

I needed to laugh, not just a laugh that happened in spite of how I was feeling, but a laugh that originated *from* what I was feeling. Nicholas always made me laugh like that. I missed his grey eyes and the confident saunter that demanded the attention of everyone in a room. If he were here with me now, he would pull the attention from me, even if it were just for a moment. A moment to recover was all I needed.

I sank to the forest floor and let the cool, damp earth hold me. Maybe I could take a moment. Just one moment. How terrible would it be if I gave up just for one, small—?

"Edmund."

It was her voice that said my name. It caused my skin

to tingle and eyes to brighten as I sat straight up and peered into the darkness toward the direction of the voice. The sound of my name on her lips reminded me why I was running. What if Joshua found me? What would he do? Kill me? Make me forget?

Why did that matter?

Because of her.

I didn't want to forget Xia.

"I'm here."

The first time I heard the voice I assumed it was just in my head, some subconscious part of my mind trying to keep me on task and focused. This time I knew it wasn't just inside me.

"Edmund."

The forest was still, but I could feel her presence as surely as I could feel the presence of demons the time they were about to descend on my childhood home in Prescott. The time I helped my sister escape. I felt the whispers in the air. They tingled down the sides of my rib cage. Instead of fear and danger vibrating through my bones, this felt playful and loving… and comfortable.

I closed my eyes, drew power and support from the planet, and turned my vision inward.

I was standing outside of my body, watching myself sit calmly on the forest floor. Xia was there next to me. Her arms were wrapped around me as her head rested lightly on my shoulder. She stroked her hands up and down the sides of my ribs lightly, and I could feel it. She whispered into my ear how much she missed me. It brought tears to my eyes.

Her timing could not have been more perfect.

"I'm here," I said again, my words thick with emotion.

"I can hear you!" she exclaimed, glancing toward the direction of my voice but looking right through me. After a few moments she gawked at my body still seated on the forest floor, confused. "Can you hear me?"

"Yes," I answered. "I can see you. I'm here… and… there."

"Where?" she asked. "I can't feel you."

I laughed, because even though the statement sounded incoherent, it made perfect sense to me. She could only see my physical body on the forest floor, but not feel it or hear it. I could only see her spiritual projection in my spiritual form. "I can feel you, but I can't see you with my physical eyes. I'm standing outside of my body, pushing myself outside of this level like I did with the hammer that one time in my dorm room. How did you get here? Are you astral projecting?"

"No. Not exactly."

She spoke to my body, whispering into my ear. I couldn't blame her because that was the only piece of me she could see. But I wanted nothing more than to have her see me clearly, look into the eyes of my soul, not just the eyes of my body, while they looked back into hers.

"Remember when you saved us from the demon in

the dorm, and you pulled us into the space between worlds and we saw Orenda?" she asked.

"Yes. You learned from that? *That's* how you're here?" I exclaimed. "You're so brilliant."

A wicked smile turned her lips. "Thank you. I couldn't do it myself but I had help. Hey, can you feel this?" she grinned and reached for my crotch... my physical crotch.

"Uh... yes..." I whispered as the feeling flooded my spirit. "I wish I could touch you. I wish we could..."

Her lips touched mine and I fell into a world of pure awareness, except the only thing I was aware of was her.

"You do touch me," she said. "All the time, in my dreams. They're real, when we're together."

"Linda Rose told me."

"I miss you."

"Don't give up on me. I'll find a way back to you."

Xia kissed my forehead and put a hand on my cheek. "I'm starting to get cold, like before. I need to tell you what's been happening."

"Okay." I didn't know what else to say. Her other hand was still on my crotch.

"Joshua knows we have your ring and has sent demons after us. We've banded together, Nicholas, Linda Rose, her coven, and me, but it's escalating." She paused. "It's worse than when you were here. We don't know how much longer we can hold them off. Linda Rose has a plan. She thinks if we can use your scythe, we may be able to control one of them."

"Yes," I said. "That's what the scythe does. Energumen can pass from their world to yours and to Orenda without using the crossroads."

"Linda Rose thinks that if we use one, she could meet you in Orenda physically enough to give you the ring back. We know you are a creature of both worlds, Edmund, especially now that you're human too. Linda Rose is sure that with the scythe *and* the ring, she could meet you and give them both back to you."

"It's too risky. I don't know how that would work. The details—"

"Edmund, I've been involved with every step of her plan. I can't explain the whole thing to you now but—"

Even as she spoke, I could feel the air around her pulse cold.

"Just trust me. It'll work," she finished.

"So you thought you'd just come on over and play with my weapon to get my weapon?"

Xia laughed. It was the best sound I had ever heard. "Is that the best penis euphemism you could come up with?" she asked.

"Well, yeah. Nicholas probably could have done better."

The smile that curved her lips was contagious. "Edmund," she continued. "You are the Angel of Death. With the ring you should be able to visit, right? That's what the Angel of Death does."

"I'm not sure, exactly."

"Well, find out."

"Here," I said, holding out the scythe. "You'll have to turn around and reach out. It's there, in front of you."

She turned away from my body and stood squarely in front of my spirit. Her eyes groped for mine in the darkness. Her desire to will herself to see me was written all over her face. She would give anything to see my spirit and body united, walking and talking as the person she knew I was.

Her hand brushed the cold metal and she flinched. For a split second, her eyes stopped searching and that wicked grin crossed her face again. "Why, Edmund! It's so big!"

"Ha ha. Very funny."

"Maybe I've been spending too much time with Nicholas."

"Well, tell him I said hello and that I'll kick his ass if he lets anything happen to you. And take care of that scythe. I don't think they sell replacements at Home Depot."

"God, it's good to hear you," she turned back to my body, still sitting on the forest floor. "And to see you. I would stay here with you if I could."

"I know. You're in my thoughts every day. But it's dangerous for you to be here. If anything happened to you—and the dogs... you do remember them?"

"I know. I know I can't come back. But if this works,

maybe I won't have to."

"I never got to tell you what I sent you over text that day. Never got to tell you in person."

"I still have the text. Don't tell me now. I want to see you when you do, and hear you, and taste the words on your lips after you say them."

I grinned. "In that case, I'll just tell you that you're one sexy lady."

Now she grinned. "I'll see you soon."

When I opened my eyes, the forest air was heavy. My body felt sluggish and I almost regretted being back in it, but I was determined and motivated. *That* was what I was fighting for. She was what I was fighting for.

I felt heavy and light all at the same time. While my body was tired and begged to quit moving, my spirit was soaring, and my mind was working overtime.

I had spent only a few moments with Xia, but the time together filled me with euphoria and excitement. I didn't even mind the silent trees, the darkness, or being alone. I *wasn't* alone. I had her.

As the campfire became visible, I was so involved with my own thoughts that I almost didn't hear my mother's voice.

"… I've been trying," I heard her say. It was the end of a sentence, of something I didn't hear. It wasn't the words that made me stop in my tracks, it was the tone.

That was fear in her voice.

The next voice was so low I was grateful that the

trees were silent. Otherwise I wouldn't have heard it at all.

"You must get him to return to Orenda. Your intuition about him is correct. He is an angel—and an important one to Joshua. Angels must be controlled. If they can't be controlled then…"

The voice trailed off there, but my mother finished the sentence.

"They'll be destroyed."

"I'm sending you some motivation and assistance. Our hunters will obey. Their lust for blood makes them perfect pets."

I shifted around a tree to get a better look at who my mother was talking to, but I still couldn't see where the voice was coming from.

"I am sending them after you and the boy. If you can't get him to return before they find you, they will kill you both."

The voice was hushed but sounded sinister. If I had my scythe I would have confronted it, but I had just given away my best weapon.

Perfect pets? Lust for blood?

"Hellhounds," my mother's voice quivered as she said the word.

Instinctively I touched my chest, half expecting to still feel the scars from the time I had walked between this world and the Level of the Body. I knew the dogs patrolled the space between levels, but this sounded like whomever this was had *trained* them.

I focused inside, toward the center of my chest where my connection to the planet was easiest to feel. It felt like a safety blanket to reach out across the planet from that point and feel the love and support of the grasses, the mountains, the rivers, and the trees.

I pushed any fear I felt down into the earth, but let the last of it convince me to err on the side of caution and not do anything stupid.

I circled around a tree trunk and found my mother sitting back where she had been when I had left, staring into the fire.

I crept out of the shadows. My mother's face looked pale in the firelight, her dark eyes not as hollow as they had been before. She looked up at me with an expression that was meant to appear fearful, but it was too calculated. It came off as nervous instead.

"You should let me go back. They have ways of tracking me," she said, this time fidgeting with her hands. She added, "You should come with me. They have ways of tracking you."

As if she planned it, as if she knew I'd overheard the conversation, a hound howled in the distance.

* * *

I didn't sleep that night, but my mother did. Her eyes were so heavy that I couldn't bear the thought of forcing her to continue onward with me, even though I knew she would be forced to if I asked. She had no choice. She was a domestic. The only reason she was out here with me now was because I had commanded her to come with me.

So I let her rest a few hours while I sat, watching her. Actually, I wasn't just watching her. While she slept, I pulled the planet's warm energy into my chest and sent it out in pulses. This allowed me to sense things deep in the forest. As the power rippled out from me, I used it like radar, feeling for something dark or malicious.

The energy of the forest was neutral. I sensed the usual animals, most of which were scared and frantic. It felt like the disintegration of the level above us was causing them some anxiety as well. I could feel other creatures, most likely the ones who had survived the fall from above. They wandered around confused and angry. They were mostly bigger than the animals of this world. Deer and moose were familiar, but centaurs and creatures I couldn't identify simply by feeling were not.

The hounds were closing in. Luckily for me, the other creatures that didn't belong here kept them distracted. With a little effort I could light up a centaur like an energetic beacon and feel all of the hounds in my sensory vision move toward it. While I was glad I could distract the hounds so easily at first, I was also concerned when I realized the reason this was working was likely because they were attracted to magic. This also meant every pulse I sent out had the potential to lead them straight to us.

They wouldn't be easily fooled for long. They were

like a dog playing with a ball; I could only pretend to throw the ball while hiding it behind my back for so long. They would only chase the invisible ball a few times before figuring out the game.

I began to feel odd as the sun peeked into the sky, staining it the usual blood red. At first I thought the feeling was because of my lack of sleep, or because the color of the sky was still so unexpectedly blood-like that it occasionally made me nauseated. As I stood and turned toward the direction of the breeze so it would cool my flushed face, my head began to swim and vertigo set in.

I lost my balance. To prevent myself from falling violently, I collapsed onto all fours. My hands clenched uncontrollably, digging into the dark soil beneath me, the bluish veins I was used to seeing in my arms turned dark.

The drumming sound in my head returned, matching my heartbeat and echoing in my veins as they thudded, black as ink. The veins were outlined so darkly that they appeared like black tattoos with every thud.

I tried to gasp, but the breath caught in my throat as if my lungs were incapable of inflating. The ground spun beneath me and I collapsed onto my side. My mother stood over me, a hard, knowing look in her eye. As dark spots encroached on my vision, she grasped my wrist so firmly that her nails dug into my flesh. A jolt of pain shot up my arm. My reflex to cry out was muffled because there was no air in my chest.

"Hold on, it's almost over," I heard her say as my

blood—blood that should have been the color of the sky but was now black as tar—dripped down my wrists and over her hand. "Just another moment, and it will all be over."

SEVEN

I registered the smell of damp earth and musty rock before my mind knew I was awake. Somewhere between consciousness and unconsciousness I was reminded of the smell, like the dank way the air smells in the *Pirates of the Caribbean* ride at Disneyland.

I opened my eyes and peered up into a cavernous ceiling. Yes. This place could totally be *Pirates of the Caribbean*.

The eyes staring down at me were familiar, but not Xia's chocolate brown. They blinked and looked away just as mine did. There was something awkward about staring into someone's eyes for too long.

"You should sit up slowly. The first time can be quite a rush," my mother said.

I took her advice and made sure to wiggle my hands and my feet first. My smoky cloak was billowing around me, light as air but suffocating. The hood was up and the opening for my face swirled so far out around and in front of me that it looked like I was viewing the whole world through an oval-shaped submarine window. I wondered if it was really the hood or if the darkness that narrowed my vision as I collapsed hadn't receded yet.

"What did you do to me?"

My mother laughed. Not the answer I was expecting. I was almost offended until the end of her laughter trilled upward and sounded more nervous than amused.

"You know," she shook her finger at me, "they didn't take all of my memories when they put this thing around my neck. They let me keep the ones they wanted to interrogate me about, including those of my husband."

She wasn't looking at me as she spoke. Instead, she was looking around frantically.

"My husband used to get fits like those. From the way you handled it, I assume it was your first? I know the first time I saw my husband go through one of them. I had the same look on my face as you did, I'm sure. He didn't know he could take me with him, then. But we figured out with just a small connection, a little bit of blood, he could bring me here."

As my head cleared, the familiar musty smell took on new meaning. I stood and saw that I was standing at the bank of a silver river. I was at the crossroads.

And I was afraid.

"What happened? Why did you bring me here?"

She laughed nervously again and stepped toward the

bank of the river, looking down it as though we were at a bus stop and she was searching for the bus coming down the road. "Oh, I didn't bring *you* here. You brought me. It happens when someone dies and you need to come… pick him or her up or whatever it is you do. I'm sure he'll be here. He'll know what to do."

"Who?"

"My husband. He's a reaper like you. He'll come."

I didn't think I could feel any sicker, but my heart plummeted into my stomach and bile took its place at the base of my throat.

She didn't know he was dead.

Worse, she didn't know he was taken.

"Mom." The word cracked in my throat as I tried to swallow it. I had been so careful, so cautious, so watchful of every single word I had said to her. How did it creep out before I even thought it?

Maybe she wouldn't notice. Maybe I had swallowed it back quickly enough that all she heard was a throaty grunt. Maybe the word didn't really break free.

But she was staring at me now, her eyes wide, her face frozen. Her expression was shocked, the only sign of movement was the color draining from her face so quickly that her lips were blue and her constricted irises turned gray.

I lowered the hood of my father's cloak so she could really look at me. I had rehearsed what I would tell her a million times, but anything I had memorized, any chance I had of making myself sound good, fled as my mind went blank.

"The Reaper is a family calling," I said. It took all my focus and strength to look her in the eye and not run away. I didn't want to see her reaction.

Her expression didn't change, but her lips parted. They didn't appear to move as she whispered, "He's dead, isn't he?"

My eyes flooded with tears and my knees wobbled. Pain and regret flooded through me, magnified by the emotion behind her question. Too much emotion. I couldn't empty it into the planet fast enough.

This wasn't how I wanted her to find out. I didn't want her to know until I had figured out a way to fix the whole situation—to save him from the energumen, to restore his memory, to bring him back to Orenda. I had to free her and reunite our family, to give back the role and responsibility of the cloak to my father and feel the relief and simplicity of being their son again. I didn't want to tell her what happened until after it was all just a story and they could smile at me like they used to on our way to the symphony.

But who was I kidding? Nothing about this was right. The level above us had fallen, our heavenly cycle destroyed. I had lived a life as a human—a life I was never meant to have lived. And I had never heard of someone coming back once the energumen took them.

I pressed my lips into a firm line, trying to compose

myself enough to say the only thing I could think to say. "He saved me," I choked out before allowing the sobs to roll through my body.

My mother ran and embraced me. I didn't expect that. The contact, the warmth of her body, the warmth of her spirit as she looked at me as her son for the first time since I was reunited with her—it was overwhelming. We collapsed together into a heap. After a few moments, I didn't know whether they were my tears or hers on my cheeks.

"Good," she said. "Then he succeeded. It was always his plan to save someone. The memory of who was taken from me, but the secret they always wanted, that I successfully protected, was that he intended on saving someone. Saving you. Good," she repeated.

But she didn't mean it. I could hear it in her voice. Her words were chosen carefully. Although she knew I was her son, her actions were based on what she believed a mother *should* do—not based on what she *felt* for me.

There was no emotional tie. She knew it, and so did I.

I released her. The look on her face echoed my thoughts and betrayed that she knew, and I knew, and she knew that I knew.

"It's okay," she said after we studied each other's faces for what seemed like too long. "I believe you. I may not remember being a mother, but I believe you. I wish I could feel the pride for you that you no doubt deserve, but I've been robbed of that. You need to know that piece of me can never be restored."

Her words were like daggers, but they weren't meant to hurt. In fact, they were cold on purpose, and behind them were hints of a plan.

She knew something.

I looked down, and then back up at her.

"Let's leave it with that for now. You have a job to do here, and we'll need whoever is crossing over to do something for us. I can't forget this conversation, and this satchel will eventually steal these moments from me."

I considered, for a moment, letting that happen. If I let her memories fade I could tell her all of this again someday when I was ready and could do it with more hope and happiness.

"No," she said, reading my thoughts. "No. I need to remember it exactly like this. He was my husband, and I'm better off knowing what happened to him. I will need my anger to do what must be done now."

"And what must be done now?" I asked as we both stood.

"I must make sure you succeed."

Just like that, I had an ally again. Even better, that ally was my mother.

I raised my hood and took a few steps toward the silver river, ready to greet whomever was crossing over. My mother's voice echoed behind me.

"What is your name? Your real name?"

"Edmund," I responded. The name tasted foreign on

my tongue. I hadn't spoken it myself in months.

There was a long pause. I thought she had finished, so I took another step toward the river.

"What's my name?"

I hadn't considered that Joshua had stolen that from her. I felt a surge of anger that was calmed only because my mother's name was on the tip of my tongue. Anger was incongruous with her name. It blasted away all sad emotions, as if it were a beacon of light among the emotional shadows of a dark night. "Mary."

I listened to her try her own name. I could imagine how awkward, yet satisfying, it would be to say. I had been Alexander when I knew nothing of Edmund, then Alexander when I wanted to be Edmund. After that I knew I was Edmund, but to protect myself I called myself Alexander. Now I got to be Edmund again, this time in front of my mother.

I grinned as I realized she was probably thinking the same thing now that she had her own name back. I wondered if her brain worked the same way mine did, connecting words with meanings in a domino effect of information. I remembered the orphanage and the foreign words that I couldn't remember learning, yet knew had meaning. I was sure my mother was experiencing something similar now. I wondered if her name connected to other words she did know, like *mother* or *wife*. I hoped that as her name ping-ponged around her brain that it was connecting to positive words and feelings.

I stopped grinning as I watched a person struggle to pull herself out of the silver river and onto the rocky bank where I had once emerged myself. Behind her was the precipice where the realm of the energumen waited to spew forth shadows with yellow eyes. I stopped grinning because I realized that they would be coming for this woman. I needed my scythe to rescue her, rescue my mother, and rescue myself.

I stopped grinning because I didn't have my scythe. I had given it to Xia.

I stopped grinning because at the same time that my mind registered the trouble I was in, it also registered that the woman coming out of the silver river just happened to have a scythe in her clutches. While I was grateful for the instant solution to the problem I was faced with, I was also confused. The woman was wearing a large sun hat and had such radiant skin that I could see how porcelain-like it was even from across the river.

I stopped grinning due to shock.

I stopped grinning because the woman was Linda Rose.

EIGHT

"Well, my child. You truly are stunning. Seeing you so soon is such a marvelous surprise. I really thought I'd be searching for days. Now, here you are. What are you doing here?"

"What am I doing here?" I exclaimed, my voice sharp. "What are *you* doing here?"

"I came to bring you this," she said, holding up my father's ruby ring. At the sight of it, my heart leapt. I could feel it pulse cold in the air around us, like it knew it was home.

My mother was at my side, her eyes wide. "That's his ring. I was asked about that ring. I was interrogated for *months* over that ring. How did you get it?"

Linda Rose didn't take her eyes off me. The smile on her face was forced. She had no idea who this woman was, and was annoyed with her already.

I laughed as Linda Rose put the ring in my hand and

cupped it with her own.

"This is my mother," I said.

"I see. Not a demon?"

"Just under the spell of a demon."

"Interesting."

I embraced her, but not entirely out of love or excitement. I wasn't happy to see her. I felt sorry she was here.

"You're dead," I finally said.

"Yes. That's why I needed your scythe. I wasn't about to cross over to end up being dragged to Hell."

"You know about the scythe? What it does?" I asked.

"Yes," Linda Rose repeated, her knowing eyes so piercing, so lovely. "I'm sure you remember the stories that Nicholas told you. I still have some sway over a demon or two."

"Why didn't you tell me? You planned this?"

"Of course! There are many people who know you, Edmund. Many people who love you. Nicholas, Xia, and I aren't the only ones. My coven knows and loves you too. We have been in this battle since the moment you left. We know what Joshua is trying to do. He's already had great success on Earth and otherwise. This was the fastest way."

"But. Nicholas? You're his only family."

Linda Rose put her hand on my cheek and pursed her ruby lips. "Oh no, Edmund. You're his family too."

The words caused a rush of warmth to settle in my cheeks, but I didn't have much time to bask in the good-feeling emotion. The wailing started and shadows quivered on the cavern walls. Soon, energumen would come for Linda Rose's soul.

The ring on my finger pulsed. My mom pushed her way between Linda Rose and me.

"Before we go," she said frantically, "there is a sprig of rosemary in this satchel. Can you find it for me and take it out? Quickly!"

Linda Rose eyed my mother carefully, looking her over for the first time. When her eyes settled on the bag that hung around her neck, the smile on her face vanished. "That spell is connected to your life. Do you know what will happen if I—"

"Just do it!" my mother snapped. Her voice sounded exactly like it did when she would snap at me as a child, 'Don't get mud on your shoes,' or, 'Don't touch the fire.' This was the first time that I had heard her sound like my mother again.

The tone, the motherly inflection, was not lost on Linda Rose. She did what anyone in the same situation would do. She complied.

Linda Rose handed me my scythe, which I gladly took from her. She then went to work on the knots in the twine around the bag. I found myself grateful for Linda Rose's French tipped manicure. Her long nails gave her leverage to pinch the thin string and work the knots loose.

When she produced a small branch of the herb, my mother snatched it with a quick "thank you," and proceeded to shove it in her mouth, chewing and swallowing.

I watched with slight amusement and trepidation. I almost laughed when my mother ate the rosemary, but was concerned over what Linda Rose said about the spell. I noticed my mom cut her off before she could finish whatever she was going to say.

"I could have done that for you," I said as my mother tied back up the bag.

"Actually, if you tried, it would have killed me. Only a human can open the bag."

"Can a human take it off?" I asked. The shadows grew more intense, driving us closer together.

I watched the wheels in my mother's head spin as she hesitated with her response. Whatever she was about to tell me wasn't going to be the full truth. "No one can take it off without killing me."

She looked at me, put her hand on my shoulder, and reached out for Linda Rose. "Let me direct us back. I know somewhere we can go."

With Linda Rose and my mother in tow, I thrust my scythe into the shadows.

* * *

The first time I'd captured an energumen with my scythe and used it to return to Orenda, I was sure there was some sort of magic involved—some law of the levels that I didn't understand that was built into the scythe. In the months since I'd been back, I'd examined the scythe closely (after all, it was a part of me). I'd come to understand how it worked.

The energumen have always had a gift. Their spiritual bodies allowed them to cross between levels. They're able to reach across the barriers, even without using a crossroads.

I had come to believe that the scythe came from their world too. It was much more spiritual than it was physical, which is how it was able to hide inside me until I needed it. Even though I knew it belonged to me, I also knew it was not from Orenda, nor from Earth. It didn't have the same makeup as the elements in either of those places. It felt different… darker.

Since the energumen were creatures of spirit, physical things passed through them, but the scythe didn't. It trapped them, allowing us to share their ability to walk through the barriers between the Level of the Body and Orenda.

At least, that's what I'd come to believe. Experiencing it again made me question everything. I should have tried to remember the transition, to find out what happened to the demon after it brought us back. Or to remember how my mother directed it to return us somewhere specific.

But instead, it felt like I had simply woken up without having gone to sleep.

The red sky was completely cloudless, but the light

breeze against my cheek breathed life into me. I knew where I was because of the woody smell of rich earth and pine. It all reminded me of a different memory, and my mind's connection to the smell would probably have been thought of as strange to anyone else. When I had been on Earth around age fourteen, I held up a red Christmas tree light so close to my face that I saw nothing else but the red glow. I couldn't remember why I thought holding a bulb that close to my face was a good idea, but the result had been that my mind emptied. I was surrounded by nothing but the smell of nutmeg from the kitchen and pine from the Christmas tree.

I sat up and looked around. Where were Linda Rose and my mother?

I was high on a trail that was surrounded by pine trees. The trail wound its way up two large mountain ridges that crashed into a narrow canyon. I had been here many times as a child in Orenda, and once as a human when I had followed a silver trail to a point where I could get Xia and Nicholas back to Earth. My heart ached as I thought of their names.

The mountain ahead was caved in. The trail that had been there was now buried in rock. I'd used my powers to try to send Nicholas and Xia to the place where the silver trail ended, and the result was a catastrophic change in the landscape.

For the first time I saw the changes the mountain sustained. Instead of two giant ridges spilling into each other with a narrow entrance at the bottom of the canyon, the ridges were twisted like an ice cream cone of multi-colored rock. I didn't even know where the trail led anymore.

The last time I was here I had been terrified. I remembered how the sound of the world had been overwhelming. All the words of the trees and plants had been jumbled in a harsh screeching noise that rendered me unable to stand. Worse, even above that awful noise, I remembered the sound of the howling hellhounds, the dogs with natural instincts to find intruders in a level where they didn't belong. The howl pierced my memory, causing my hair to stand on edge.

Then, I realized the howl wasn't in my memory. It was on the trail ahead of me.

I found myself on my feet as a bolt of adrenaline hit me. My heart quickened as I ran, a guttural scream tearing from my chest. "Mom!" I yelled, my feet carrying me toward the howl, against the advice of my mind that wanted me to run the other way.

I flew over the rocky terrain until I ran around a bend and found myself surrounded by towering canyon walls. How far had I run? It couldn't have been far enough to get into the canyon.

"Mom!" I yelled again, turning back, deciding to retrace my steps.

I was met with a solid wall of rock.

"Linda Rose?" I yelled.

I put my hand on the rock that blocked my way back. It felt cool, but solid enough to be real. It wasn't some trick of the mind or illusion. What was going on?

A howl from within the canyon spurred my feet into action again. I couldn't think of anything else but getting to that howl. I didn't know why, but I was sure I'd find my mother along the way—find her in danger.

The hair on the back of my head prickled as I ran deeper down the narrow path, barely missing collisions of rock with my shins. I squeezed as fast as I possibly could between boulders that left a gap barely large enough for me to fit through.

It didn't take long for the feeling of hopeless dread to settle into the pit of my stomach. Everywhere I looked I could see nothing but tower upon tower of stone. The winding path that weaved its way in front of me was so narrow that I couldn't see more than ten feet in front of me.

I didn't know how long I sprinted down the trail, but the sun started to slip behind the cliffs. While the tops of the rocks glowed, the bottom of the cavern floor was claimed by shadow.

I thought about turning back. Just as I was about to give up, I caught movement out of the corner of my eye.

Everything was eerily still. Even if there were plants or trees speaking, or voices carried on the wind, the air where I was standing was deadly calm. I could hear my heartbeat echoing off the rock walls as I looked down and saw a print in the dirt—a hellhound's paw print.

I put my back to the canyon wall, materialized my scythe, and inched forward.

I saw Linda Rose first. Her white sundress stood out like a beacon against the rusty rock. She had managed to climb onto a ledge caused by a fracture in the wall. She clung there helplessly, just out of the reach of the hounds circling below her.

My mother was on the ground, a hound poised on top of its prize, the black hair on its back standing on end.

My mother wasn't moving.

My blood boiled so hot I saw the steam rise in front of my eyes.

The adrenaline in my system turned fear into rage. Before I could command my feet to move, I was running toward my mother. The hound lunged toward me and I buried my scythe deep into the soft portion of its underbelly.

The blood looked black in my red-tinted vision, but felt warm and sticky as it splattered across my face.

To my surprise, the dog did not go down. Instead, he used the force of his lunge combined with the powerful swing of the scythe to roll sideways, ripping the scythe from my hands.

With one smooth motion of his powerful jaws, he twisted his neck, latched onto the handle, and pulled the blade from his stomach. He threw the scythe to the side while still in midair and landed on all four paws, perfectly poised for another attack.

He looked at me with eyes that were dangerous—dangerous because he was afraid and hurt. I knew that if he attacked, it would be with the strength of a cornered animal fighting to survive, fighting to live, fighting to kill or be killed.

By the time I registered the shift in his tense muscles, it was already too late. This animal was smart and vicious. He had given me no sign of his calculated plan until it was already put into motion.

I blinked—that must have been what he was waiting for because in that tiny fraction of a second, I found myself hitting the ground as the beast tackled me. Somehow I managed to get my arms under his neck, holding the rows of sharp teeth at bay as they snapped so close to my face that I could smell the putrid, sulfur stench of the animal's breath.

My arms felt like elastic. They flexed up and down as the animal bounced on them. No matter how hard I tensed my muscles and pushed against the weight of the dog, I couldn't hold him far enough away to give me any leverage. I was pinned. The muscle and bone in my arms wouldn't hold against the hound's weight.

Beyond the snapping sound of powerful jaws, I could hear screaming. I hoped the screams were from my mother, because if she was screaming that meant she wasn't dead.

A warm pool of blood from the hound formed

beneath me. I had spent plenty of time on the ground in a cooling pool of blood. I wondered if that would always be the first vision—the first memory of my life flashing before my eyes—every time I was about to die.

It's funny how time slowed down when death was inching close, how fast the mind had to work to keep up. Maybe time was just an illusion and all of it was relative.

The hound's eyes were close enough to my own that we peered into each other's soul. I could feel his burning hatred, his disdain for being here, his pain from the wound in his stomach. I could also feel how alive he was. The wound I inflicted wasn't mortal. Not as long as he could kill me. Not as long as…

I realized the thoughts in my head weren't my own. They were his.

I knew how to kill him.

I watched a thin wisp of smoke rise in slow motion from the pores in my arm just as time rebounded like a slingshot to its normal speed. With a push of outward energy, I unfolded my wings. Each and every one of the feathers solidified into a razor sharp dagger.

I didn't even know I could do that. The hound had shown me. It was what he feared from me.

I folded the wings into myself, and as I did I was bathed in blood. The hound exploded as I tore him into countless pieces.

He registered no pain. He was totally eviscerated before he even knew what hit him.

I sputtered on the wave of blood that washed over my face before the head of the beast landed painfully on my nose and rolled off to the side.

I wiped my face, although the blood only smeared. Then I stood and turned to face the other dog. I spread my wings, letting loose a growl that ripped from the pit of my stomach. It came from that pool of dark energy that had found a home there, a part of me that didn't mind being smeared in blood and enjoyed the terror that my blood-covered face inspired.

The dog turned and moved so fast it disappeared. As it vanished into the canyon it let out a howl that sounded more like a whimper than a war cry.

My mother's face was ashen. When I got to where Linda Rose was kneeling over her, I was relieved to see her chest rise and fall in regular rhythm.

"Was she bitten?" I asked, careful to make my voice calm and even.

Linda Rose glanced up at me, but quickly looked away. "No, I don't think so. She collapsed. The hounds didn't seem interested in killing her. Just me."

I kneeled down to check, but as I reached for her, I realized my hands were caked in crimson.

"You look terrifying! Like something from my nightmares. You should find a place to wash up." Linda Rose's eyes flickered toward me, but still didn't reach my face before they fell away again.

I threw up my hands, motioning emphatically at the

narrow canyon we were in. "I don't think there's water anywhere near us. If I so much as pissed, this place would have a flash flood."

Linda Rose's cheeks flushed the same color as her lips. "How is it that such a young, well-mannered boy such as yourself could be dead for just a few months and in that time lose all sense of class. You made me feel so joyful upon seeing you—after my own death, I might add—but I'm infuriated by your *total* recklessness and lack of *tact*."

She practically spit the last word. Even in anger, I had to admit she maintained her sense of propriety.

"I've been under a bit of pressure," I said, trying to soften my tone, but not succeeding. I heaved my unconscious mother over my shoulder at the same time, illustrating my point. "Did you know I'm now responsible to save everyone who dies?" I asked the question while walking further into the canyon, turning around to let my facial expression be noticed. "Everyone," I emphasized. "It isn't just about my family anymore—"

"Speaking of, do watch her head."

I swerved my mother's limp body around a rock that jutted from the canyon wall.

"It's now about *all* you people. I have to find a way to save the angels who died and fell to Earth. I have to save the humans who have died and should go to heaven but have been snatched away by creatures that were my childhood's equivalent of the bogeyman. I have to figure out a way to free my people from enslavement that's caused by a spell contained in a bag I can't touch. I have to figure out a way to put the walls of the levels back together, and return the centaurs to their world—"

"I'm sorry, do you really mean centaurs?"

"Oh, and let's not forget I have no clue what Joshua is doing, or why my mother brought us to this rock maze that I'm pretty sure was commissioned by David Bowie."

I couldn't help it. I started laughing. It didn't take long before Linda Rose was joining in.

"David Bowie. That was good," she cackled.

I had never felt laughter like this. It came from manic amusement, the dark place my soul had settled, not humor. It felt good to laugh, of course, but it didn't make the tasks seem any lighter. I was laughing because I didn't know what else to do. Right now, the only thing I *could* do was to carry my mother while putting one foot in front of the other.

That was until I turned a corner and was greeted by another dead end.

"End of the road?" Linda Rose asked, a lingering curl touching her lips.

"Looks that way." I checked the dirt path below to see if we had veered off one way or another. "Well," I set my mother down against the rock. The path was so narrow that she didn't even slide down to a seated position before her feet hit the other wall, "I do have wings. Maybe I could fly up and take a look?"

"You can fly?"

I had never actually tried, but what else were wings for? I shrugged.

"Wouldn't you at least need to be able to get them fully extended? I don't think they'd fit in here."

She was right, unfortunately. I couldn't even extend my arms to the sides without touching rock.

"Okay. Right." I scratched my head, but not because of confusion. It actually itched. "We can go back to where the dogs attacked. That space was more open. Unless you think maybe we could climb?"

Linda Rose's sun hat was shadowing her face, but I could still see the glare she gave me.

"We go back then."

Linda Rose started heading back. I collected my mother, whose face was still flushed, her eyelids vibrating like she was dreaming. I was grateful for the jarring movement because it was a powerful sign of life. She wasn't injured, and I could almost convince myself that she was mysteriously sleeping.

I had just flung her over my shoulder when Linda Rose's face appeared inches from my own. I jumped backward. "Geez, warn a guy before you sneak up on him!"

Linda Rose's cheeks looked as rigid as the stone of the canyon walls and her eyes were wide. "I can't explain it, but the way is blocked by another wall of rock."

"What?" I asked, although I already felt claustrophobia setting in.

"We're trapped!"

I set my mother back down and allowed her to slide back down to her slumped position. I headed back the way we came. There was a turn I didn't remember taking when we had come, and then nothing but solid stone.

Linda Rose was right behind me, her arms crossed. "It's cold over here." The skin on her arms pricked with goose bumps.

I touched the wall, feeling a tingle race through me. The feeling settled right on my breastbone.

"Can you feel that?" I asked.

"Feel what?"

"Magic."

Linda Rose shrugged.

"Do you remember the conversation we had in the coffee shop when we first met? You asked me what it was like to *feel* the spoon? Those goose bumps on your arms aren't from feeling cold, they're from feeling magic."

"I did expect to feel connected to this place. But I also expected blue skies and nature speaking to me. I expected the birds to sing songs that I sang with my coven. I expected it to be simpler... more heavenly. I didn't expect to hike through canyons in my favorite pair of Louboutins."

"Next time die in sweat pants and tennis shoes," I smiled. Both my hands were on the wall, trying to sense where the power that was surging through it was coming from. Whoever put this wall here had to be close, had to know we were here, and had to be watching us.

"Orenda isn't exactly what I remember either," I continued. "Things have changed. I know Joshua is to blame for a lot, but my connection to this place? I don't know if he's to blame, or if I am. Was the time where it was natural to have every day of my life full of magic and connection real? Or were my memories of this place partially fueled by childhood fantasy? I really can't say for sure anymore."

"Was the sky always that awful color? It reminds me of a bad glass of Merlot I once had in Italy. It's so ugly I can taste it. Would it be too much to ask for heaven to have blue skies?"

I laughed. "The red sky is new… and it isn't good."

If this wall of rock was listening to someone with power, driven and motivated by magic, then that meant that it could listen to me. I just had to convince it to.

How had I done it before? This whole mountain had listened to me once, when I sent Nicholas, Xia, and myself out of this world and back to Earth. I had been scared then, convinced I would die, and hadn't thought to ask the mountain for help, only thought to send my friends to it… to the place where the silver thread and moonlight became one. There was a powerful place our ancestors considered sacred around here somewhere.

That had to be where my mother wanted us to go. It was the only reason I could think for her to bring us here.

"Where is that place now? How do I get there?" I

whispered. I wasn't asking Linda Rose, or anyone in particular. I was asking the wall.

I knew that the wall was there to protect something. I didn't know if that fact just clicked and made sense in my head, or if the wall had given me the feeling. Either way, I knew we were close.

That meant someone was trying to protect that place; that someone was also nearby.

I felt a stab of fear. Would the energumen know of the ancient ruins my people considered sacred? Would Joshua have sent someone here to watch and make sure no one could get close?

"Who is it?" I whispered again.

I shuddered as a memory washed over me. It felt like the canyon was alive around me, glistening in the pale red light. I couldn't tell if there was a wind in the canyon or if it was just my memory. My nostrils flooded with the scent of spring grass as my childhood words fluttered back to me in the air. *Ask them to grow*, I had said. *Ask them all to grow.* Then, for Hailey and Ralph I hastily added, *I will meet you at the ruins.*

Breath caught in my throat as I realized the color of this rock wall in the pale red light looked exactly like the color of fire… the color of my best friend's hair.

Now I knew who was following us. I knew who was changing the canyon walls, who was protecting the sacred space, and who would want to make three strangers feel trapped.

"Ralph," I whispered as my gaze traveled upward. At the top of the cliff I saw a mop of flaming hair that burned in the evening light. Two icy eyes glared down at me.

NINE

For the first time in months I was sleeping deeply, dreamless and submerged in darkness. At least there were no images of Xia being murdered, or sex-crazed electric skin. There were no yellow eyes chasing me around in the utter blackness of oblivion either. I was just floating among the whispers of the trees. It didn't matter what they were saying, it was all just static anyway, like the sound when the wind blows through quaking aspens.

I was content on the verge of utter obscurity, but the problem with realizing where you are when you're supposed to be obscure is that all the worries of real life start to flood in, pulling you back to reality. Worries are like winches, like the ones on the front of those tough looking Jeeps, strong enough to lift the entire vehicle up a mountain.

What if the Jeep doesn't *want* to go that way? What if I didn't want my worries to wake me up?

It was no use. I was winched awake. And now I really wanted a Jeep.

I opened my eyes just as Ralph pushed the door open to the bedroom. From the flickering light that spilled in from behind him, I could tell it was still very early. The sun wasn't even breaking over the mountains yet.

"Hey," he whispered. His voice was rough. "She's awake, but we don't know for how long. You'll want to come see her."

I didn't hesitate. I swung myself out of the bed and padded toward the door.

I wish I could say my reunion with Ralph was everything I'd hoped for, that we were able to pick right back up where we were when I had left Hailey and Ralph on that hillside when we were ten, but we were no longer kids. Technically, I was now ten years younger than him since I had died and started over again on Earth.

It was all very confusing, and I doubted he trusted me, even if he believed I was who I said I was.

Hailey was tending to my mother in the kitchen. They had turned the handcrafted dining room table into a temporary hospital bed because it was close to the kitchen fireplace—the warmest place in the house.

"We think someone messed with your hex bag," I heard Hailey whisper to my mother, whose eyes looked back at Hailey. I couldn't tell if she comprehended the conversation.

Ralph slipped his arm around Hailey's waistline and

pressed his lips to the side of her head. "You should get some sleep. The sun will be up soon. I know you don't sleep well when it gets bright outside."

Hailey nodded in agreement and shifted her body so that she could catch his lips with her own. As she stepped past him she froze and met my eyes.

"I always wondered what it was your family did that was so important it had to be hidden from the rest of us. I suppose knowing the location of a crossroads would be dangerous even by today's standards. Still, it suits you. Angel of Death," her lips curled.

I didn't know how to respond. The mage society had been reduced to the point where only dozens were free. Hailey and Ralph had managed to make it to the ruins where the few who escaped banded together and formed a small village. Hailey was appointed healer because of her exceptional mind and knowledge of science. Ralph protected the village because, as it turned out, Joshua was in his family line and Ralph's family had always been privy to the secrets of the Level of the Spirit. Who could make a better protector from an onslaught of energumen than a member of the family that was tasked with their control to begin with?

I had always known Ralph had a gift for knowing when someone was possessed. Now I knew why.

As it turned out, my whole childhood in Orenda was filled with secrets. Every interaction seemed so normal, our society so communal, but deep down, everyone hid what they truly did. Everyone lied about their jobs, and we were divided more by bloodline than I had realized. Somehow it had worked. That was just how we had functioned.

Maybe that was why Ralph wouldn't look at me right now. I had broken the code and told him exactly who, or what, I was. He made it apparent very quickly that revealing that I knew the location of a crossroads (even though technically I didn't) was something I should never speak of again except to my children who would need to be taught to take my place.

That was the only conversation we had had.

Now he stood with his back to me, his red hair illuminated by the firelight. He clutched my mother's hand, but wasn't looking at anything other than the wall as far as I could tell.

I approached from the other side of the table.

My mom's head rolled toward me and she smiled. "There's my son," she said. "You have the ring and the book. He'd be so proud."

I could only assume she was talking about my father.

"It works through death. The darkness. The trees. The plantings. He has the trees now doesn't he?"

I wasn't exactly sure whom she was talking about, but she wasn't strong enough to answer questions, and I couldn't bring myself to show any confusion. "Yes, he has them."

"They don't belong to him. They belong to us. They

belong to our family. That's how it's supposed to work. That's why he changed his mind."

"The trees belong to us?"

"No, no. Not the trees. *All* of them belong to us. Not to *them*. Not like that."

It was too early and the sentences too incoherent to make any sense of what she was saying. Finally I looked up at Ralph, who still wasn't looking at me.

"Do you have any idea what she's talking about?"

"She's been mumbling about *trees* and *gardens* and *them* and *us*, but I don't know. Hopefully when the fever breaks she'll be more understandable. Would you stay up with her? There's a sponge here to keep her lips moist, and some broth by the fire if you can get her to eat anything. Hailey will just need a couple of hours. The children will be up with the sun anyway."

"Of course. Get some sleep."

He hesitated for a moment. The discomfort in his shoulders made it obvious he was debating whether to turn away from me so he wouldn't have to look at me, or to turn toward me and risk having to acknowledge I was there. Turning the long way would have been painfully obvious, so he turned toward me.

I didn't give him the satisfaction of averting my eyes. I locked them right onto his.

I read so much on his face. The spark in his eye rekindled the emotions we had together as children—the fun, the hope, the anticipation for our next big adventure—but responsibility and loneliness had squared his jaw, and the dimples on his cheeks were almost faded from lack of smiling. Each muscle placed his facial expression into a carefully constructed mask. It was obvious that their relaxed state habitually formed a stern scowl.

The playfulness was gone.

I raised my eyebrows at him—an invitation for him to sit and talk, to get to know me again, or to stare into my own face until he understood all the things I had been through. Beneath that controlled expression I saw a flicker of curiosity before he finished turning and stomped off to bed.

"Looks like it's just you and me," I said to my mother, whose eyes were open and staring at me, a giant smile plastered on her lips. In the dark, the expression was frightening.

She didn't respond.

I hoped that it wouldn't be long for Ralph to speak to me again, to sit down and really speak to me. His curiosity would get the better of him, and he certainly wouldn't let Hailey and I have that adventurous conversation without him. That was against his very nature, and I knew his nature. After all, he was still Ralph, and I knew him. Didn't I?

* * *

The next time I opened my eyes, my forehead hurt from having slept so long on the table. There was a puddle of drool between my feet. My mother's breathing was deep but regular. She looked comfortable and peaceful. Even a little color had crept back into her cheeks.

A boy with wide-eyes, no older than four, woke me by setting a cup of steaming liquid next to my head. His complexion was like his father's, but Hailey's darker hair tempered his. The result was a cherry-wood colored mop that fell carelessly over, but couldn't hide, his icy blue eyes.

When the steam hit my nostrils, I was taken back. My childhood in Orenda sprang into my mind with vibrant definition. This was the tea I wished for when I could get neither it, nor coffee. This was the tea my mom used to make in the mornings. I had names for some of the spices now—nutmeg and cinnamon—but the leaf that was used in the brew had a citrus taste that defied explanation.

"Thank you," I said sincerely, taking the cup and pressing my lips to the rim.

"The chickens weren't willing to let any of their eggs be eaten today," the boy said, so articulately that I couldn't hide my surprise. The sentence also illustrated how the Orendan people thought, in contrast to the humans. "Ms. Beth usually prepares some sweet bread for breakfast at the pavilion."

I couldn't help but smile, "Is it any good?"

I thought I was being funny, but the boy was taken aback, "I wouldn't have told you about it if it weren't any good." He gave me an expression of, *What do you take me for, an idiot?* and took a step back as his father walked into the room.

At least Ralph looked at me this morning.

"Good morning, David. Thanks for making the wake-up-tea."

Wake-up-tea? The cadence with which it was said was familiar, like when you say the same phrase over and over again and it becomes almost one word that takes on its own meaning, like 'Cup-of-Joe.' It was exactly how my parents used to say it. I needed to hear it *said* like that to remember what it was called.

Ralph continued, "Your sister started in the gardens a half-hour ago. You're supposed to spend time with the horses in the fields today too."

David sulked out the back door of the small stone house, bursting into a run as soon as he thought he was out of sight, but Ralph called after him, "And stop harassing the chickens in the morning. They'll never want to give up their eggs. You know we only eat them on special occasions."

David took a moment to turn around and argue, "Oh, Dad. They're not even fertilized yet! I think every day should be a special occasion if they're just going to go to waste!"

Hailey appeared in the kitchen doorway, looking amused. When Ralph noticed, he threw his hands into the air and scoffed. "He's your son."

"He's exceptionally smart," I said while Hailey poured herself a cup of tea.

She took a sip and looked after him from the window. "Actually, he's behind in his studies."

"Behind? The kid talks like he's a college graduate," I said, surprised.

Hailey faced me and leaned back against the sink. She shook her head with a wry smile on her face. "How long did you live as a human, Edmund?"

The question seemed out of place, but I answered anyway. "I was 21 when I died."

"So you went through human schooling?"

"I was in my junior year of college..." I didn't finish my thought because I wasn't sure whether to say 'when I died,' or 'when I was brutally murdered by Joshua... again.'

"What do you remember of your education here? Before..." Now she trailed off, I'm guessing for the same reason.

"Not much, really," I said honestly. "I remember playing with all of the kids together. I mean, the Elders were there, and there were some lectures. Mostly, I think we had a lot of time with each other."

"That's how it works here," Ralph jumped in. "We don't teach in classrooms or lecture halls. There aren't predefined lessons or facts or data we teach our children. We teach them to develop their connection to the world around them. The world becomes the teacher."

"Like when they used to send us to gather food," Hailey interjected. "We were a gathering society. The best way to learn to gather was to go out and do it, not to be taught in a classroom where the blackberries grew, or the best place to find mushrooms. We learned by experience."

"And you," Ralph said, looking at me so sternly that his conviction made it impossible to look away. "The trees taught you. You were *their* student. You always had a connection with them. With all forms of physical bodies, actually."

"The spirits taught Ralph," Hailey said. "That was his gift."

"But you," I finally spoke to Hailey, because what she said reminded me of what she was like as a child. "You were always drawn to physical sciences, math, and chemistry."

"Which I learned by studying geometry in nature, Edmund. I didn't learn chemistry in a classroom. I learned it by studying the world."

"Oh, be honest. You learned geometry hustling humans playing pool," Ralph laughed.

Hailey blushed. "It's still real world experience!"

Ralph grinned. For the first time since our reunion, his shoulders relaxed.

"We were ten, Edmund. Ten," Hailey continued. "We took a horse and a cart overnight. We had a responsibility to the town. We were already educated enough to navigate, to problem-solve, to care for each other and the horse.

Tell me if a human classroom compared."

"I suppose children who grow up in rural areas or on farms are used to that sort of responsibility, but you're right. Humans value the innocence of childhood. 'Growing up too fast' is not a good thing there. It usually means your childhood had difficulties. I don't remember my childhood here very well. Only that last day. Before that, I only remember fragments. And I didn't remember any of my childhood as a human. Once I put the ring back on, it was like I'd died the day before. The twelve years I had been on Earth prior to that were completely erased. It wasn't until after I died again and came back here that I remembered even fragments of those twelve years. Even now it all feels like bad dream."

Ralph read my face, his shoulders tensed to his ears while I still formed the question I wanted to ask, the question he knew was coming.

"How many survived?" I asked.

"Well, I'll show you." By the way his gaze fell from mine and didn't meet my eyes again, I knew the number was low. He turned toward the door and motioned for me to follow.

"I'd like to let Linda Rose know that I'm going out with you. I don't want her to wake up and be alone."

"She's already out in the meadow," Hailey said, following Ralph out.

I glanced at my mother, who was still sound asleep, and had a second thought about leaving her here alone.

But the pull of reuniting with my family, my whole magical family, was too great. I had been waiting for this moment, to be among my people, living as they once did. Living free.

TEN

The sun kissed the spot where the blood red sky met the majestic peaks of the ancestral mountain range. The light spilled down the jagged walls of rock into a small valley that was made up of one grassy meadow split in two by a wide river. My eyes scanned the wildflower-covered bank back toward a small patch of trees, and further to where the water tumbled down the rock in an impressive waterfall. The hiss of the cascading water almost made up for the silence of the air by filling the light breeze with white noise. The air tasted of morning dew. Although the valley was small, it felt more like home than the town where the men had taken over.

There were only six visible structures laid out in a half-circle against the mountain. Most looked like small dwellings, either built from natural woods or, more commonly, hollowed out of the rock with a front façade constructed of river stones. In the center of the circle was a covered pavilion attached to an enclosed room with a spire. On Earth, I would have recognized it as a church of some kind, but remembering the culture I was in, I realized it was a new parliament building—the towers reminded our government to always look upward when making decisions. Not to God, but to the higher purpose, the higher road, the kinder goal.

Ralph led me to that building now.

Inside there were ten benches, five on each side split by a central aisle. The duality in this new village struck me as a feature that wouldn't have been tolerated in Orenda—the meadow split in two by the river, the benches split in two by an aisle. The implications of being divided caused me some anxiety. I shook it out of my mind. I was being overly observant and judgmental.

Hailey took a seat on one of the back rows. I followed her while Ralph walked up to the front.

A quick head count revealed twenty-three people in the building, including myself. I didn't recognize anyone immediately, but I was staring mostly at the backs of their heads, so I couldn't be sure.

"Thank you all for coming this morning," Ralph said. There was an altar up front with an elevated seat, most likely reserved for the patriarch. Ralph headed toward it at first, but then opted to pull a wooden chair away from the wall. He sat at the front of the aisle on our level. "I trust the children are out taking care of the physical needs of the village, and have been instructed to leave us to attend to our business for a bit of time today?"

A few heads nodded.

"The news that I need to bring to everyone's attention today concerns Mary Gavel."

I heard a rumble in the crowd. Hailey took my hand.

"Our houses have been incomplete, without a representative with knowledge of the Level of the Body. She, above all others—"

Ralph purposely buried his gaze in the crowd so he could avoid mine… again.

"—has the knowledge to help us piece back together our heritage. Maybe, with her help, we could figure out how to bring those who have fallen back."

The murmur turned to excited chatter.

"How was she found?" I heard a young man ask.

"That's what I wanted to talk about. Hailey is an accomplished healer and has been taking care of our medical needs with precision. Unfortunately, Mary's spell satchel is still intact, although recently meddled with."

"We've been through this before," the young man spoke again. He stood now, all eyes trained on him. "No one survives."

"I don't need to tell you how important it is to save Mary. To have someone of her age and experience, with her specific knowledge, would make all of us feel safer. I'm hoping we will pull together and give our focus to Mary so that there might be a different outcome. I'm hopeful that this time will be different. The satchel already had the rosemary removed. We've had her sedated and sleeping until now. If we work together, our power might be enough…"

This was the first time I heard that Ralph and Hailey sedated my mother. I thought she was drifting in and out of consciousness on her own. I didn't like that they had kept this bit of information from me. Or maybe Ralph was trying to cover for her condition, making it seem that it wasn't as bad as it was? I couldn't be sure.

"Who removed the rosemary?" the man asked, accusingly.

"Someone who recently crossed over," Ralph answered. I felt a bit of tension leave my body. Linda Rose had removed the rosemary. Maybe there was hope that we could dismantle the spell and save not only my mother, but also all the enslaved mages.

"A human?"

My mouth pursed and I was about to answer when Ralph's gaze burrowed deep into mine. It was so unexpected and forceful that my voice caught in my throat. I almost missed how hard Hailey was suddenly squeezing my hand.

"No," Ralph's voice boomed.

I wasn't sure what he meant. Was he saying 'no' to me? Like 'no, don't talk?' What did he mean 'no?' Of course a human had done it. Linda Rose untied the bag and took out the rosemary. My mother said only a human could. Otherwise…

"That person is out in the meadow now. She doesn't remember, but she's my aunt."

I heard an uproar from the crowd, but it was all background noise to the revelation that was forming in my head. Occasionally, one of the raised voices would break into my thoughts but I was so frozen that my hearing was selective.

"She's as good as dead," someone said.

"No one's ever survived." That one felt like a punch in the gut.

"We should trade her to Joshua for information."

That one had me on my feet. My father's cloak didn't just appear around me, it erupted and filled the entire room with black smoke. As it did, all sound was pulled from the air. All voices were silenced.

Either that, or everyone was stunned.

As the smoke returned to me, swirling around my body, all eyes fixed on me. Faces that I didn't recognize drained of color, some with mouths that hung agape out of fear or awe. I wasn't sure which.

"On a lighter note," I heard Ralph say sarcastically, "Mary's son, Edmund, has also returned. He rescued my aunt from the energumen."

I spent the rest of the morning explaining how the Angel of Death was the duty and domain of my family. The knowledge that it was the Gavel family's responsibility to bring the dead to Orenda was known by the mages, but the details on how that was done had never been discussed. It seemed like the secrets from the various levels, while being shared among the group of survivors more openly, were still not being fully explained. I kept my eye on Ralph, whose expression helped guide me as to which parts I should keep quiet. Like the crossroads. I knew that was off-limits. Ralph had already told me I shouldn't repeat anything about that.

I learned about Ralph's family and more about his relation to Joshua, which made sense because he knew the secrets of that level. I learned that Samuel, the Elder who was still in Orenda, was considered the proper Elder over the Level of the Soul, but that his knowledge of the Death of the Soul gave him access to the Level of the Mind. He had sixteen grandchildren who escaped Joshua's attack, while people with knowledge of the Level of the Spirit made up the other seven.

My heart dropped into my stomach when I realized that all the living mages were sitting in this room, and all of them had been either children younger than I was or teenagers at the time of the attack. I knew none of them by name.

I recognized the names of some of their parents, or aunts, uncles, and cousins. They were teachers, family friends, and Elders. Growing up, I knew of seven Elders, one for each of the seven levels of existence, but this was the first time I was hearing about which death each Elder knew about, and what knowledge each one maintained.

I wanted to know what the seven levels were, because

I could only remember four: the Level of the Spirit, the Level of the Body, the Level of the Soul, and the Level of the Mind. I knew that there were three deaths: the Death of the Body, the Death of the Spirit, and the Death of the Soul. I didn't know how they related to the levels, or why the remaining levels didn't each have their own death. This was the first time I had been somewhere it was being discussed openly.

In my time, it was all a secret.

My questions were dodged, but I was able to piece together that all seven levels were accessible through three houses: the body, the spirit, and the soul. Orenda was a soul level, but there was crossover with the Level of the Body. All levels above the Level of the Body *had* bodies.

There were crossovers, from what I could tell, from every level into the level above and below it.

But, it all gave me a headache. The levels weren't linear. A spirit, for example, contained a soul even though the Level of the Spirit was below the Level of the Body and the Level of the Soul was above the Level of the Body. So how did a spirit have a soul but no body? I wasn't sure how much of the truth about things like my father's book, ring, and role of The Reaper to divulge, or how much I could offer the conversation when I couldn't even answer why a spirit didn't have a body if it had a soul. Ralph still looked at me like I couldn't be trusted.

There was also a consensus that no one actually knew what the Death of the Soul required. According to them, no one had experienced it before or after Joshua.

It was almost as if *my* people had died with Joshua's plan. Of the twenty-three people in the room, Ralph and Hailey were the only two I would even consider trusting. At this point, I wasn't even sure I could do that.

When someone asked me about the ruby ring that pulsed cool in the air, a pulse that could be felt by others in the room, I simply responded, "It's a family heirloom. It belonged to my father."

"Your father, the Elder who had a secret job to help the dead cross from the Level of the Body to Orenda?"

Maybe I had already said too much.

"Have they not had any humans come to Orenda since he was killed?" the same man who had spoken earlier asked. I didn't like him. He seemed to want all of the knowledge for himself. He wanted to lead, but his style of leadership was oppressive. He reminded me of Joshua.

"I don't know," I answered shortly. "I wasn't there."

"How did you maintain your memory? We know from our knowledge of the spirit realm, from the boastings of the energumen, that the fallen of our race don't remember who they are."

The man's blond hair and brown eyes made the confused look on his face appear even more out of place. I couldn't figure out which 'house' he belonged to or to whom he was related.

So I lied. "I don't know. I could make up an answer if you would prefer."

The man scoffed. "Don't think you're better than we are just because you lived life as a human and managed to make it back. Joshua killed a lot of people. No one here likes him. The fact that he killed you doesn't make you special."

"You're right," I said, making my voice as even as possible, "but the fact that I made it back here *does*."

The man's eyes narrowed. "I hope you're right. I guess we'll see. I hope having you here will help us fill in the gaps and make it possible to restore our people, but I doubt it. It makes me feel suspicious of you, more than anything. You know why? Because you didn't restore Ralph's aunt's memories, and you haven't yet saved your mother."

I wanted to lash out. Everyone expected me to. The tension in the air wasn't just between this man and me. It was so that I could almost see it like an oppressive cloud in the room.

I didn't want to be here. I expected my reunion with the mages, the angels, to be one of great joy and peace. I expected us to bond over our common trials and stand united as a powerful army—an army of biblical proportions.

But everyone here was broken, just like me. Everyone was too busy pointing fingers and identifying what they lacked to make any sort of progress.

I didn't know the real reason why the trees had stopped talking, but at this point, if I had to venture a guess, it would be because they didn't want to talk to us anymore.

I didn't either. There was no point in being where I didn't want to be, so I left the big black cloud of oppression and fear by making my way to the door. I stepped into the sunlight. No one stopped me from leaving.

As I walked toward the house, I noticed children through the window. My mother had been propped up and the children were spoon-feeding her gently. Her eyes were sunken, but she ate eagerly. That was a good sign.

I didn't want to deal with any of that, didn't want to see her or talk to her or get strange looks from the kids. Even if they weren't rude or accusing looks, they would be awkward, questioning ones. I didn't want to interrupt her eating, or risk the possibility that my presence would change her mood, make her worse, or cause her to expend energy she didn't have.

I walked past the house, past the meadows, past the shadows of the mountains that were cast by the afternoon sun, and into the open field. I kept walking until I ran into the bank of the river. Hesitating for a moment on the bank, I watched the deep water bubble. I thought about wading through the water and continuing my trek until I couldn't go any further. Should I be determined and stay my course, or turn up the bank, and walk against the direction of the river's current? The question dealt with much more than crossing a river.

Maybe it dealt with where I was psychologically. The direction I would go was the most important decision I could make. Right now it was a decision about where I would walk with the river, but I knew there was a deeper direction I had to choose as well.

I was done fighting. The river flowed. It wouldn't be stopped, changed, or forced to reverse direction. Why was I trying to steer the river?

Turning, I went with the flow.

After a half-hour, I happened upon a large sun hat, a flowered dress, and stiletto pumps sitting on the bank of the river. The way they were carelessly flung about caused my stomach to clench with a stab of concern. Linda Rose was meticulous. If she had taken them off, they would've been folded in a neat pile, tucked away under some bush.

"Edmund, you really *must* learn how to relax. Even with everything you have going on, you can't miss out on life—or is it death? Life after death? Yes, I think I'll go with that one. You want more time to get things done? If you take your time, you'll have more of it."

The voice was behind me and… above me? Spinning and cocking my head toward the voice, I burst into laughter.

Linda Rose lay on a smooth tree branch suspended over the river. She was lying exactly like those nature shots of a puma in a tree, complete with her arms and legs dangling over the water. Stark naked.

At first I didn't see her because, although her white

skin contrasted with the branch, looking at her against the bright sky made her almost disappear. She looked at me with childlike excitement, then rolled off the branch and crashed into the water below, laughing.

Paddling over to the bank where I was standing, she stopped just short of getting out. "You know, one of my favorite things, the part of your story I made Nicholas tell me over and over again, was the brilliant connection you once had with nature here. I only wish I could have heard the story in your words. Nicholas pays astounding attention to detail, but I don't think he knew how to capture the connectedness, the oneness of everything you felt as a child."

I crossed my arms. I didn't mean to feel defensive, but I did.

"I could not *wait* to experience that for myself. So here I am." She raised her eyebrow in that way that made her face look asymmetrical and off-putting, but the expression was also playful. "Throwing all propriety back to whatever damn human decided to be proper, and reconnecting with myself."

"Sometimes that's the only way to get the answers you seek," I repeated, the words coming back to me as an echo from my earlier teachings.

Linda Rose paused before looking at me, as though she were forming her words carefully. "Then why haven't I seen you spend any time with yourself, with nature and the natural parts of you that were once all part of the *same* you?

Have you forgotten? Are you... too human?"

If my arms weren't already folded, I would have folded them. How was it that I was standing in front of a naked woman, yet *I* was the one who was uncomfortable?

It was because she was right. When I was a child here in Orenda, if I would have been as hot and sweaty as I was now from the sun and the walking, I would have stripped off my shirt and pressed my bare back against the base of a cool tree. I would have lain in the grass and let the wind caress my body. I would have taken a nap on that same branch that Linda Rose had been on. When Hailey and Ralph decided to wake me up, they would have pushed me into the river. I wouldn't have cared. I wouldn't have been mad. I would have *experienced* it all.

I couldn't get my shirt off fast enough. Linda Rose was right. I had to get out of my favorite red Converse shoes and feel the mud at the bottom of the river squish between my toes. I had to float and feel the water on my back and the sun on my stomach. It was time to let go of everything that held me back. At this moment, that meant letting go of my socks, my pants, all of it!

Jumping into the river, the shock of the cold water raced up my spine and left a wave of goose bumps on my skin. The mud at the bottom was exactly as I knew it would be—warm, therapeutic, full of life. In the cool water and the warm mud it was easy to open the connection I had with the planet. All my frustrations, responsibilities, fears, and pain drained into the river. Just like she had always done, Mother Earth swept them away.

Linda Rose and I didn't speak for the rest of the afternoon. We let ourselves float, experiencing the river. We didn't fight the currents or steer where they would take us. We didn't care about where we had left our clothes or worry about how long it would take us to get back. We floated in silence, sharing each other's energy, and listening as the wind and water whispered to us.

'Go float in the river for a few hours,' would have ben something my mother would have told me to do when I was younger and felt disconnected or frustrated. Not because she would have been tired of me and wanted me out of the house, but because of the lesson I would have learned.

I didn't know how I had forgotten something so simple, so necessary, so angelic.

I felt a universal current pulling me from the river just as the sun set. The hush of twilight was blanketing a small thicket of trees we had floated into. The trees grew around a large rock, and I ached to feel the roughness of the rock on my skin.

Linda Rose was right behind me as we heaved ourselves onto the rock. It had two perfectly formed divots that were tailor-made for us to sit in. Our legs dangled off the edge a few feet above the damp soil beneath us. The color of that soil was so vibrant that I could see the shades of orange and blue that combined to create the fertile brown. Even though the light was fading, the entire world awakened. The green tree leaves glowed, and numerous fireflies twinkled so often that I felt I was in a magical place drawn up in the imagination of a surrealist artist.

On that thought, I paused. This was Orenda. It *was* a magical place. It *was* surreal.

Folding my legs and sitting cross-legged, I stole a glance at Linda Rose. Her skin was radiant. It caught the light from the rising moon and fluoresced. Seeing her like this would convince any man the moon was shining only for her.

Linda Rose caught my eyes and pursed her lips. "How are you now, my child?"

"Much better, thank you."

"I think this is how I would like to spend all of my days here, don't you think?" she sighed.

I didn't know how to respond. Yes, spending my days like this would be wonderful and relaxing. But no, I wouldn't want to only experience wonder and relaxation. There were many other emotions to feel, emotions that I felt reconnected to. While this was wonderful and relaxing, it would eventually get lonely.

Linda Rose still looked at me. Her eyebrow twitched in anticipation of an answer I wasn't going to give. When the moment grew beyond the reasonable time for an answer, she added, "Well. What else would I do? I always expected heaven would be filled with family and friends—not that you aren't a friend, or family, mind you—but it's emptier than I expected. I think I have more questions than answers as well. Shouldn't there be a big billboard somewhere titled 'Life's Top Ten Questions Revealed'?"

I laughed. "You didn't get the orientation?"

Now she laughed, the grin on her face beautiful.

"I suppose," I continued, "that they didn't expect you'd need one, since you've been here before."

"Ah, yes. Ralph's aunt, I've been told," she said.

"You knew?"

"They told me this morning. I'm not sure it matters or that it means anything anymore. Do you think I'll stop feeling human some day, and start feeling like an angel?"

I couldn't wipe the grin off my face. "I think, one day, you'll realize you are both."

"What do you think it means for your mother, that I'm not human and untied her spell bag?"

"Well, you said yourself that you feel human. That must count for something. I saw her this afternoon. She was awake and eating. I think she's on the mend."

I wasn't sure if it was the tone of my voice, or whether Linda Rose heard what the mages said earlier today: that no one ever survived. She looked at me in a way I'd never been looked at before. She pitied me.

"What if she doesn't recover? Will you forever blame me for that?"

"No. How could I? You didn't know," I said, shocked and alarmed. This was a jarring conversation after spending the day releasing emotion. Now I was suddenly attacked by it.

The look on her face remained unchanged as she reached out and cupped my cheek. Her skin was warm, the touch tender. She kissed my forehead, before turning away and saying, "I did know."

There was a new emotion—one I *had* felt before, but I couldn't isolate it among the flood of gentleness, pity, guilt, fear, love, anger, and now… confusion. "What?" The question was both for her, and for me. What was I feeling?

Linda Rose looked down at her French-tipped toes and flexed them. I could tell by the sharp look in her eye that she was not going to dodge the question. Instead, she was buying time as she put together the best—gentlest—way to say what she needed to say. I wasn't going to like this.

"When I was younger, an inexperienced witch, married to Nicholas's adopted father," she began, "we practiced some dark forms of magic."

She pushed a blond strand of hair out of her eyes and tucked it behind her ear as she stared at me. Her eyes pleaded with me to understand. Her whole face begged me for forgiveness for something that I didn't even know I needed to forgive her for.

"I am intimately familiar with demonic spirits, Edmund. After you were gone—"

"Please tell me you haven't been conjuring demons. Please tell me you didn't get Xia involved in conjuring demons."

"They know things, Edmund. They know many secrets of their world. They know your story. They know what happened to you after you died. They know about Joshua—they love him even…"

She was talking too fast now. I had interrupted her perfectly planned thought process, and now she was dodging my question by rambling. "They also know how to lie," I said.

"Not to me!" Her voice was hard. She was…*defensive.* "I know about the three deaths. They told me who you are. How do you think I knew about Xia's dreams, and that you were the Angel of Death? How do you think I learned about the power of your scythe? I planned my death to get your father's ring back to you, after knowing all the details to make sure I would be able to get to Orenda, with you, to you. All of that information came from them."

"And what did you trade for that information? What did they make you give them? More children? Xia's children? Nicholas's?"

I don't know whether I meant the words to hurt, but I was hurt. I was hurt because Linda Rose had been talking to my enemies, but also because she had involved Xia. *Xia*!

And I wasn't there to protect her.

That thought turned my pain into anger, but what could I say? It was already done. "I don't appreciate you putting them in danger. Either of them. Nicholas may be your son, but he is my friend and I feel responsible for him."

"The price was mine to pay, not theirs."

"What did you pay?"

"My life. The demon I worked with, the one I had the closest relationship with? She killed me."

"But she didn't get to claim your spirit at the crossroads," I said. "How is your death a prize without your spirit?"

"Oh, I imagine they will come for me."

"Either that or they'll take it out on the people you love."

Linda Rose wasn't looking at me anymore. She knew I was right, although we both hoped I wasn't. Finally, after flexing her toes again four or five times she said, "I know what your next step is. I know how one dies spiritually."

"How?"

"It's possible for a human to become a devil. Did you know that? Think of someone you know, someone whose eyes are vacant, who is nothing but a shell, who walks around as a human but whose body is ripe for possession."

"I don't know anyone like that."

"Don't you?"

I remembered Henric's eyes, dark and hollow on the day Joshua possessed him. It was a murderous, empty look. I realized that while his eyes weren't always black, even before the possession, they were often empty. Vacant.

I also remembered Joshua's eyes. They were sharp, quick, powerful, and calculating when he murdered me. I couldn't forget the sneer on his face or the gleam in his eyes when he knew he had the upper hand. As quick and sharp as they were, there was also something missing in them. They were soulless.

"Murder," I said in barely a whisper. "Murder is how one kills their spirit."

"What happens to the spirit that dies?" Linda Rose prodded.

"It is reborn, of course. As an energumen."

"That's how Joshua gained power over the spirit level. He became one of them." Linda Rose looked at me with a pained expression. Her watery eyes gleamed in the moonlight. "It is the only way to learn their secrets. The demon that told me this knew of no other way."

"There's always another way. Now that I am back here, with my people, maybe I won't need to experience this death."

"Have you ever read *The Art of War* by Sun Tzu?"

"Can't say I have."

"There is a quote often misattributed to him, mistranslated, for sure, but I believe in its truth. 'To know your enemy you must become your enemy.' "

What she said made sense. The second death required murder. The second death required letting a part of you die that couldn't be resurrected. The second death was a cycle itself. If I was going to have any chance to follow in

Joshua's footsteps, to gain the power he already had, to complete my father's work and save my family, my friends, my people, and my world, I was going to have to become one of *them*. I was going to have to kill someone.

If Linda Rose knew she wasn't human and heard my mother say that a mage untying her satchel would result in death, why would she have done it?

Unless Linda Rose was setting up my mother to die. Unless she was setting her up to be the person I would kill.

ELEVEN

I woke up to my own blood-curdling scream. In my dream, I was back in my tiny apartment in Orenda. My mom had woken me with a fresh pair of sheets clutched in her arms and her customary greeting: 'You were thrashing again.'

The greeting had come to symbolize that I was really awake, that the shadows in the corners of the room and the electric current running over the surface of my skin were real, but that the nightmares were not. When I bumped into Xia's warm body in the bed with me, my heart skipped a beat. How had she gotten here? Was she dead? I rolled her over and peered into her beautiful face. She looked peaceful, her eyes closed like she was sleeping, a rosy cheek accented by the blue moonlight cascading over her.

She drew in a painful breath as her eyes snapped open.

"You did it!" my mother laughed as Xia's hot, sticky blood poured out around the protruding handle of the knife lodged in her stomach.

In the deep pools of her eyes I could see my own, glowing yellow.

I shot out of bed and surveyed the darkness around me as I gulped in deep, cooling breaths. I tried to decipher whether I was really awake now, or whether I was still in a dream. The sweat on my forehead tickled as it ran into my eyes, blurring my vision, making it easier to convince myself that the movement in the darkness around me was real.

The moonlight streaming through the window was pink—the color of the sky diluted by the blackness of night and then lit again by the moon, like a flashlight through a glass of diluted wine.

My skin crackled, but as soon as my feet hit the dirt floor beneath me I felt an instant connection to the planet. Waves of calming energy wafted over me.

My float in the river with Linda Rose helped with my connection to nature. At the thought of her name, I felt a quick stab of anger, which then was robbed of intensity by the waves of comfort and peace emanating from the planet. I allowed the cool ground to take all my negative emotions. I was tired of feeling angry and afraid.

After a few minutes, I pulled on a pair of shorts and made my way out into the main living area. The night air was cold. I found my mother propped up in a large wing-backed chair close to the fire. At first I thought she was asleep, but as I sat in the chair next to her, she turned toward me.

"You were trashing again," she said dryly. By the heaviness of her voice I knew, this time, I was awake.

"Sorry for all the sets of sheets I've destroyed over the last few months," I forced a smile, half apologetic, although I wasn't taking responsibility.

"How often are you able to sleep through the night, comfortable and dreamless?"

"Not very often," I admitted.

"I'm sorry," she sighed. The apology felt bigger than sympathy.

"None of this is your fault."

"Hmmm…" she cooed, letting her eyelids drop for a few seconds. They looked heavy.

I was used to seeing the firelight dance on her face. Under the orange glow she looked healthy and vibrant, although the fire accented the shadows beneath her sunken eyes.

"Linda Rose came to see me a few hours ago, while you were sleeping."

A twinge of guilt pricked me. When I returned to the house my mother was asleep again, and I didn't feel it fair to wake her. I hadn't taken an opportunity to speak to her at all since she fell ill.

"I'm going to die. You're preparing for that, I hope," she said, her eyes still closed.

"I'm not going to let that happen. I was talking with the rest of the mages today in a town council meeting. They're certain that with us here, we can find a way to break the spell. We have the power of all three houses now, someone who knows the secrets of each of the deaths. They said that together, we'll find a way."

My mother opened her eyes and looked at me. "The houses?"

"Yes. The House of the Body, the House of the Spirit, and the House of the Soul. With all three houses united, they said every spell could be undone." Okay, maybe I was exaggerating a little about what they'd said, but she didn't need to know that.

My mother shook her head, calling out my lie. "There is no way, Edmund. Linda Rose is not human."

"I'll find a way. We have to keep you safe and alive for the time being. Until I find a way, I'm sure we can keep you alive."

"Do you know how happy I was when I found out you that were my son again?" my mother asked, changing the subject abruptly. Her eyes glimmered in the light, which made them appear less sunken. "Do you know what it's like to feel the memories return?"

Actually I did—although 'return' wasn't the word I would have used to describe the experience of having my father's ring slam memories back into my head. Had that been why my mother was sleeping so much? She was recovering from remembering? My head hurt just thinking about it.

"I remember the first time I held you. I remember watching you play with your friends. I remember your first steps and your first outing to gather food. I was so worried about you. But I knew that Orenda would care for you and bring you back to me."

My eyes stung with tears.

"I know our society is different from human society. Family is different here, so much bigger, but the one thing that is the same between our world and theirs is that a mother's love for her child is a force so powerful, so fierce, that there isn't any stronger connection. You will understand love like that one day, when you have a child of your own."

"I want you to be there when I experience that."

The look on her face wasn't exactly skeptical, but it definitely said that she knew better; she wasn't going to lie and pretend.

"I'm proud of you and what you are doing. You're too young for this responsibility, even by our standards. There is still so much for you to learn before you should be saddled with this work."

"And you'll be around to teach me—" I said.

She interrupted me, firmly. "Edmund. Stop. I am your mother and you are no longer a child. We must speak honestly about these things."

"So you want me to just give up on you?" The darkness in me ignited, causing my temper to flare. I hated feeling incapable—I didn't want to hear that I couldn't save her. "You want me to let you die?"

"A mother will do anything to protect her child," she responded with extra softness in her voice to counteract the rising pitch of my own. "You mustn't allow Joshua to win. You cannot die again in your current state. You must descend into the shadow world and conquer the Death of the Spirit, but you cannot do that without your memories. You must enter as one of them, Edmund, otherwise all will be lost."

The gravity of her words sunk in. If there was anyone I wanted to murder at the moment, it was Linda Rose. "You want me to kill you?"

"A sacrifice must be made. I'm going to die anyway, slowly, and painfully. I would rather see you kill out of mercy, not out of fear, power, or malice. It's the price of entry. You, of all people, know death is not the end, that it's not as serious as it seems."

"Not serious?" I exploded. "Not serious? Of course it is serious! You will lose everything. Those memories that are coming back, you'll lose those! You will lose your son, lose me forever!"

"Edmund, I have already lost your father, my friends, my family. You are all I have left."

"Exactly!" She was proving my point. "Even more reason for me to save you. Together, we can figure it out. Don't you realize that you're all I have left, too?"

"I am dead either way. Even in our normal cycle we

145

are not meant to remember forever. I would rather have my death mean something. I don't fear death. It's better than being a slave to this curse. It's better that my death propel you forward, instead of holding you back."

"No. I will not sacrifice the only family I have for power. That is what the energumen do."

"That is what Joshua did," my mother urged, her voice carrying much more motherly authority than I had heard since I was a child. "He sacrificed us all. He still sacrifices. He steals the spirits of the humans, of the mages, and now of the creatures from the levels above. He made them fall so that they could be slaughtered and given to the energumen. When he runs out of spirits on Earth, in Orenda, and in the level above what do you think he'll do then? He will continue until he destroys every single creature that has ever existed. One life to save many—and by many I mean an infinite number of souls, Edmund. You are the only one left who holds the keys to the Death of the Body. You are the only one who is close enough in power and progression, close enough to stop him."

"You are part of my family. You also hold the keys to the Death of the Body, and two heads are better than one."

My mother was frustrated, but did not give up, "There isn't time for me to go to Earth, to live a life with my memories intact, and to come back here. I don't know where the crossroads is, or the secrets it contains. I only know how to get there when *you* take me. That was a job for your father, a job that was always supposed to be passed on to you. I have been with you, and I've been with him, but I can't get there on my own. I already lost your father. Please don't make me continue on, living with the possibility of losing you. Not when my death could *save* something so important—save our people. Save *you*."

"I won't do it. I can't do it," I said with all the conviction I could muster.

Then my mother did something unexpected. She reached up, snatched the satchel from around her neck, tore it loose, and in a fit of fury tossed it into the fire.

"I am your mother, and you will do as I say! I now have twenty-four hours to live. Prepare yourself. Do not let my death be in vain."

TWELVE

It must have been intuition that told me to follow the river to find out where it originated, although maybe it was the river that told me while I was letting its cool waters carry me the day before. I set off at dawn, just before the dew started to bead in the fields. I traced the river back through a forest of pines that climbed up the base of the mountain. The trail came to an abrupt end at a wall of rock, but I knew better than to trust the walls of rock here. I found a hidden trail by looking to the trees, all of which seemed to point to it without saying anything.

The climb was steep and dangerous, the trail barely wide enough for one person. At times, I had to cling to the rock and sidestep my way onto the next ledge, all the while perfectly aware that if I slipped, I would be swept away by the river below, which roared angrily among the rocks.

It took me almost being knocked off the ledges by two sizable waterfalls, and another few hours, to find the cavern. It was hidden so perfectly just to the inside of the second waterfall that I would have missed the crevice opening had I approached from the other direction.

Inside, the cavern had the familiar smell of damp earth and rusted metals, a result of water seeping through layers of sediment and redistributing heavier substances in long rocky points that clung to the ceiling and reached up from the floor. The cavern also had a familiar feel: one of power and mystery. I registered that this place was another crossroads before I even thought about it, because it *felt* just like the one where I had met my father. The only difference was that this one didn't feel like home. It didn't belong to me.

It was more claustrophobic than the one I was familiar with as well. The openings were tighter and the walls arched inward in a threatening manner. I was a skinny guy, but had to turn sideways to follow the path to where the cavern finally opened, revealing a familiar scene.

The river of water converged here with a river of light. It was exactly the same color as the silver strand I had followed with Nicholas and Xia on our trip to Orenda. It rolled and broke into shadow like the one that had taken me from Earth and deposited me here. And, just like the other crossroads, there was an angel guarding the way. He was not alone.

Samuel stood at the edge of a precipice with a group of three people. I made my way around the cavern, sticking behind some of the larger rock formations, until I was in a position where I could hear them talking.

"You are all ready to embark on a new life," Samuel said. "A life you helped plan and prepare. I'm pleased and excited for the learning experiences you are about to have on Earth—it's a marvelous place."

This was where he came to send people back to Earth? That must mean that there was a Going to the Level of the Body here, which made sense, since this would have been where I somehow managed to get Nicholas, Xia, and myself back to Earth when we were here together. The silver trail had led us to the crossroads that could send us back.

The silver river didn't just mingle with the water here. I noticed from this angle that it also had a small tributary that split off and tumbled over the cliff.

"What's at the bottom?" the young boy in the group asked.

"No one knows for sure," Samuel answered. I could tell by his voice that he wasn't being entirely honest. "Some say that there is no bottom, that the crevice extends all the way into the next life."

It was kind of him to say such things to comfort the boy, but I knew better. I knew how people got to the Level of the Body and back. They had to experience the Death of the Body. The crevice would kill them, one way or another.

"The transition is perfectly painless," Samuel continued, trying to be as comforting as possible. The words sounded rehearsed. It was obvious he'd had this conversation many times. "It's just a small step, and a slight fall, like the kind you remember feeling when riding roller coasters—"

"I hate roller coasters," the woman in the group interrupted.

Samuel laughed gently. "It won't really matter. As soon as you take a step, you won't remember taking it anyway. You've done this many times before."

"How many?" the boy asked. He sounded fascinated by all of this.

"This is your sixty-seventh jump, my boy. And every time, you're the first to do it. No doubt one of your first lives made you a brave man. You'll get to be that brave again. On death row you won't even cry or beg. You'll be dignified as you smile and accept your punishment for all of the wicked things you are going to do to women."

The boy stuck his tongue out at the woman. "This is going to be fun. See you in a few years," he chuckled, jumping.

There was no screaming, just the sound of everyone at the precipice drawing in a breath as the boy's hair hung in mid-air, a puff of sandy blonde seeming to defy gravity before it became the last vision of him.

"Your turn, my dear," Samuel said, placing his hand in the small of the woman's back. She stepped to the edge willingly, but turned back with a nervous expression on her face. As she did, Samuel used his leverage and pushed her over the edge. She screamed.

Samuel looked at the last man and smiled, "She *never* goes easily. Always with doubt. Sometimes overcoming doubt can only be accomplished by going through something quite horrific to teach you faith. Hopefully, this time, the lesson will stick."

The man laughed. "I'm excited to know her again. Hey, when was the last time you jumped?"

Samuel's grin didn't fade, but shifted into something a little more jeering. "I'm not human. I don't jump."

"I heard lots of angels were jumping now."

"Please don't call us that. It's derogatory. An invented name given by humans—creatures who don't really understand us. Calling us 'angels' is like using one of those derogatory names you humans assign to your races."

So mages didn't like to be called angels? That was interesting. I had no idea.

"I'm sorry," the man started to say, but with a quick flick of Samuel's wrist the man went flying, headfirst, into the pit. The roll of the 'r' in the word 'sorry' echoed, but turned angry as he fell.

Samuel wiped his hands on his cloak, as if trying to clean them off, when I stepped out from behind a stalagmite. When he turned and saw me he took a step back in surprise, and almost slipped into the precipice himself.

"Mother Earth, Edmund! Don't sneak up on a guy so close to a cliff!" he exclaimed after steadying himself.

"Sorry," I chuckled.

Samuel winked at me and put the grin back on his face. "I'm assuming you found what is left of our people. How did the reunion go with Hailey and Ralph? They owe you their lives, you know."

"Not as well as I had hoped, to be honest. Things are… different."

"Yes. The mages have decided that due to the limited number remaining, sharing the secrets of each family is more ideal than how we used to perform our duties. I think there was a reason that each family only had to be responsible for their own gifts. Each gift is meant to remain separate from the rest. Trying to learn it all creates confusion for most."

"And makes others power hungry," I added. "I noticed a lot of your family survived. How did they get so lucky?"

Samuel's expression soured. I'd hit a soft spot.

"Honestly, I traded my life for theirs. Because I was willing to remain the keeper of this crossroads, under Joshua's supervision, my family got some advanced warning."

I had to admit that I was furious that he was able to make such a deal, to save his lineage while I had none. But instead of showing that anger, I controlled my expression and changed the subject, using this time to learn all I could. Bridge burning could happen later. "So this is how it's done, huh? Sending people back to their next life. You fling them over a cliff."

"Well, we used to have a big party—orgies complete with dark robes, blood lettings, sacrificial daggers—really dark stuff," he said it in a way that I couldn't tell whether he was joking, "but this way is cleaner."

"But it doesn't matter where they die, right? I mean, I didn't die here, and I still went to Earth."

"True," Samuel answered, his eyes studying my expression, debating what to tell and what to keep secret. He must have decided to trust me, because he finished. "The silver river will guide the dead here anyway, but processing them at the edge of the cliff ensures they don't meet any dangers along the way, get lost, or somehow manage to elude the pull and stick around. Some people have the ability to stay if they choose. I'm not sure why. Ghosts, the humans call them."

It must not have been love or determination that allowed people to stay, I decided. I had tried to stay on Earth, to stay with Xia, but the pull of the silver river had been too much.

"So this is your crossroads?"

"Yes, it belongs to my family."

"What are its Comings and Goings?"

Samuel gave me that look again, determining whether or not to trust me.

"Well, obviously there is a Going to the Level of the Body, as I'm sure you've already figured out. There is only one Coming from the level above us, which seems quite pointless now. But around that bend there you can see the red-tinted sky from the Level of the Mind. Of course, now you could go outside and see it anyway, so it's not that spectacular."

He grinned. I did, too, even though mine wasn't genuine, just manipulative. I wondered if his was the same.

"But there is another Going here," he said taking a step closer, "in case you might need it." He gave me a knowing look, but I wasn't sure how to interpret it. "It is a one way road to the Level of the Spirit. They can't come through this crossroads, but we could *go* from here. Not that they need a crossroads to come and go as they please these days."

"Why not?" I asked.

"No one knows. No one is even sure whether something changed or if it was always one of their gifts. Level Walkers, we once called them."

I had heard this term before. It sounded familiar, but I couldn't recall the memory. The last time I had heard words and could only recall darkness around their meaning, I had woken up in a Catholic orphanage. I didn't like the feeling.

"Not all energumen are able to do it… cross between levels without a crossroads, but it seems more and more have figured it out. My guess is that it's their growing power, thanks to a certain friend of ours."

"Joshua is *not* a friend," I snapped.

Samuel didn't look surprised by my outburst, but

crossed his arms defensively. The mixed signals I got from him were exhausting. Friend or foe? I might never know.

"Well," he said, "my work here is finished for the day. I wouldn't stay too long on your own here, my boy. Crossroads can be dangerous places, especially when they don't belong to you."

I didn't know what to make of his warning. His eyes glanced behind me, toward a rock formation that partly hid a heavy slab of rock that was carved to look like a table. When I looked back to where Samuel had been standing, he was gone.

"Samuel?" I asked, but the cavern only echoed my own voice.

I walked over to the slab of rock, which looked darker than the stone that made up the walls. It seemed as though water had deposited all of the rust in the limestone onto this one slab, but it didn't stand tall like the other rock formations in the cavern. It also didn't come to a point.

Nature couldn't have formed such a perfectly flat surface. Our ancestors must have carved this table.

As I got closer, the color of the rock took on new meaning. The rusted red stains became evident.

The rock had a slight slant to it, allowing liquid to fill a channel. There was a drain near one end of the slab.

"Blood-lettings," I said aloud as Samuel's words came back to me. I followed the trail of rusted red off the slab and down a shallow channel to where it spilled out over the cliff.

The channel was wide enough for me to sit in. It was clear of rock, sand, and debris. I didn't know if it was insensitive to sit here or not, amongst the bloodstains of countless people, but it was a nice square place to sit and feel secure with my feet dangling over the edge of the cliff.

The thought crossed my mind to jump. I could return to Earth and, in fifteen or sixteen years, set off to find Xia. I had my father's ring, after all. I wouldn't forget. I wondered if the cloak and scythe would come with me, if it would materialize on Earth as I was born into another body. Would I keep it inside of me, hardly remembering it was there?

In fifteen or sixteen years, Xia would be pushing forty. I would still love her, but by that time she would have moved on, maybe even had children of her own; children that could end up around my age.

I shuddered at the thought. I would have to find another way to get back to her.

I allowed myself just a few more moments holding the vision of her in my mind. I tried to recall what she felt like, but the only place I could remember her warm skin was when her cheek was pressed against mine in the forest just a few days ago. I remembered holding her in a dusty hotel room while she cooed into the nook at my chest, but I couldn't remember what it was like to have her breath against my skin, or the taste of her kiss, or the floral scent of her shampoo.

My visions of Xia conjured disappointment because I couldn't remember our time together clearly, so I forced her from my mind, focusing on my mother instead. Today was her last day alive and the best plan I had was to follow the river? Why had my intuition led me here? What was here for me to find that could save her? What kind of monster did she think I was? Her own son capable of killing her? Did she really think she held the moral high ground, putting me in that position?

I didn't understand her desire to die. I didn't understand how death was better than trying to break the curse. What I did understand was her desire to become a sacrifice, a martyr. Maybe that ran in my family—my father had obviously done the same.

Could I ask them both to sacrifice their lives for me? Was that what parental love was all about? I understood sacrifice for protection, maybe I could even understand her trading her life for mine if it came down to that, the way my father had. I didn't understand why she would sacrifice herself to help me on some unnecessary quest for power.

I had already made it back to Orenda. I was home with my people. Together, we would unite and stop Joshua. I was sure of it.

So why wasn't she? Why was she so sure I had to kill her, *and* become the thing I was brought up to fear the most?

How could I sacrifice everything I was, everything I

had become, all the answers I now possessed, to become a demon?

When I heard footsteps behind me, I didn't turn around. Whoever entered the cavern could push me off this cliff, if they so desired. Part of me wished they would. At least then I wouldn't have to face this problem. It wasn't even a decision because the answer was simply 'no'— I would not trade my life for my mother's. I would not become a killer.

So, person behind me, go ahead and push. I didn't fear death. At least not my own.

I refused to admit that my mother didn't fear her own, either.

There was no pushing. There was no other noise. I sat, expecting someone to say or do something, for much longer than was comfortable, feeling someone's gaze on the back of my neck.

When it became obvious I was *not* going to turn around and address this person, they sat next to me, also hanging their feet over the cliff.

The woman next to me wasn't my childhood friend, even though her hair was the same color and she went by the same name. Hailey had barely spoken to me. She took every opportunity to avoid being in the same room with me, except for the small amount of time we were together in the town meeting. Having her here, sitting inches from me, made me anxious.

She didn't look at me, even after I finally glanced at

her. It was like she was giving me the same treatment I gave her when she walked in, letting my eyes study her while she sat, unmoving. I wondered if she was considering that I might push her over the cliff.

I wondered if she was afraid of death.

"When we were kids," she finally said, her eyes still trained on the black chasm below us, "when we wanted to play house, do you remember that place our parents would send us to spend the night alone?"

"Actually, no," I answered honestly.

Hailey's face remained expressionless. "That place was intense. We didn't get to play like the humans do. Everything we did had to be a lesson—had to mirror a larger part of our reality. Ralph and I fight about that all the time. I think playing house should be more about imagination and less about teaching our children how to survive on their own for a night."

"Humans put a lot of stock into imagination. That's how they shape their world, really. They don't have the world shaping them so much," I said, trying to put into words the difference between them and us, trying to explain the dissonance I felt in myself. "It makes them—us—." I couldn't decide which to use, so I gave up after tripping over my words for a few seconds. "Humans are great creators thanks to the things they imagine. What they pretend becomes real, but they forget to live. They influence their experiences, but forget to allow their experiences to influence them. It's a struggle for control.

Will the world control you, or will you control the world?"

"You've always understood both—shaping your world but getting feedback from your creation. Your connection has always been better than mine." Hailey looked at me, the ice in her eyes had something hidden behind it. Maybe a bit of jealousy.

"Not better," I said. "That's a bad word. No one is better. Everyone plays his or her part. All are important."

Somehow she had steered the conversation here, because she snatched up my words and responded quicker than I expected her to. We finally arrived at the real reason she was here. "Your mother understands that too. She has a role to play."

"*Et tu, Brute?*" I whispered, not to chide her, but to chide myself for thinking we were having a real conversation.

Hailey didn't get the reference. She stared at me blankly, but softened her tone. "Humans are selfish. They don't understand sacrifice for the greater good."

"Humans understand every life is important, and exchanging one for many is not about the greater good. The greatest good is what is best for all involved."

"I think the humans call that way of thinking Utilitarianism," Hailey said. I think she was trying to show off a little. "It's a flawed mentality. We don't understand that way of thinking," she said. I wasn't sure who was included in that 'we.' "Sacrifice can't be avoided; it's never easy."

"Would you kill Ralph if you were in my position and he was in my mother's?"

"You mean if he were going to die, and I was choosing to sit at the edge of a cliff and sulk instead of spending our last hours together?"

Her words hurt, but she stopped there. She closed her eyes for a few seconds while she reconstructed her thoughts.

"I would spend our last few hours together and hold on to our memories," she continued. "But yes, I would do what needed to be done. If I were in your situation, I would save our people."

"Do you understand the cost? Because I don't."

"Maybe not," she said, pensively. "I think I understand the logistics, but Ralph understands the process. He's waiting outside to talk to you next."

"What is this, an intervention?"

Hailey grinned. When she did, I could almost see her childhood facial features. She lit up, just like the sun in the wagon lit her up when we were ten. "I don't know what an intervention is, but by your tone, I'm guessing this is one."

She turned to leave. I could tell by the look on her face that she didn't expect to see me again.

"Wait," I said. "How does Ralph understand? Has he ever killed anyone?"

Hailey froze, turning back to me. "We have all done things to stay alive here. Before we were able to hide ourselves, we fought off human invasion and guarded ourselves against mages who were followers of Joshua. We've all killed to survive. Haven't you?"

I scanned back on my life. With all of the death that surrounded me, I had to admit that none of it was by my hand. "No," I finally answered, astonished.

"It used to be a rite of passage for Ralph's family—for the House of the Spirit. To understand spiritual death, they used to kill on their twelfth birthday. Once our society grew, not everyone was expected to endure such a trial."

"Did Ralph?"

"Ralph killed his first human on the night of the invasion. We were outside the city, just to where the walls had vanished over the hill, when two humans approached us on the road. We tried to duck into the fields, but they found us."

It felt like she was leaving out many important details of the story, but she was leaving them out on purpose. They must have been painful.

"He saved me," she said in a whisper, her eyes distant and dewy in the dim light.

"Is that when you knew you loved him?" I asked, because the look on her face had shifted from pain and discouragement to something more content.

"Actually, no," her expression shifted again; now it looked more like longing. "But that is when I knew that I would give my life to him and allow him to love *me*. Honestly, I always thought I would end up with someone else."

Her gaze fell away from mine too quickly. She walked out before I could ask her to explain.

When Ralph came in, he didn't avoid my eyes. He didn't stare into the abyss, or even get close to it for that matter. Instead, he stared directly at me, intently and with purpose, sitting on the edge of the rock slab that was used for sacrifices. He wasn't here to talk about the weather, so I couldn't help but bait him with less meaningful conversation.

"You never asked me about my life as a human," I grinned. "In fact, no one seems to care much."

Ralph grinned too, but it felt condescending. "No mage has remembered their life after descending to a lower level, and as for the Level of the Body, no one *does* care. Human lives don't mean much, which is why Joshua was trying to find a way to break their cycle, to stop us from being responsible for them. What could you tell me about your life that I haven't already heard from someone else?"

"I want to know about your life since I've been gone. I want to hear about how you and Hailey got together, about how you escaped that night, how you and the others found each other and have been getting on since. I want to know why the trees stopped talking and why this place feels so much less like home. I want to know about your plans for retaking Orenda and—"

"There are no plans to retake Orenda," Ralph interrupted. "As for the rest, I'm not sure we can trust you.

I mean, I don't even know if you're human or mage anymore. All I know is that you don't think like us."

He didn't take any time getting to the point. By commenting on how I thought, he was directly commenting on the fact that a mage would have killed my mother for the greater good. I still didn't understand how that was moral.

Ralph had often picked up on my thoughts. This time he was so spot-on he surprised me.

"Morality is a human construct," he said, his gaze icy. "We've always understood that right and wrong are less about morality and more about perspective. Killing someone who is already dead is not immoral. It's opportunity. Sometimes it's compassion. It's why your doctors have been arrested for assisted suicide and you execute prisoners. Compassion and opportunity serve the greater good." Ralph held his hands palms up, and moved them up and down in alternate motions as if weighing compassion and opportunity on a scale.

"I'm not sure you're helping."

"I know. I told Hailey I'm not adept at conversations like this. I'm putting it into perspective for you. You are the only one I know who has experienced physical death and remembered your life before. Do you remember any of your lives before that?"

"No," I answered. "But this isn't about *me*."

"Of course it's about you," Ralph responded.

He wasn't going to listen to me.

"It's about you because you carry the cloak and the scythe. You claimed a role that comes with great power. You have a greater understanding of who you are and the cycle that we now all exist in, and have the ability to bring that power with you through levels of existence that most of us will forget about after one lifetime. I will forget when I die. Hailey will forget when she dies. *Joshua* will forget when *he* dies."

This last sentence caught my attention. "What is your plan, and what does it have to do with my mother?"

"I know what kind of power taking a life gives you access to," Ralph said. The muscles in his neck rippled as he swallowed after saying so. The swallow acted like a period, accenting and defining the words, giving them more power and meaning. "There is an exchange, of course, like with any power. It's dark, mysterious, and a little dangerous. But it is the only way to recognize and tap into the darkness of others."

"It's how you are always able to recognize an energumen—"

"Yes. Even before I killed anyone, I had access to the power because I *would eventually* kill someone. It's a darkness that transcends time… at least, transcends a lifetime. You didn't have that darkness before, but you do now. That means that you will kill before you die again, Edmund. I can see it in you as easily as I can see an energumen."

He continued, "Killing a human is different than

killing a mage. Few of us have had to kill one of our own. Joshua used it as a means to enter the realm of the spirit. He's able to do more there because that's the realm that's at the base of everything. He is using possession and spiritual manipulation to change the physical worlds. To stop him, someone has to challenge his power."

"Why does that mean I have to kill my mother?"

"Killing another mage will give you the doorway. Doing it here, at this crossroads, will give you access to the energumen's world."

"Why haven't you gone? Why haven't you sent someone else?"

Ralph looked at me like I was stupid. He studied my response for a long time before crafting his own. "Do you know what power *consists* of down there?" he finally asked.

"Yes," I said. It made perfect sense to me. The only reason Joshua would trade the spirits of humans and mages alike to the energumen, was if that would somehow guarantee him power. "Spirits. Souls. People," I said.

"And who owns the spirit?" Ralph smirked.

"The person to whom it belongs," I said. I didn't get where he was going with this conversation.

Ralph laughed so hard he almost fell over. His laugh was manic, like I had said the most amusing, yet dumbest, thing I could have ever said.

"If that were true," he choked out between rolls of laughter, "then a human would be able to bring *himself* to Orenda and save *himself* after death."

"What?"

"*YOU* are responsible for their souls. *The Reaper* decides how many to give to the energumen and how many to allow to continue their cycle of learning." He was still laughing, but now it sounded like he was powerless, laughing at me because he didn't know what else to do. "You are the judge and the jury. The souls belong to your family. That's why Joshua had to wipe you out. Only The Reaper has any true claim to the spirits of the dead. No one here has any authority to claim them. Joshua has no authority to claim them. It can *only* be you."

"I understand this," a new voice called from the entrance to the cavern. It was a voice that was strong and recognizable. I responded to it in the way that a son responds to his mother.

She stood in the doorway, looking frail and weak. I had no idea how she made the climb. She was dressed in a white nightgown, her skin so pale that she looked translucent, like a ghost. I knew that it wouldn't be long before she really was one... a spirit on its way down to the Level of the Body—a spirit without her memories. This was going to happen whether I did something about it or not. She was going to die. Her strong voice didn't match her withering body.

I was on my feet before I realized it. What was she doing here?

"Leave us, Ralph," she commanded.

He slipped a dagger out from his back belt loop and

laid it on the altar. Then, he did something I didn't expect: he walked over to me, flung his arms around me, and pulled me into a tight embrace.

"We will catch up soon enough," he said. "I will tell you how Hailey and I got together, how we escaped that night." He smirked again. "I'll even ask you about your human life and pretend I'm interested. Promise."

Watching him go was harder than watching Hailey leave. Ralph had always been more than a friend. He always looked out for me. He had saved me from burning alive. I missed his cavalier demeanor and warm sense of humor, even though it had to be buried underneath layers of hardship and mistrust. Watching him walk away without breaking down that barrier and experiencing the warmth I knew was inside made my throat burn and my stomach ache.

They left me alone with my mother.

Her hand was pressed to her forehead and her eyes were closed. I stared at her in silence, comparing her features with the woman I had known. When I was a child, her soul was vibrant and excited. She had the ability to connect with people and make them feel like everything was going exactly as it should. It seemed like every act she did was somehow tied to making people feel warm inside—whether that was cooking her five-star soups, stirring up her delicious hot chocolate recipe, or drinking alcoholic beverages that my father said were good for nothing but warming people from the inside out.

After the invasion, she had spent her life in service. She cared for people, performed chores they didn't want to do, watched after them with motherly care, and still found time to be by my bedside every morning with a fresh pair of sheets, even when she didn't know I was her son.

She rubbed her temples before looking at me, smiling softly. "The memories have almost all returned," she said.

"It hurts when they do that." I was concerned. I could tell she was in pain, but she didn't mention anything about the headache.

"It's worth the joy of remembering you. I can finally relive what it was like to watch you play with Hailey and Ralph. They were always your favorite of the children. I can remember your father in ways that had been stolen from me. I remember us all going to the symphony, and the pride I felt in you the first time you heard the planet singing along and realized that the conductor did nothing more than help the instruments keep up with the planet's song. It's almost like," she paused, the words catching in her throat, "almost like my life is flashing before my eyes. But slowly, so I get to savor each happy moment."

"Please don't make me do this," I said.

My mother waved my words away with a flick of her wrist. "My son. It's already done."

"You can't come back into my life and then force me to take you out of it. All this talk of morality and right versus wrong—it's wrong for you to ask me to do what you are asking me to do."

"Help me over to the altar, Edmund," she cried. Her command was barely above a whisper, her face twisted in agony.

"I will not." I stood my ground, squaring my shoulders. The time for me to be her little boy and do what she said without reservation had passed. I was no longer a child. I was a man.

I saw pride in her eyes at my defiance. Her lips curled in a knowing smile. She struggled to move forward, but made it clear she was going to attempt to reach the altar herself. Her knees shook as she tenuously placed one foot in front of the other. With each step, my heart broke a little bit more. Why was she doing this?

"Stop," I said, tears streaming down my cheeks. "Let me save you. Please?"

My mother's knowing smile widened as she responded in a weak voice, her words choked by emotion. "I will not."

I opened my connection to the planet and poured out my emotions as quickly as the earth beneath me would receive them. How could this be happening? How could I watch my beautiful mother, now so weak and decrepit, shuffling to her own death? How could she still be so defiant?

When her knees failed her, I watched her fall in slow motion. It was like a small part of me was falling too. I had a flashback to the time when I was close to death and my knees buckled. I hadn't been able to stop my fall, and I remembered how painful it was to catch the weight of my limp body with my face. I remembered wishing for my mother or father to be there to comfort me. If I were at that time and place again, I wouldn't want to fall alone.

I caught my mother before she hit the ground. I don't know how I moved so fast but it must have had something to do with time, which was standing still. I laid my mother down on the altar. I had no intention of fulfilling whatever master plan she, Hailey, Ralph, and even Linda Rose had concocted, but her limp body felt heavier than it should have felt. It took all my strength to not drop her frail frame.

Sitting on the altar, I rested her head in my lap and pushed the hair out of her face. She looked at me with bright, clear eyes. I remembered what it was like to die, to start that death with tears. Eventually her body would do what mine had; it would rebel, refusing to let her feel, refusing to let her continue crying.

My mother pushed something cold and hard into my hand. It was the dagger Ralph had left behind.

"No," I said, pushing it away. But her intentions were clear.

She made her arm rigid with whatever strength she had left. She tensed every muscle, so pushing the dagger away was impossible without hurting her.

"Please," she whispered. "You know what this will mean for me. I want to start over. I want the chance for a happy life. I want to be slave to none. I want to feel the sun on my face and know I am free. Send me to the Level of the Body and let me experience joy. Take the power you need to save me someday."

I didn't know what to do. Even though I had no intention of using it, I took the dagger so she would relax.

"I'm so proud of you," she said, her words so quiet that I couldn't be sure she didn't just mouth them.

"I love you," I said.

"Save your father from them."

I knew she meant from the energumen. I also knew she left this last piece unsaid until now for a reason. There was only one way I could do that. I had to go into their world to claim his spirit myself.

My hand closed around the dagger.

"Do it!" she said.

I wrapped my arm around her, pulling her tightly into my body. She grew cold, her body slowing down. I wanted her to feel the warmth of my protective arms. I would always protect her.

I raised the dagger.

"I love yo—" she said, but the last word cut off in a groan of air and blood as I plunged the dagger into her chest.

PART TWO—THE HELL OF THE DAMNED

THIRTEEN

The death of the spirit ends much like the death of the body, with the feeling of being lost within the swirling blackness of oblivion. At any moment, I expected my consciousness to cease and the awareness of any knowledge of what was 'me' to drift into the vacuum of nothingness. I expected there to be no more 'me.'

All deaths are deaths of the senses, or the senses as humans and mages have gotten used to them. While some people go downright mad in the face of sensory deprivation, losing all connection with the ego, all a dead person has to do is remember what life was like and he or she can find the connection to their soul again.

Maybe I was waxing philosophical because I was insane. As such, I didn't feel like I could be blamed for the way my emotions pieced together thoughts while I experienced a fleeting moment of extinction.

The world started to fall back together again when I

realized that extinction wasn't extinction if it *had* a 'fleeting moment.' I still existed.

It began with beautiful stars that twinkled in the black universal fabric. They weren't moving, but appeared in tight collections of formed shapes like diamonds, spheres, and cylinders. Wave upon wave of sparkling star-like diamonds.

There was a word for this…

…Chandelier.

Hell had chandeliers?

I was in Hell, wasn't I?

I remembered something I had heard long ago. My memory was fuzzy, but it was something about how angels didn't like to be called angels. The thought was humorous, and it made me wonder if Hell didn't like to be called Hell.

The rest of the room took shape as I focused on who I was and how I came to be here. It was an arduous process, like waking up out of anesthesia. I was running in a dream, exerting energy but getting nowhere. I had to relearn how to feel my hands and feet. My body felt different; everything felt lighter and disconnected.

I was in a dusty lobby that smelled of old books and burning electrical wire. Huge windows looked out over nothing but darkness to one side. On the other side, heavy wooden doors looked warm in comparison to the black walls.

Near the center of the room was a massive fire pit. Towering, wing-backed chairs were dispersed throughout with designer care. A person sat in one of the chairs, but I couldn't make out her face beyond a basic outline, because her skin was so black that her features vanished against her shadow-like body. Another shadow woman sat in the corner of the room by the windows. Her hands were buried into her kinked hair as she peered downward at a chessboard on the table where she rested her elbows. I noticed that there wasn't another player. All of the pieces on the board were black.

"May I help you, sir?" a voice called from behind me. I spun around to find myself standing on one side of a large cherry-colored reception desk, but I was more surprised by the woman who stood behind the counter. Her piercing yellow eyes danced inside her midnight face and stood out like two full moons against a starless sky. Something about the color of those eyes made me uncomfortable.

"Are you here for a room, Mr....?" she asked politely.

"Uh," I said, trying to buy myself time to get my bearings. What was my name again? Why did I feel worried about giving it? "I don't think I have any money."

"Money!" the girl scoffed, following with a bell-like laugh. "I wouldn't have guessed that you came from Earth. You're more... *pronounced* than most humans we get here."

I didn't know what she meant. My head was too foggy to ask or to care. I was glad she dropped the issue of my name for the moment.

"You must be new. I can get you a ground floor

room for the cost of one a night. We can run a tab for a month, but then you have to square up if you want to stay."

"I'm sorry? One what?"

The bell-like laughter rang out from her again. I didn't like it. It felt too cheerful and I could tell that it was drawing attention to me. I felt more than one set of eyes on the back of my neck.

"One soul, silly."

She was too cheerful. All I wanted was to get away from her and bury my head in the sand where I wouldn't be seen for a few days.

"Fine," I said, unsure of what I agreed to. "I'll take the room."

"Great," the woman said, the pitch in her voice high enough to have sung the note with the precision of a soprano. She handed me a piece of bone and gestured down the hall. "This is your room key. You're number thirteen, on the right there."

"My key?" I asked, doubtful.

"The finger bone of a virgin," she sang. "No two are alike."

I grimaced, but thanked her and took the piece of finger.

I found number thirteen down the hall to the right, just like the woman at the front counter had said. The door was made of heavy, warm-colored wood. The number was painted in blood. A single, bare light bulb illuminated the doorway with a harsh arc of light that looked like it was meant to strike fear into my heart. It worked.

"Lucky number 13," I mumbled, inserting the bone into a hole under the rusted knob.

Inside, the room was macabre. There were no electric lights, but the room flickered with dozens of burning candles. The floor was dirt. The candlelight made the objects in the room quiver with shadows. Despite the sea of tiny hot flames, the air was ice cold. The walls ran with a black, tar-like substance. I couldn't tell if it was actively bubbling down the walls, or if my vision was so blurry that I imagined the dribbling. My eyes were so tired I couldn't hold them still.

When I walked into the room, movement on my left startled me. At first I thought someone else was in the room or that the moving shadows had leapt out at me. Upon closer inspection, I realized it was my own reflection in a mirror. I tried to convince myself that there was nothing to be scared of, but my heart continued to race.

I was startled with good reason. In the mirror, staring back at me, was one of those dark shadow people like the woman in the lobby and the one behind the desk. My skin was as dark as night, so black that it looked as if I had been dipped in the tar that coated the walls. My eyes were the same shade of yellow as the part of the fire that danced above the candlewicks. They flickered like a flame.

I touched my cheek, surprised it felt as solid as it felt

when I had been on Earth and in Orenda. I found this discomforting because I remembered this was the Level of the Spirit. I felt solid, but I saw my skin moving, floating around like smoke tightly contained in a human-shaped vase.

The mention of smoke brought back the memory of my father and his enormous coat of smoke. As soon as I thought about it, my skin crawled and my body erupted, covering me with the cloak. My black face blended in so well with the rest of the robes that peering into the hood revealed nothing but darkness. I had to search hard to find my two glowing yellow eyes.

I shivered. The image in the mirror was too dark, too powerful, and too unlike the person I wanted to be.

I looked away from the mirror and allowed the heaviness of my eyes to convince me I was tired. The bed looked like it had already been slept in. Even though it was unmade and covered with stains that resembled the shape of a human body, I couldn't resist the temptation to lie down. The second my head hit the lumpy mattress, I fell asleep.

* * *

I didn't remember dreaming. In fact, falling asleep in this place was as close to oblivion as I could have experienced. There was no thought about fading away, what would come next, or even what it was like to disappear forever. Instead, I was awake a moment after I closed my eyes, but time had somehow slipped between those moments unnoticed.

A knock at the door startled me.

Getting out of bed, I gave myself a quick glance in the mirror. I wasn't sure why I was concerned about my appearance. I guess I wanted to appear presentable in case Lucifer whisked me away to the depths of the underworld. My hair was messy, as usual, but I thought it had that perfect 'wake-up' vibe to it. I noticed my jet-black hair perfectly matched the rest of my jet-black body. The monochromatic coloring, while foreign, wasn't as terrifying now that I was rested.

I had the same features as I did with a body, with the same thin, but muscular, build accented by the fact that I was shirtless. Was there a clothing store in this world? At least whatever put me here had the decency to give me pants fashioned from iridescent raven's feathers. They reflected the candlelight with an eerie greenish-black sheen.

I opened the door and found a young woman standing on the other side. She had the same messy hair as I did, only hers was longer and stuck out about six inches in a ratted mess. She wore the same type of clothing, but her feathers were constructed into an intricate cocktail-length dress with a neckpiece that made her head look like it was floating.

Her stance was rigid, but relaxed a bit when she said,

"Hi."

"Hello," I responded awkwardly. I hadn't relaxed my stance.

"So. You're new, right?"

"Yeah, I guess I am," I responded.

She ran her hands through her hair, ratting it further.

"Hey, you're the girl that was in the lobby when I got here. You were playing chess."

That comment caught her off guard. She put her hands down and her eyes narrowed. "You're observant for a newbie. Most of us take a few months to tell each other apart."

"Well, you looked familiar, and the hair thing you just did with your hands gave you away."

"Oh," she grinned. "Nervous twitch, I guess. Anyway, I wanted to stop by to wake you up. I know they tell you at the desk they'll give you thirty days, but what they don't tell you is you'll end up sleeping all that time off at the beginning. The transition here is exhausting."

"I dunno," I rubbed the back of my neck, "I feel pretty good, but thanks for stopping by."

"How long do you think you've been asleep?" she asked, raising her eyebrow in a way that I suspected was a challenge.

"A few hours?" I responded.

Now she grinned, the whites of her teeth splitting the black smoke-skin in a way that was jarring and unnatural. "Try seven days, Alexander."

I was so stunned that my jaw dropped open.

"See? Told you. The amount of time you sleep when you're new is crazy. You'll get used to the pattern soon. You'll learn we don't get tired the same way you did when you were alive. Going from awake to tired is pretty instantaneous."

But that wasn't why I was shocked. I was shocked because she called me by name. "What did you call me?" I asked.

"Well that's your name, isn't it?"

"How did you know it?" I said, taking an aggressive step forward.

The girl matched my step by taking one back. "Chill out. I must have heard it at the desk when you got here."

She was lying. I remembered with perfect clarity the woman at the front desk. I was worried about giving my name, not knowing which one to give. When she didn't ask, I was relieved. So where had this girl heard the name Alexander?

I gawked while I put the pieces together in my head. I knew she looked familiar—was that because I'd seen her in the lobby when I got here? Or was it something else? Besides that, she knew me as Alexander. That meant she knew me in the Catholic orphanage on Earth, and *only* in the Catholic orphanage on Earth *before* Father Michaels died. Finally, she was playing chess…

"Is your name Ruth?" I took another step forward.

This time, the girl didn't step back. She just dropped

her hands to her sides as her shoulders relaxed. "You remember me?"

"Of course I remember you!" The excitement of having her here, standing in front of me, alive (sort of), transformed my emotional state from suspicion to friendliness. "How did you…? What are you…? Why are you here?"

She threw her arms around me and kissed my cheek. "That's a lot of questions. Want to chat about it over a cup of coffee?"

My eyes widened in disbelief, "You have coffee here?"

"We have coffee here."

"Like actual, same as on Earth, real coffee?"

"Starbucks on every corner."

"Seriously?"

"No. No Starbucks—but coffee, yes."

"Are you sure I haven't died and gone to heaven?" I joked.

The smile on Ruth's face vanished, her eyes hard and serious, "Alexander, you're one of *us*. This place *is* heaven. The only people who think of it as something else are dumbass humans."

The way she said the last part of her sentence, with absolute dismissal, caused a twinge of fear. To dismiss humanity so offhandedly was so… demonic.

Or was it?

I felt the darkness in the pit of my stomach flare,

contending with my humanity. I didn't know why, but it was comforting to know that the darkness had survived and had been reborn. It was good to know it was part of my deeper spiritual makeup.

My thoughts about humanity crept up from that pit. What connection did I have to them, anyway? I didn't owe the human race anything. What had any of them ever done for me?

I had been born an angel.

Now I chose to be a demon.

My trip into humanity was nothing but an accident. No one defines who they are because of an accident.

FOURTEEN

A giant woman who was wearing way too little for her size and who looked more like a big ball of mist from far away, placed a steaming French press on the table. "Can I get you two anything else?" Her voice carried throughout the building's café. I decided to call the building The Hotel, because it reminded me of the Eagles' song, 'Hotel California.'

"Would you like anything else?" Ruth asked me politely, repeating the woman's question. Her hand was over her forehead like she'd lost patience.

"Seven days sleeping and I haven't eaten. Shouldn't I be hungry?"

"We'll take three baby hearts," Ruth said to the server, grinning.

The woman laughed, although it sounded like she was hacking up a lung. "He new?"

"We'll just stick with the coffee, thank you," Ruth

answered the first question.

The woman grunted and waddled away.

"We are demons, Alexander. We can eat and drink what we please and when we want, but we can't die from hunger," she laughed a condescending laugh.

"You know," I said, taking the opportunity to fill her cup, "after I left the orphanage, I changed my name to Edmund. I'd prefer that, if you don't mind."

"Oh really?" Ruth asked, adding sugar to her cup. "Why the name change? Didn't like what the nuns assigned to you? I'm sure they went in alphabetical order. Poor kid before you was probably named Zeus or something."

"Zurishaddai," I laughed.

"What?"

"The last Z name in the bible, alphabetically. Although I suppose you could claim it was Zuzim. I'm pretty sure Zuzim was a name for a group of people though, not an individual."

"What?" Ruth repeated.

"Zurishaddai. The father of Shelumiel? Never mind."

Ruth's eyes widened and her face paled. "You kept up with that religious crap?"

My cheeks went hot, but I hoped the black swirls of my skin would hide my embarrassment. I raised my cup and said, "I like being informed," before pressing it to my lips.

"Wait. So how did you end up killing someone if you

were all… holy?"

Her question was nonchalant, so casual that she didn't look up from her coffee when she asked it. She must not have expected me to be surprised, but the implications were painful.

When I didn't answer right away, she set her cup down and put both hands flat on the table. She leaned forward and rolled her eyes. "Oh, come on. You've *at least* figured out that's the reason you're here as one of us and not one of *them*, right? We kill people."

One of them? She must have meant humans. I could tell by the way she spit out the word.

"Please tell me you're not going to be one of those sulky demons pining for human affection. Those are the ones who end up with no souls, wandering around until the end of time instead of gaining power, exploring dimensions, making friends, and having fun."

There was so much in that one sentence I wanted to ask about. I decided to not answer while I organized my thoughts. I needed sugar. I reached for a spoon but hesitated.

"Seriously, Alex… Edmund. What's up?"

I shoveled a few spoonfuls of sugar into my cup. "The last time I had coffee, I had a bad experience with a spoon," I chuckled.

I think Ruth was assessing my mental health, because the look on her face was somewhere between annoyance and concern. I let her stew a minute. I didn't know why, but I enjoyed getting her ruffled. I almost burst into laughter as I remembered she was dressed in feathers.

"Sorry," I said, taking another swallow of coffee. It wasn't nearly as good as I had remembered. A bit too earthy in a bad way—like dirt. "So we like being called demons?"

Ruth sat back in her chair and crossed her arms. "You have some weird priorities. Yes. We like being called demons. The word inspires something—fear, maybe? Respect? It works well at keeping people in line and getting us what we want. So why change it, you know? What would you rather be called?"

"Well, 'demon' inspires images of little red-horned devils in my mind, but 'energumen'—"

I froze as Ruth's demeanor changed. Her smile faded, making her face look angry. Her lips pressed into a firm line and her back went rigid. "Where did you hear that word?"

I searched my memories. I had known Ruth in the orphanage for a short amount of time. She must have remembered that I woke up one day calling myself Edmund. She would have heard rumors and stories from the other children about my being from Orenda. But had I ever talked about Orenda in front of her? Had she seen any of my magical abilities? Did she have any reason to believe I was something other than human?

She wasn't in Sister Mary Elizabeth's class when I caused the water to spill from the granite desktop. She wasn't with us during the exorcism. Had I used my magic in front of her at any other time?

I couldn't recall. Was she being nice to me not because I was a fallen angel, but because she thought I was a fallen *human*?

I chose the safer route. I didn't bring up who I really was… yet.

"I'm sure I heard someone say it. I thought it was a neat word. Why?"

Ruth eyed me with suspicion. I wasn't sure she bought my explanation, but her shoulders relaxed. "There are other creatures. Mages…"

She misread my intense, interested stare as I hung on her every word. She thought I was giving her a look of confusion, an attempt to focus on something I didn't understand. She must have, because she clarified: "Sorry. You would know them as angels. Like, from heaven? Anyway. They call us energumen, or what's left of them."

She smiled. "But don't worry about all of that. There's plenty of time to learn about the other worlds after you learn about this one."

I wanted to kick the loud, fat waitress as her voice blared from behind me. "You kids okay? Your bill's ready whenever you are. It'll just be one."

"One?" I barked, angry mostly because she interrupted our conversation. I felt like I was just getting somewhere with it. "Isn't my room one a night? One for coffee seems a bit extreme, isn't it?"

"Well, Mr. I'm-A-Big-Demon-Now, whattaya gunna do? Split it?"

The woman and Ruth laughed hysterically. They laughed for so long that I became uncomfortable and worried that the hilarity at my expense wouldn't stop. Ruth's laughter was quiet and attractive. The way she scrunched her nose uncontrollably as her body shook with laughter was endearing. The spiraling of server's hacks in my ear gave me vertigo and made me want to vomit.

"Well, yeah. Why can't you split it?" I asked, sending them into a second fit of laughter.

Ruth fluttered her hands as she choked on her breath, somehow managing to control herself until she was able to speak.

"You can't split a human soul, Edmund."

"Or an angel's!" the server exclaimed, her words coming out like a punch line.

I couldn't look at them. Instead, I stared deep into the black liquid in my cup until I saw my own yellow eyes reflected back. I was going to be sick.

Ralph had told me that spirits were power here. Now I knew how. Spirits contained souls. Spirits were currency.

This cup of coffee had cost a soul.

FIFTEEN

Ruth didn't say anything when I pushed back from the table and walked away. She also didn't follow, which was a good thing for her and for me. I left the café and made my way back to the lobby where the woman with the high-pitched laugh had been working the desk when I got here. She looked up as I approached.

"How do I get out of here?" I asked abruptly.

She stared at me for a moment before closing the magazine she had been reading. "Look, I know you're new and you're used to certain pleasantries from Earth, but you can't stop being a demon any more than you could've stopped being human before. While I understand suicide was an option as a way out, we don't have that option here. I suggest you give yourself some time to adjust—"

The more she rambled, the more uncomfortable she looked. I cut her off. "I don't mean out of *here* here. I mean out of this building. Outside."

"Oh good," she breathed a sigh of relief. "Sorry, some new people—"

"I don't care about new people. Where's the exit?" I snapped.

I expected her to be taken aback by my outburst (did I always feel this angry?), but she wasn't. She didn't look surprised or upset with me. Instead, her lip twitched upward and she pointed down the hall to her left. She looked amused and said, "Take that hall to the end and turn right. There's no real door like you're used to. Just trust me and keep walking."

I followed her directions and headed down the hallway. This side of the building was more upscale than the side of the hotel where my room was assigned. This hallway looked like I would expect a hotel to look, with green and gold paisley-patterned carpet and gaudy brass fixtures. The doors were made of the same wood, but the numbers weren't painted with blood; they were made of metal and fastened to the center of the doors with small brass nails.

It was sad that I used the word 'upscale' to describe styling that would have been popular in the 1980s, but compared to the blood painted doors and dusty bed sheets, even the 80s looked comfortable.

I turned to the right when I got to the end of the hall, into another hall that looked the same. After a few steps, an eerie feeling caused me to stop and pay more attention to where I was going. I had been concentrating so intently on getting away from Ruth and getting some fresh air that I didn't noticed that I couldn't see the end of the hallway. It didn't look like it stretched on forever. Instead, it faded out, as if the end of the hallway were covered in black mist that hid the full length from view.

I spun around. The hallway leading back to the lobby intersected with this one, which stretched in front and behind me as far as I could see. It plunged into darkness in both directions.

Was I crazy? Did the hallway extend forever, or was the black mist my own mind playing tricks on me, trying to make sense of where I was, or of what I had become?

I pushed that thought out of my mind as quickly as it entered. I knew I hadn't dealt with what was going on. I purposely hadn't thought about my mother, or her dying words, or what I had done to her body after she was dead and I had gone insane.

Maybe I hadn't come back from that; maybe I was still insane. Maybe the green and gold colors and the endless hallway that faded to black were nothing more than my imagination. Was it telling me that no matter how fast I ran, I would never escape this place I'd put myself in?

What was wrong with me?

I shouldn't have paused to think. Had I just kept my head down and moved forward I could have been outside by now. As my feet moved again, I almost ran into a little boy.

I gasped and stopped myself. His pale blue eyes and ivory-colored skin were a shocking sight in this world full of black and yellow. Had white faces always been this ghostly looking, or had I become so accustomed to seeing yellow eyes that this kid's pale skin looked otherworldly?

"Have you seen my brother?" the boy asked innocently, but the question sent shivers down my spine (or, quivers down my central smoke stack? I was really going to have to figure out this new body of mine eventually).

Before I could answer, the temperature dipped. It was a cold that came on so abruptly that I couldn't help but notice. It was also not a normal cold. Not like the ice that's in the air before the first snow, or the crispness of Halloween night when the chill brings a living excitement. This was a deadly cold. This was sentient.

The lights flickered as the mist rolled in and condensed. At first it looked like black fog billowing from the air currents. The fog rolled itself into the shape of a man-sized cigar, finally materializing into a fully manifested energumen.

"He's mine," I heard the voice in my head before it echoed around me. Another pair of yellow eyes burned into my own. The demon stood just behind the boy, a dark shadowy hand on his shoulder, claiming him.

The figure had a dangerous sneer on his face and his posture made me skulk backward. I didn't know if this demon was really that much bigger than I was, but what mattered was how small I felt.

"What's a little Mammon like you doing here?" his voice boomed.

I instinctively took a step backward—a motion that wasn't missed and caused the demon's eyes to burn brighter. His lips curled from sneer to wicked grin.

"I asked you a question, *boy*." He last word was spit with a condescending tone. "Has no one taught you to bow to your superiors, to cower before us? To service us?"

"I'm just looking for the exit. I needed some air," I responded, the evenness of my voice surprising. My eyes flickered toward the pale-faced boy.

The demon's eyes followed my own, but he continued to speak. "Still thinking like a human, are you, Mammon? Do you think you're still breathing air?" he laughed, deep and guttural. "Do you still feel pain, too?"

He lashed out. The tips of his fingers were filed down to sharp claws. His hand moved so quickly that I didn't see it coming for me. A flash of shadow and my cheek was stinging.

The demon laughed as I coddled my cheek. The last time I had been struck like this I was twelve years old in an orphanage in the middle of Los Angeles. Mary Elizabeth had struck me out of some sick form of Godliness. This demon did it out of some sick form of devilishness. Either way, the rumble of anger bubbling up inside me was the same. When the anger hit the dark void at the pit of my stomach I wondered how much of a demon I was inside. Maybe I always had been when I was angry.

"Do you want the boy?" the demon challenged. "Take him from me if you dare. Do you need this one soul to save yourself from descending below, Mammon? To save yourself from being cast out, a slave to the sky? Would this one soul save your own?"

I wasn't sure what this creature was talking about, but with each word my anger lurched higher. It was in my throat now, begging to be released in a war cry. What was driving me to challenge this creature?

"I will trade him to you for one year of service. One year as a slave will teach you many things you can use once you are free."

"I am slave to no demon," I let the words escape, but it didn't assuage my anger, just released the building pressure.

My father's ring pulsed hot on my finger—another small amount of pressure released as the air around me heated.

The demon looked as though he had been struck with my fist, but didn't back down. The challenge made him even more confident. I watched as he flexed his muscles and pushed back on me with his coldness.

"I will take whatever Mammon I wish as a servant. You would do well, *human*, to remember that we *all* serve *someone*."

I didn't know if it was the way he accused me of

being human, or if it was the word 'Mammon' (which I finally realized was used as some low-level insult). Maybe it was the idea of being slave to this demon or any other. Or perhaps it was my inability to relate to or distance myself from my own humanity. But darkness pushed up from the pit of my stomach, through my throat, and exploded into my head. My body of darkness refused to contain all I was inside. The Angel of Death erupted from me. In an instant, I doubled in size, driven by the darkness swelling within me. My large black wings were made of the same incandescent feathers as my shorts. The cloak was so large and deep that I was sure it hid my yellow eyes. My father's scythe… no… *my* scythe was swinging before it had even fully materialized, and was buried into the neck of the demon instantly.

The slice of my scythe as it made connection felt good, just like it had felt good to bury the sacrificial blade into my mother's chest. Only this one thrust, this one *thud* rumbling from the blade and reverberating up the staff and into my arms and body, was enough to quell the insanity. I was satisfied with the surprised and fearful look in the demon's yellow eyes.

"I am no slave, and no human," I said, not sure if I was addressing the demon, or myself.

I always heard it said that where there was smoke, there was fire. I didn't realize how true that was until the skewered smoke at the end of my scythe burst into flame and vanished.

I didn't know what had just happened, but after the burst of flame I grew scared that someone might have seen what I'd done. The emotional high was over, relieved by my outburst. I quickly withdrew the cloak, wings, and scythe back into me while scanning the hallway.

Everything seemed normal. The dimly lit corridor once again terminated in hazy black mist. Even the young boy had mysteriously vanished. I half-expected dozens, if not hundreds, of yellow eyes to appear out of the mist and come for me. I felt that exposed.

As the adrenaline withdrew, paranoia and exhaustion set in. I slumped against, and slowly slid down, the striped wallpapered walls.

I hugged my knees to my chest and breathed heavily. I didn't care that the demon told me I didn't need to breathe. So what if thinking about my breath was a human habit? It made me feel better. I breathed because concentrating on the motion calmed me, but not enough to shake the feeling that everything happening was a dream.

My mind had a hard time accepting this reality. I longed for the days where the world felt real after waking from a good night's sleep. Maybe I was disoriented because I hadn't seen anything but the inside of this hotel. Maybe I needed to get out into this world and see it for what it really was.

I could even accept Orenda as real—it always was, even when I was a human on Earth, I could feel the realness of the magic around me. Now Orenda felt far, but still real; it felt more real than this place.

If I could accept the reality of Heaven, why was I having such a hard time accepting the reality of Hell?

I took one last breath and stood up. I still wanted fresh air, to get out of this building so that I would feel less claustrophobic. That was going to have to wait until I slept.

I understood what Ruth was talking about now. I understood what it was like to fall from alertness to instant exhaustion. I could barely convince myself that the walk back to my room was necessary. I hoped that I wouldn't run into a single set of yellow eyes on my way back.

Unfortunately, that hope was dashed as I reentered the lobby. Ruth came toward me.

"I was coming to check on you. Are you all right? Forgive the expression, but you look like hell."

"I'm fine. I needed to get some air, but halfway down that funhouse of a hallway, I got tired."

My explanation should have been enough for her to go away and leave me alone. To my horror, she followed me.

"You know you don't need air, fresh or otherwise," she said.

"Yeah, yeah," I said, lifting my hand to wave her off. But it was so heavy that it ended up flopping around a bit.

"I'll come wake you up in another seven days. We really need to talk about how you pay for your room, and make sure you have enough time on your lease to…"

"To what?" I chided. "Harvest enough souls?"

I didn't know why my tone wasn't enough of a hint that I didn't want to be followed, but Ruth stuck there beside me anyway.

"Well, I'm glad you're a quick learner, observant enough to figure stuff out. But seriously, Edmund, you're going to need to understand."

I was back at my room, sticking the bone into the lock under the knob. The door didn't open.

"Great." I tried the lock again.

"Did you get yourself mixed up?" Ruth asked, trying to be helpful.

"Ruth, I don't go around with a bunch of virginal bones in my pocket."

She sighed, picking up on my frustration. "Well, go see the front desk then. They're going to charge you three to replace your lock. It will cost you one for the cost of doing it, and two because they'll have to find another virgin. Back when the Aztecs used to sacrifice them it was no big deal, but now they're harder to come by."

I gawked at her, but by the look on her face she didn't think she had said anything abnormal. She looked like she had said the most natural thing ever.

"What?" she asked. "You can't blame *me*. It's just how it is."

I groaned, heading back down the hall, through the lobby, and to the front desk. My feet felt like they were going to fall off. Ruth followed me the entire time.

I put my key on the counter as the girl eyed me with suspicion. "My key isn't working," I said, letting my frustration creep out.

She pulled out a large, bound reservation book and slapped it on the counter. The cover was made from some sort of skin. I allowed myself to believe that it was old, cracked leather.

"I thought you were going out," she grinned, flipping through the first couple of pages slowly and without looking at them. She was taking her time on purpose.

I rubbed my forehead. "I got tired before I made it down the hall."

"I see," she said, placing her finger on the page and sliding it down.

Had she actually been looking at the page, and not directly at me, I would have believed she was searching for something.

But then her finger stopped. She finally glanced downward. She flipped a few pages and looked at me with wide eyes.

"Well," she said, the word coming out breathy, like she was impressed. "It seems, sir, that you've been upgraded."

"What?" Ruth and I said at the same time, although mine was a question and hers was an exclamation.

The woman at the desk took my bone off the counter and slid me a new one. "It seems you're now down the *left* hall, left at the fork, up to the fifth floor. You're the last room on the right."

"A *fifth* floor, *east*-facing, *corner* suite?" Ruth said, looking shocked. "How can you afford that?"

"There must be a mistake." I addressed the woman behind the desk while I gave Ruth an eat-shit-and-die look. "I'm supposed to be down *that* hall, in the crappy first-floor, non-corner room."

The girl behind the desk looked at me with incredulity. "We don't make mistakes."

At this point I could barely keep myself standing up, so I focused my energy into smiling at her and said, "Fine. Thank you."

What did it matter? I was living in a dream world anyway. I was becoming more convinced that whatever reality existed here was nothing more than a nightmare created in my own head, my own personal Hell. Any moment now, I would wake up. Any moment this world would reveal itself as an illusion and I would find myself, where? Back on Earth, maybe? Orenda? The real Hell?

I had to wake up.

Hopefully that would be after I slept.

SIXTEEN

Before my eyes opened, my nostrils were flooded with a pleasing, masculine scent that my mind went to work unraveling—mint, cedar, suede, and citrus with a bite of spice. Bergamot, if I wasn't mistaken. It not only smelled good, but also made me crave a hot cup of Earl Grey tea.

I opened my eyes to a strikingly designed ceiling, complete with a raised checkerboard pattern carved out of the molding. I sat up and surveyed the room. The linens I was sleeping on felt crisper than Egyptian cotton. The comforter was filled with down feathers.

The heavy drapes were drawn and stretched all the way from the crown molding to the plush carpets. My yellow eyes burned back at me from a dark corner where a floor-to-ceiling mirror was next to the door.

I yawned, swinging my feet over the side of the bed before noticing something in the room wasn't right. Although I moved, the yellow eyes staring back at me from the corner hadn't.

I gasped, turning toward the figure next to the doorway.

"Pardon my intrusion. I was freshening up the room. Some of the other patrons complained they could smell the sulfur from lower-class demons below."

"How long have you been standing there?"

"I just finished my work. I meant to slip in and out without disturbing you, like I've done for the last sixteen days. I didn't make any noise, but certainly beg your pardon if I woke you."

"How do I request that no one be allowed in my room unless I specifically ask? I would imagine *we*," I emphasized the word in hopes of convincing this demon I was someone important, "occasionally prefer our privacy."

"Yes, of course. I will speak to the front desk on your behalf. Again, please pardon the intrusion. Excuse me."

He didn't wait to be excused. I couldn't tell if he gave me a short bow before exiting, because all I saw was the shadows shift as he slipped out the door.

After he left, I twisted the lock on the door to make sure it was secure. In the back of my mind I knew it wouldn't matter, though. No doubt he had a key.

I turned back to the room. It was dark enough in here that a human would've had difficulty walking around without bumping into things. As a demon, the darkness didn't bother me. The small flicker of a few candles I lit on the dresser satisfied any craving for light. The light caused the shadows to dance around the room and caught in the crystals of a chandelier that hung over the bed. The crystals made a beautiful pinging noise as invisible air currents moved them ever so slightly. They knocked against each other, sounding like a soft wind chime, but more subdued and relaxing.

Ruth had sounded so envious of my—how did she put it?—fifth floor, east-facing, corner suite, so I pulled back the curtains and checked out the view.

Behind the curtains, the windows stretched taller than I was. The glass was so clear I worried I might fall off the ledge and out into the night. I didn't get more than one curtain pulled back, though, because I was immediately enthralled by what I saw.

Seeing the sheer size of the building reminded me of the aerial shots I had seen of New York's Central Park, where giant buildings ran up against the park boundaries. I always believed that one day, one of the buildings would get tired of being crowded and step off into the open space. The difference here was that only one massive structure wrapped around three sides of a giant central garden that was much larger than Central Park.

I had no idea why Ruth would be jealous of a fifth-floor room. I could see dotted windows towering above me in all directions. There had to be at least one hundred floors in this place.

I could only imagine the view from the one hundredth floor, east-facing, corner suite. Being on the fifth floor did have its advantages, though. I could make out the garden's odd-looking black plants, twisting in perfectly manicured rows offset by fountains running black with blood. I envisioned energumen in the garden, tending to plants and fountains, although I could only make them out by first finding their glowing eyes against the blackness.

The light outside didn't come from any sun. Instead, its source was a giant fireball that roared on the far, open edge of the garden. It was too far for me to make out what was burning.

Barren mountains stretched beyond the fire, their jagged rock structures devoid of life. They looked like they belonged on the moon, not part of a life-bearing planet.

Then, beyond the mountains, framing the whole scene, was the sky. I was convinced someone was playing tricks on me, because although there were dots of bright stars, the whole sky looked like it was moving and breathing. I saw it inhale and exhale with an undulation. I couldn't watch for long before I became motion sick.

There was something about that garden, though—the way the energy of this level moved through it. I was drawn to it the same way I was to the river where Simon had drowned at the orphanage, or to the foggy mountains in Carlsbad, California. I hadn't been able to drain feelings here like I could when I was connected to the planet. Instead, my feelings exploded in fits of anger. I'd buried my scythe into the neck of a demon. Finding the source of power in this world, the connection to nature, had to become a priority before I exploded again.

Stepping out of my room, I paused. If I wanted to find my connection to nature, I was going to have to respect her. I went back inside and tore the comforter off the bed. I had already given into the demon too much. I had allowed anger and darkness into my soul. I had committed murder. I couldn't lose myself here.

"Hey. You know, I never caught your name," I said, dropping the comforter onto the front desk.

The woman behind the counter was exasperated to see me, but smiled politely. "Lilith. And before you ask, bow, grovel, or whatever it is some of the other demons have tried, I am *not* the Lilith of Jewish mythology. There are plenty of demons named Lilith, you know."

I grinned. "I won't ask then. Although had you not said something, I would have been curious."

"You and everyone else." Her gaze slid to the comforter. "What's wrong with that?"

"Ever watch the PETA video about down filling? I'd prefer a regular blanket, please."

Lilith looked as if she had nothing to say that I would have liked, so she replied, "Okay, sir."

I smiled and thanked her as I walked down the hall to the left of the desk, taking a right at the fork. I kept walking until the dark mists in the hallway gave way to the outside.

There were no doors, just a wall of air that marked

the transition.

Outside, the air was crisp and clear. Stepping into it put my mind at ease. I was overcome with the spectacular wrought iron fences that edged out a garden so large that I could see the fence running into the horizon in both directions.

Spaced at regular intervals that lined up with the entrances to the building, were large archways that permitted entrance to the garden. Heavy vines as black as night accented the arches. Their thorns were the size of my hand.

The thorns were perfect for catching the Spanish moss that drooped overhead and swung in the light breeze. The air alternated between refreshing chilly gusts that woke me up and made my mind feel sharp, and warm air that enveloped me like a lazy summer's day.

Stepping through the archway, I made my way down the path. As I did, my breath caught at the beautiful plants growing inside the garden gates. To my left was one of the most knotted-looking black rosebushes I had ever seen. Its flowers had hundreds of petals, not dozens. To my right was a broad-leafed plant I couldn't compare to anything I had seen before. Its leaves snaked inward on themselves and had two jagged points that looked like fangs. I didn't dare touch them for fear they would bite.

All of the plants were black, but I appreciated and connected with the macabre twistedness of the plant life. All of the vegetation seemed normal, except for their blasphemous shapes, patterns, and black color.

I wasn't paying attention to the path when I turned the corner. I had been tracing the vines of a plant whose leaves looked like human hands when I bumped into another demon on the path. I hit him at my full walking speed. In a hurry himself, he hadn't bothered to slow down either.

Profanity escaped both our lips when we collided, but he was larger than I was. Without a second thought, he shoved me as hard as he could.

He barely gave me a glance as I stumbled backward and fell into the hand-shaped leafed shrub. I heard him laugh and swear at me as he continued on his way.

"You've got to be more careful," a familiar voice said. "You could end up running into the wrong demon."

Ruth peered down at me with a smirk on her face. Her hand extended to help me up. It took me a moment to distinguish her hand from the leaves.

"What? Are you following me now?"

"Actually, yes," she admitted, withdrawing her hand and folding her arms. Her hair was, as usual, disheveled and a single white feather clung to her tendrils, much the way a stray leaf might fall unknown into a hiker's hair. "I was hoping to find out where you were keeping yours. You owe me one for that cup of coffee you made me pay for."

"What are you talking about?" I pushed myself up and smoothed my feathered shorts to make sure I wasn't exposing myself.

"Oh, come on, Edmund," she said, looking hurt. "You were only here for seven days. Seven days! In that time, while most newbies sleep, you somehow managed to rack up enough for a *fifth-floor* suite. With *windows*! What's your secret? Did you find some unknown limbo? Have a trick to hunting? I didn't know you knew how to travel to the other side yet. So what was it?" she asked, taking a step closer so she could get into my face. "Like, did you find a crossroads or something? Did you blow up a building with a bunch of people inside and take them all? Seriously."

"I don't know what you're talking about," I said, not knowing how to phrase it any clearer.

Ruth raised an eyebrow at me, pursing her lips. "What are you doing in the garden, then?"

I threw up my hands. "I'm out for a midnight stroll."

"Yeah, right. A midnight stroll in the Garden of the Damned to tend to your precious souls. One of which you owe me." She poked her long index finger into my shoulder. "Unlike you, I don't have many to spare."

"Wait," I said, the gravity of her words like a slap to my face. "What do you mean tending to my 'precious souls'? Here, in the garden?"

Ruth crossed her arms tighter and eyed me with suspicion. "What game are you playing? You steal the souls from the worlds above and enslave them by planting them here in the garden. That's how you get them to show up on the books so you can *pay* for a cup of coffee for someone you *thought* was a friend. But you know this,

213

because you're spending more souls on one night in your room than I have spent my entire time here!"

I relaxed my shoulders and stared Ruth squarely in the eye. For some reason, I wanted her to believe me. "Ruth, I have no idea what you mean. Are you telling me these plants are *souls*?"

She looked defeated and unsure of herself. "Well, manifestations. Representations of the soul planted beneath. Like that one you landed in. You can tell it is human by the hand-shaped leaves, and the one over there with the fangs was probably a centaur or griffin. It will sprout a nice hellhound for the owner in a few more weeks." Her tone changed, "But you have to know this. You *have* to."

I was in utter shock. Horrified, really. "I had no idea."

"Then explain how you own so many."

"I have no idea." I said again.

"You *have* to know," she said, meeting my repetition with her own. "How could you have so many and not know where you put them?"

"I don't know how I got so many to begin with. How do I find out? How do I find out where they all are?"

"You've *lost* them?" she asked with an incredulous giggle.

"Is that bad? Can they be stolen?"

The question took her off guard. She took a step back. "No one steals them. Joshua would cast you out to the ships if he found out someone was stealing souls."

I froze. That was a name I was not prepared to hear.

When I didn't respond Ruth continued, "You know. The ships? You don't know about the ships?"

I still felt dazed from the punch of Joshua's name. The name brought with it a realization, a memory of a conversation that I had with Ralph moments before I came here to this world. I had forgotten that Joshua was here somewhere.

Ruth pointed up toward the sky. "Those ships?"

I followed her finger upward because I didn't feel prepared to do or say anything else. It seemed like every second here I had more questions.

When I looked up, I had even more.

"What the…?" I asked, my eyes widening.

I had seen the sky from my room and noticed its undulation. It looked like the whole world expanded and contracted with an invisible breath that I could feel in the air around me, cold then warm. What I hadn't noticed was that the sky wasn't really a sky at all, but a giant ocean. The undulation was the rise and fall of the oceanic current. To top it off, way over my head were ships in the sky. Ships that sailed on the waters.

SEVENTEEN

My hands shook around a hot cup of Earl Grey Tea that the plump server woman had set on my table. Ruth ordered two cups of coffee, making sure to clarify that I would be paying.

"However you got the souls must have happened that day. Try to remember what you did," Ruth said.

I already figured that part out. The demon that confronted me in the hall—the encounter that ended with my scythe buried in his neck—was the only explanation. Somehow, whatever I did transferred his souls to me.

"Come on," Ruth prodded. "When we were having coffee the last time, did you know then that you had so many?"

I shook my head, answering her question with one of my own. "I'm able to remember my past life, and so are you. We came from a higher level. Why do you think we're able to remember?"

I'd surprised Ruth so much today that she must have been out of the emotion, because her face remained relaxed. "You know a lot about the way things work. More than you should. I only learned that Earth was above us and that humans don't remember after they come here by watching some of the other demons. I didn't have anyone here to help *me*," she said. Even though her face didn't show any emotion, her tone was frustrated. "I learned by sneaking around and watching others."

"I'm grateful you're here for me," I said, keeping it short so she wouldn't be able to use something else I said to dodge the question.

"Yes," she finally answered. "Becoming a demon, choosing this life from the higher level. The price it takes? Killing? Included in that is the price for keeping your memory."

"Who did you kill?" I asked, allowing the truth that Ruth had to have murdered someone to finally sink in.

"You ask a lot of questions and don't give many answers," she snapped.

"I'm sorry. Is it an inappropriate question?"

"Not at all. Most demons gloat about it. Most killed more than one before coming here."

"So you only killed once?"

"I thought I had, but then thought I didn't. Turned out I really did," she replied with a cryptic answer.

"Sounds complicated," I pushed, taking a sip of my tea to seem nonchalant.

Ruth's eyes looked sad, which was an expression I had never seen on an energumen before. "It was Sister Mary Elizabeth," she blurted out. "God, how I hated her."

Now I was confused. As far as I knew, Ruth had died before Sister Mary Elizabeth.

"It was after the massacre. Somehow I survived by hiding under one of the altar tables in the chapel. I wasn't supposed to be in the chapel without supervision. When I came out, Sister Mary Elizabeth was there in the aisle. She was bleeding badly, but alive. When she looked at me, I knew how much trouble I would be in, assuming she got better and could discipline me. Somewhere in the room, a voice told me I could escape. All I had to do was take the pillow someone had kneeled on during mass and hold it over her face. She didn't struggle."

"But that doesn't make sense," I said after Ruth fell silent. "I saw her. I talked to her. Father Paul told me she had survived."

"That's what I thought, too. I remembered seeing her on TV, doing interviews about the massacre. I was certain she would come after me for what I had done. Eventually, she did."

"So you didn't kill her?"

"I did. I killed her that day in the chapel. But Sister Mary Elizabeth had a secret, Edmund. She was a killer herself."

"She was a demon."

"She *is* a demon," Ruth corrected. "In college, she

came for me. She told me she wanted my heart for what I had done. She forced me to stage my own suicide."

"How horrible! Was that the last time you saw her?"

Ruth laughed an uncomfortable laugh. "No. I see her every day. I'm her familiar. I'm enslaved to her."

I fought the urge to turn around, to check behind me, just to make sure Sister Mary Elizabeth wasn't standing in the doorway. The thought of running into her again made my skin crawl. I lost the fight with myself, and quickly scanned the room.

"You'll soon learn, Edmund, that the souls you take are never your own. The ones you own won't stay yours. Eventually you'll find yourself indebted to someone and you'll work for him or her. They'll give you an allowance and some living expenses and, depending on how wealthy they are, you can exist here quite comfortably. Even if you don't, the deal made with Joshua gives him access to the entire garden anyway. He could knock on your door tomorrow and demand them all. It's a good idea to make friends. That way slavery isn't so bad."

At the mention of Joshua's name, I scanned the room again. "It seems like the demons got the raw end of whatever that deal was," I chided.

"At least the wealth trickles down now. Joshua opened a crossroads to us. A crossroads is a place where a normal human would go after they die," she explained. "Joshua killed the family that used to take the humans to heaven and, as a result, we get all their souls. That was a huge influx of power down here. He's sending others now, too. We'll have to expand the gardens soon."

"What is he doing with all that power?" I wondered aloud.

Ruth knew the answer. "Right now he's using it to collapse the levels above us. As many as he can, from what I've heard. The more upper levels he can get to fall, the more souls will forget, and the more souls we'll have to plant."

"How successful has he been?"

"Only one as far as I know. We started to get some weird animal creatures that I've never seen before. Creatures from mythology."

"You'd make a mighty fine harpy, if I do say so myself," I laughed, and reached for the white feather in her hair. Maybe it came from one of those damn down comforters. "Here, see?" I said, plucking it from her tresses and balancing it on the tip of my finger.

Ruth laughed, blowing on the feather so it drifted across the room.

"Now, your turn. Who did you kill?" she asked.

The question caught me off guard, not because I didn't expect it (I had asked her after all), but because it came on the heels of laughter. It caused a stab of pain in my chest. "My mother," I said, shortly and honestly.

"Wow. Your birth mother or adopted mother?" she asked, leaning forward and setting her elbow on the table. She rested her chin in the palm of her hand.

"My birth mother."

She looked impressed, "So you found her, then?"

"Something like that, yeah."

"So why'd you kill her? Were you that mad that she left you in that awful orphanage?"

I forced a laugh, but it came out insincere. "Actually, she asked me to."

I wasn't prepared for Ruth's shocked look. Her face was so emotive, and she was a master at catching me unprepared with her expressions. Usually, however, I was unprepared because of her demon-like attitude toward everything. This was the first time she expressed surprise that matched the reaction I expected from a human.

"How…" she paused, "…inhuman of her."

I laughed, this time sincerely. The look of shock returned to Ruth's face. What an odd conversation this was. "Actually, that would make sense," I answered.

The confusion on Ruth's face deepened.

"Well, you see, my mom was an angel."

Ruth's face went slack. All of her did, because she dropped her coffee cup and it shattered into hundreds of ceramic pieces on the table. The hot liquid spilled into her lap, but she didn't flinch.

"Ruth? Are you okay?"

It took her a few minutes to blink, then she shook her head and looked around. We'd attracted the attention of the large servant woman. She rushed over with a rag and mopped up the mess.

"Good lord. Now why'd you go and do that?" she scoffed.

"I'm so sorry, Josephine. I don't know what came over me," Ruth said, her voice barely a whisper. She looked directly at me while continuing, "Please put this on my tab, Josephine. I'd appreciate it."

"No," I said, "I was supposed to…"

But Ruth pushed her chair back and briskly walked away.

I didn't have much time to decide to follow or not, but I knew what I'd said had set her off. I figured if Sister Mary Elizabeth and Ruth were so close, then Sister Mary Elizabeth must have filled her in about me.

Catching up to her, I asked. "Sister Mary Elizabeth doesn't know I'm here, does she?" I could barely keep up with her.

"I haven't told her yet."

We were now running down the hallway. "Are you going to now?"

She fished her key out of her pocket. Turning abruptly, she shoved it into the door.

"Ruth!" I exclaimed, concerned that I said something that was a mistake.

"Edmund, shut up! Don't *ever* tell anyone that again, do you understand? Don't say it again. Don't bring it up again. Don't talk to me about it again."

She was in the door, closing it on me. I stuck my foot in the way so she couldn't shut it.

"Why does it matter? Talk to me, Ruth."

"I should have stayed mad at you," she said, her face pressed into the small space where the door was still ajar. "Why would you put me in this position? I can't tell her. I can't tell anyone. If I do, they'll come after you. Edmund, they'll *all* come after you."

With that, she kicked my foot out of the way with amazing accuracy and strength. Then she slammed the door in my face, the sound of the lock reverberating through the hallway.

EIGHTEEN

I slept for a few more days. It had been a long time since I had dreamed. I was almost to the point of believing that demons didn't dream. Maybe they did, but blackness was all they dreamed about.

Tonight, I became aware of the darkness. In it, two yellow eyes watched me sleep. They approached silently, but as they drew closer, their intensity dimmed until they changed into a chocolate brown.

It looked like someone finally turned on some lights, twisting a dimmer switch on the wall. Xia stepped from the shadows and the world around me exploded into a fury of Earthly color. The room I was in was still my bedroom, but the white carpet, furniture, and bed coverings looked different in the light. White had many shades, some bluer, some more yellow. As a demon, I had forgotten almost all of them.

Xia stood at the foot of my bed, her black hair

cascading over a blouse so red it made me forget whether red even existed in this world. She raised a leg, seductively positioning her foot on the edge of the bed. Her skirt was so short that I pushed myself down deeper into the mattress. The view from a lower angle wouldn't hide any part of her.

She unbuttoned her shirt, her eyebrows rising playfully while her ruby red lips grew irresistible with each button. When the last one fell away and her blouse hung loosely on her shoulders, I couldn't contain myself. I had to touch her.

I would have leapt from the bed, except she shook her head and wagged her finger at me. She wanted me to stay exactly where I was; she wanted me to enjoy the show. I was drinking her in. I wanted to remember her satin skin and ruby lips when I woke up. The color of her skin that was slightly lighter between her breasts. I wanted to be reminded of it all, to experience her in all the ways I was robbed from being able to experience her every day.

When she pulled the blankets off me, I almost protested. I didn't like her seeing me like this. I was ashamed and self-conscious that I lacked my physical body. I looked more like a shadow than a man.

But none of that mattered when she walked to the side of the bed and took my hand in her own. I forgot about all of my protests the moment I felt her warmth, because all I wanted was to feel her skin against me.

My mind dizzied as she picked up my hand and

placed it on her inner thigh. My heart thudded and I licked my lips as she directed my hand upward with a light touch. I had forgotten how warm and smooth her inner thigh was. Grateful as I was for the spot where my hand ended up, I was already considering how much better it would be if I could use my tongue instead.

While I might have forgotten what it felt like to touch Xia, I did remember how she tasted.

Xia climbed on top of me, running her fingers softly up my chest, to my shoulders, then down the insides of my arms until both her hands clasped mine. She pulled my hands above my head and pinned them there as her ruby lips settled on mine.

Except those weren't Xia's lips. Xia's lips always tasted like peppermint and cherry lip balm. Xia's lips were soft and playful. This kiss was hard and tasted rotten.

"Told you it wouldn't be too hard to get into his head," Xia said. Except it wasn't her voice.

And I wasn't dreaming.

Laughter pealed throughout the room. I struggled to get up, but the demon sitting on me was heavy. It was Josephine, the gluttonous server.

"Show him your tits again. He liked that part," one of the other voices said.

"Did you *really* want to *taste* her?" another voice smacked, followed by irreverent laughter from a group.

"Shut up!" Josephine bellowed. "I've had plenty of licks in my day, thank you very much."

The laughter erupted again.

"Get off me," I said through clenched teeth.

"Aw, come on, baby. We were just getting to the good part," she said.

Someone else took hold of my wrists, someone even stronger than Josephine.

"Just let me back into that head of yours," she continued, tapping her finger on my forehead as I struggled to get up. "That girl of yours was quite a peach. I can play her. I'll get you off in ways that slanted pussy hasn't learned yet."

"What do you want?" I asked, my jaw still clenched. It was that or spit in her face. I decided since I still wasn't sure how many of them were in the room, I wouldn't take my chances… yet.

"Besides a good ride?" Josephine cackled, bouncing up and down. "It's always the girl that can be used to get to you chaps, isn't it? Well, unless you're a chap who likes chaps. You got one of them floatin' around in that head of yours too, don't ya? I almost had a hard time deciding which character to play. Minyak over there woulda had to do the kissin', on account of having the right parts."

"Get to the point, Josephine," a voice said. From the exasperated sound of it, I would have guessed it was Minyak.

"See, there's been some talk about you," Josephine said, her voice changing. It was less playful, lower in pitch, more dangerous. "How is it that a wee little pup managed to set yourself up in this fancy room in less than a month? At first we thought you must have been all tied up with a devil, but we've been asking around, and are pretty sure you're not connected."

"Maybe I am the devil," I replied coldly.

The room burst into laughter again.

"Oh, you got some fight in ya, I can tell. Some power too, methinks. Most people can't see past me in their dreams so fast. But you ain't no devil."

She leaned closer, her yellow eyes burning into mine. I could smell her hot breath on my face. It smelled of rotten eggs and tuna fish. "Now, we don't care about whatever secret it is you're hiding, see. We just want a cut. So you're going to work for us now, or we'll start talkin'. The people we'll be talkin' to won't be as generous as we were by letting you play a little with your girlfriend and all. Though they'll still be after your balls, if you catch my drift."

Josephine patted my cheek, but got off me.

"You know, maybe I'll put myself up in a room like this. Next door, even. That way we can have these little chats as often as I'd like. Why don't you go see the front desk right away and make sure I get upgraded, if you wouldn't mind."

"If I ever see you in here again," I said as the hands around my wrists loosened, "I'll kill you, and any of the little friends you bring with you."

Josephine cackled again. "Kid, you can't kill a

demon."

"You sure about that?" I challenged, although I wasn't sure myself. When I used my scythe against the demon in the hallway, he vanished in a fiery show. I didn't know whether or not he was dead, or what death even meant here.

It didn't matter. No one was there to hear my challenge. Somehow, they'd already disappeared.

I went to the front desk right away, but not to get Josephine a room next door to mine. When I arrived, I peeked into the café. Josephine was nowhere to be seen.

"Hey, Alexander," Lilith said, surprising me. She wasn't usually the one to start a conversation.

"Hey, Lilith. I was just coming to see you."

"Find the extra down comforter in your closet?"

I laughed. "No, not exactly. Hey, the other day I woke up and there was a guy in the room cleaning up. How do I ask for a private room? I don't want anyone else to have a key."

Lilith smiled. "We're spirits, Edmund. The rooms exist only to divide the space. The locks are flair for the newbies. For a while, we all laughed at you fiddling with your bone," she said, shifting her gaze to something more lascivious.

"So I can just walk into any room I want?"

"Well, yes. Technically. I wouldn't suggest it, though. If you walk into the room of someone more powerful than you, or someone who has an employer that's more powerful than you, you'll regret it. For the most part, we respect each other's privacy."

"Are there any laws? Someone I could talk to if this guy keeps coming back?"

"The big, bad demon that replaces your candles and washes your windows?" Lilith smirked.

I rested my hand on the counter and leaned forward, donning a lascivious expression of my own. I was young, right? I knew how to flirt. "What can I say? I don't like people touching my things."

Lilith bit her lip and scanned the room. "Look. There's talk about you. I've tried to keep it to myself, but I'm curious. How did you end up so wealthy so quickly?"

"Maybe I have some demons working for me."

Lilith eyed me with suspicion, but her face didn't lose the spark that told me she was interested in what I had to say. "How would someone like you get so many demons to work for him?"

"Why don't you come to work for me and find out?"

Lilith blushed. "I don't know if you're playing with me, flirting with me, or being honest. Whatever the case, my current employer wouldn't like it if I started *working* for someone so much younger than him."

I rapped my knuckles on the counter. "Well, the offer's on the table." I turned to leave. I got two steps when I thought of one more question I wanted to ask. "Oh, one last thing. If I wanted to upgrade, how much more a night would it take me to go up a floor or two?"

"The floor isn't based on how much you can afford a night, although the cost is proportionate," she said. "They're based on an average monthly quota. Fifth floor means you bring in at least 50,000 souls a month. Considering you've been asleep more than half that time already, I would guess upgrading to the tenth floor next month shouldn't be a problem for you."

"So the 100th floor—"

"—not just for demons who *have* a million souls, but *bring in* a million souls a month," Lilith finished my thought.

"How do they manage so many?" I asked, honestly curious.

Lilith shrugged. "They have a lot of employees."

"Still, it doesn't seem there would be enough souls to sustain that for very long."

"The mortality rate on Earth is 150,000 a day," she rattled off, expertly. "If we claim all of those souls, there's enough for all seven—" she froze. "I got suckered into telling you that, didn't I?"

I pointed at her with a flirtatious grin. I didn't want her to feel like I was using her, and that dream with Xia had me noticing the women around me. Lilith was pretty. "What can I say? I've always been bad at math."

Seven. There were seven demons on the top level. If there were only seven apartments on the top floor, they had to be huge.

More importantly, these seven demons had to be the

ones that made the deal with Joshua. There would be no other way that they could have gained so much power.

Most importantly, those seven demons were the source of Joshua's power here.

I wasn't worried about Josephine or the others. They were itching to get to the fifth floor, so I doubted they had the power to sway anyone important. Now I knew it was also unlikely that they were even employed by someone who was employed by someone who was employed by the top seven.

Josephine could have my room… when I moved up.

If I had millions of souls, I wouldn't work the garden myself. Of course, I would have the same demons that worked collecting the souls work the garden for me. I might even let them believe some of the souls they planted for me were theirs. That's how I would set up the system, if it were up to me. "Plant your souls in this garden," I would say, while in the back of my mind knowing everything they planted was really mine.

Ruth told me she learned her secrets by watching other demons. I was going to learn from her and do the same, but hopefully on a larger scale.

I walked into the garden with greater purpose and the seeds of a plan forming. I didn't stop to take note of the moss hanging above my head, or the intricacies of the plants that looked as black as oil. I knew each plant was a representation of a life, of a creature that had been taken by an energumen and now fueled Joshua's power.

It took me a while to reach the center of the garden, but I appreciated the fact that I had no muscles that got tired or lungs that felt breathless. I carried my quick pace, almost floating over the surface of the walkways.

At the center courtyard, there was a fountain that looked inspired from Greek and Roman art, only this fountain paid homage to demonic conquests. In the middle stood a bronze figure of Joshua. Surrounding him were scenes of dark demons in various poses of dominance over angels, centaurs, and humans. Seven dark demons.

The fountain sprayed blood high into the air, which then painted the bronze statues as it dripped back into the pool. The whole scene was accented by the large ball of fire that was becoming visible on the other end of the park. It was the perfect fiery backdrop.

To be honest, I found the scene impeccable. As a demon, I appreciated the wickedness of it all.

As I suspected, this place was a hub of demonic activity. Some bathed in the blood of the fountain while others rested on benches that lined the large courtyard.

I turned back to the building to get my bearings. The sections of gardens too close to the building would not be easily visible from the higher vantage point of the top floors, but I had a direct line of sight from here in the courtyard to the highest windows. Even if these demons had employees and workers, they would want to keep watch on their investments.

When I had been a child in Orenda, on the night before I was killed there, I met an energumen. I allowed his words to echo back in my mind now:

How odd and how strange that I would find three little mages while seeking for men. Its voice had said, strangely sweet and alluring. Quiet, like a whisper that sounded like a song. *Perhaps I will take you back to my realm, and leave the men be. A great reward for one mage; imagine the prize for three!*

If an angel's soul was somehow worth more, I had no doubt they would be planted here, near the back, near the ball of fire, where they would be illuminated and visible to the upper windows. If my hunch was correct, the further out from the building, the more important and powerful the soul.

"Hey, you," I said, stopping a demon passing me. "Can you give me a hand here?"

"What's in it for me?" the demon turned, eyeing me carefully.

"A lot, if my employer is happy. I'm supposed to do some work on his angels back there somewhere," I motioned, "but I can't remember where they are."

At the mention of the word 'angels,' half the demons in the square turned and looked at me.

"Who's your employer?" the demon asked. The vacant look in his eye told me he knew as little as I did where the angels were located. Damn.

"The last time I told someone, he made me sleep on the first floor for a month," I grinned, controlling my facial expressions carefully, but not stiffly.

I got a rumble of giggles from the demons within earshot, plus a few nods of understanding.

"You're the newbie, right? The guy who got promoted to the fifth floor in just a few weeks?" one of the other demons sitting next to the fountain asked.

Bingo. This was the guy I wanted. "Yeah, that's right."

"Is that how you did it? Went and got yourself some wealthy benefactor?"

"Ah come on," I joked, playing up the part. "You've all got an angel or two under your belts by now, don't you?"

The first demon that spoke to me grumbled. "We don't get to keep any of *those* ones."

I slapped him on the shoulder in a friendly manner, but addressed the demon behind him. "Can you show me?"

"Depends on who your employer is," he prodded. "But they're all back there."

"I'll tell you," I eyed the other demons who were now all looking in my direction, eavesdropping, hoping to learn a secret that could hold some leverage over whoever my rich benefactor was. "But only you."

"What's your name?" the demon asked. I wasn't prepared for that. This guy was smarter than I thought.

" 'New Guy' works fine for me," I grinned, looking innocent. "It's what everyone calls me anyway."

The demon in front of me, the one who I'd talked to first, laughed. I recognized the laugh. He was one of the demons in my room this morning with Josephine. I took mental note of his sharp jaw and crooked smile so I could recognize him again. I was sure this wouldn't be the last time I'd see him.

The demon that seemed like he knew more about the angels motioned for me to follow him. He stepped out of the courtyard and down a path toward the flames. I followed until I was sure we were out of earshot.

He spoke first. "It would be helpful to know who your employer is, or at least who he works for. This area is the start of the Royal Gardens. There are seven sections, as I'm sure you already know."

I watched his gaze slide over to me as I stepped up to his side. He was wary of me now, but still curious. I was sure he was certain he could handle me if I were lying, but something I said or did made him cautious; I could see suspicion in his eyes. "Which of the sections do you tend most often?" I asked, not feigning curiosity.

The demon stopped and faced me. "I think it's time you give a little information before you ask any more questions."

"Fine," I said. "I'm supposed to find someone in particular. I need to confirm that a certain plant is being cared for as intended. It's a special case—someone who had great importance to the work and who took a long time to gather. He was the keeper of the crossroads, the same crossroads we now use to claim the souls of humans who die."

The demon sneered. "You're looking for the Angel of Death. Why?"

"I'm not *just* looking for the Angel of Death. I'm looking for him *and* his family."

The demon was more comfortable now that we were talking. He started walking again with me by his side. "My question remains," he said. "Why are you looking for these particular angels?"

I told him the truth. Not that it would matter much in the long run, as long as my plan went according to… well… plan. "I want to make sure the entire line is present and accounted for. Joshua made certain promises regarding this family, promises to my employer and his employer, related to the control of the crossroads. I don't think we can be satisfied until the entire family is accounted for, do you?"

The demon looked back at me, his eyes hungry for power. Whatever he was going to say next was key. It would reveal his real reason for helping me. "What do you know of this family that the rest of us do not?"

Inside I jumped for joy, but I controlled my expression so I wouldn't reveal my excitement. The information about my family must not have been shared throughout the demonic world, or they would have known my mother and I were unaccounted for.

"I know that he had a wife and a son."

"And you are looking for their plants?"

"Yes."

"What if I told you I knew they were not here?"

I was taken aback. He knew more than he was letting on. "Then the line is not under our control. That's a problem my employer would like to solve."

The demon stopped. "Well then, I've already done your work for you. As I said, I am certain that they are not here. So now you've wasted my time and your own. Tell me the name of your employer so I can request payment for my lost time."

"You're going to blackmail me?"

"Of course. I didn't lead you to a place where we could be alone for no reason. Since you have no idea where you are or where you are going, I doubt you are employed for someone as important as you say. Otherwise, you'd have known that we passed the plot of garden you should be familiar with twice already. I will give you one final chance to tell me the name of your employer, or I will have you stripped of rank and power and send you off to the barges where you will work for me forever."

I didn't doubt he could do whatever he said he could do, although now I wished I had more time with him to ask about the subjects he brought up—about stripping others of their power and rank, about the barges, which I guessed were somehow connected to the ships that were sailing across the ocean… or sky… or both?

But the look in his eye was determined. It should've

inspired fear. Instead, I smiled. "Fine," I said. "Edmund. Edmund is the name of my employer."

The demon's head cocked to one side as he processed the name. "I don't know of any devil named Edmund, but it is familiar. Why do I know that name?"

"I don't know," I stated, the blade of my scythe slicing into the demon's neck. "Oh wait. Yes I do."

The demon burst into flame.

I knew what would happen. This demon would be missed. News of his disappearance would spread through the lower ranks—I just wasn't sure how fast.

I hoped I had caused enough of a scene in the courtyard to convince the demons that I was employed by one of the higher-level demons, because as news spread to them of someone hired to steal the spirits of other demons, I wanted there to be finger-pointing and blame. I wanted the demons to fight among themselves to discover who my employer was. I wanted that fight to go all the way to the top.

If I were right, based on what I had learned about the hierarchy and secrecy of this place, there would be dissension in the ranks. Dissension that would reach all the way to the top seven.

Let one of them come down and find me.

Let one of them come ask me who my employer was.

NINETEEN

I was upgraded to the fifteenth floor that night, but flirted enough with Lilith to convince her to give Josephine a room on the tenth floor, leaving me on the fifth. I didn't do this for Josephine's sake, but because it worked in my favor to get her off my back. It also took some suspicion off me. Anyone who figured out I was responsible for the death of the demon would think my employer took the lot of souls. Staying where I was helped support the rumor that I worked for someone higher up.

I wanted panic and chaos at the thought of a demon hired to steal souls from other demons. After all, how would a 'new guy' know how to do such a thing, or have the capability of doing it? I was just 'Alexander,' poor human orphan employed by some big bad devil and taught how to burn demons. Not the most foolproof plan, but I only needed it to work for a little while. If word made it to Joshua, he would know what was happening. I hoped the chaos I caused would sufficiently give me enough time to weaken his hold over the garden before he was aware of it.

I didn't know what I expected when I went downstairs the next morning. Perhaps I was hoping for mayhem and chaos. I expected upturned tables and a lobby in shambles, but that wasn't the case.

Instead, I was disappointed to find everything perfectly normal. Lilith was at the front desk, her feet propped up on the counter with her usual magazine in her hands. She glanced at me as I crossed through the lobby.

"Did you think these girls were pretty, on Earth?" she asked, holding up a picture of Angelina Jolie on the cover of People Magazine.

I walked over to her and shrugged. "Brad Pitt seemed to like her. At least he did when I died. She's pretty. She has nice lips."

Lilith scoffed. "In my time, girls like Josephine were more desirable. Humans are too skinny now. You must agree."

"Why's that?"

"Well, you chose to give her an upgraded room instead of…" she stopped.

"Instead of?"

"I don't know. Some other girl."

My eyes narrowed. "You didn't want to come work for me, remember?"

Lilith laughed. "I don't think you'd hire Josephine either. Whatever she did to gain your favor, I'm sure I

RICK CHIANTARETTO

could do better."

"She threatened me," I replied honestly. I didn't want her thinking Josephine was doing *me* any favors.

Lilith leaned back in her chair and put her feet up on the desk again. She held back a grin. "So why didn't you have your employer take care of her, then?"

Either she was playing with me, or word had spread. I gave a neutral answer that could work either way. "Best not to rock the boat."

"Mmmhmm," Lilith hummed, raising an eyebrow at me. I didn't know what she did or didn't know.

"How long have you been here?" I changed the subject to something safer.

"Oh, about 400 years."

"A Renaissance girl, huh?

"Something like that."

"How did a girl like you get to be the front desk keeper at the Hotel California?"

She didn't get the reference, but closed her magazine and got the gist of my question.

"I was in London in 1665, but from Eyam originally. When I was a girl, my father offered me to the men in the village. I fled to London when I was thirteen. When the plague hit, I was illiterate, poor, and without family, so I became a searcher of the dead. Do you know what they did?"

"They got paid to help keep records of those who died in the plague," I said, remembering the term from a history class.

"Well, I got infected." Her gaze dropped. "I figured if I was going to die, I would at least bring judgment to the town full of men who abused me. I left London and made my way back to Eyam. My vengeance resulted in eighty percent of the village falling to plague."

"You wiped out an entire town?"

"Now I work the front desk," she said without emotion. "What did you do to earn yourself a position of such luxury?"

"Tell me this," I said, carefully justifying my query so she wouldn't suspect it. "Did you kill your father?"

"Of course!" she spat.

"Why?"

"Because I hated him."

I nodded. "I killed my mother."

"So what? There are many demons here who are of lower status who have done much worse."

"Yes," I said, letting my stare burn into hers. "What is more cruel? Killing because you hate, or killing because you love?"

Lilith crossed her arms. "Do you think that matters?"

I shrugged. Maybe it wasn't enough to convince her, but it was a good start. "I don't know," I admitted. "I'm just the new guy."

I walked away, grinning.

Lilith sat, looking tongue-tied. She didn't want me to go, but it was to my advantage to leave her wanting more.

I used my newfound *friendship* with Josephine to have coffee and a strawberry tart delivered to Lilith. That was the closest thing Josephine had that was from the Renaissance. I hoped the thought would make up for any lack of authenticity.

Josephine wasn't as accommodating as I hoped, considering I'd upgraded her stature. I half-expected her to make the delivery for free; instead, she charged me double for the coffee, plus extra for the time it would take her to waddle across the lobby.

Making my way back out to the garden, I debated whether I should go toward the back. Those demons would be worth more, but maybe staying up front and picking off a few lower-level demons would be a good idea. I didn't want to cause panic only in the back of the garden. It was a bad idea to bring attention to a place where more powerful demons could be dispatched to protect the crops. But I knew it was the higher-ranking demons that had the knowledge I needed, and the power to make noise. Yes, I needed power.

Besides, it was quieter in the back. The last thing I needed was someone noticing who I was and what I was doing.

I made my way past the courtyard and toward the back of the garden. The pathways here were narrower. They were less traveled, but the plants were denser. It was no wonder I was able to walk around in circles when I was here last time without noticing.

The plants were so tall and the pathways so narrow that the only way I could keep my bearings was to repeatedly check for the source of light—the giant burning ball that lit up the seafoam green sky.

Sticking to the edges of the paths, I walked carefully. I wanted to take someone by surprise, not because it would make stealing his or her crop easier, but because I actually hoped to run into someone I could observe for a while, unnoticed.

Turn after turn, row after row, pathway after narrowing pathway, I grew more discouraged. I was so close to the fire that I could see flames leaping above the contrasting oily plants. The air around me started to heat up and dry out. My smoky skin reacted to the heat in an odd way, swirling faster and billowing within the confines of my spirit body.

Someone had to be here. I felt a familiar domineering presence, a presence that filled the area with a sense of observance, a sense of knowing. Someone was watching me. I wondered if I'd made a mistake. Now the stalker was becoming the stalked.

Turning a final corner, the feeling of being watched intensified so much that I didn't doubt someone would be standing in the pathway. I was prepared for a smoky, dark body dressed in iridescent feathers, with strong yellow eyes. I was prepared for something new, something more powerful, something darker than an energumen. Whatever was here was throwing a deeper and stronger energy.

Instead, I found nothing but a long pathway that dead-ended in fire. The pathway was otherwise empty.

Still, the draw of the presence was all around me. It pulled me down the path, toward the flames that now rolled upward and leapt into the pathway, charring the plants at the edge of the garden.

I peered between branches and leaves as I walked, expecting to see a flicker of shadow or a glimmer of yellow. It would be easy for a demon to hide in the plants.

As I neared the flames, wisps of smoke escaped from my body. They curled and danced in the still and heavy air, like fine tendrils of smoke dancing from the tip of burning incense. The reaction created a curious sensation as it ran through me, like when sweat would run down my forehead, except this sensation covered my entire spirit body as the wisps streamed from my pores.

The rolling ball of fire was so bright that it surrounded me in its orange glow. The seafoam green edges had faded, the light so encompassing that I couldn't see the top windows of the building anymore. I was engulfed in orange sky, contrasted with black plants at the edge of the garden.

I lost myself in the mesmerizing flame. The way it rolled in unison made it seem as if there was a single source, a point where the flames originated before exploding into a ball of fire. But the black-planted souls still hid the source from my view.

Suddenly, I was drawn to the last plant on the corner

of this pathway. Its odd, delicate leaves shook violently with every step I took, no matter how softly I walked. Then the fire in the sky changed so that each flickering flame directed its flow and attention to the plant.

The heavy leaves of this plant hung from fragile stems, which made them catch every breath and rustle in wind that could be created with something as subtle as waves of thought. As I drew closer, the shape of the leaves became distinguishable against the orange background. Small, sickle-shaped blades hung from razor-thin stems.

Without thinking, I touched the plant. An electrical current flowed through my body, confirming to my spirit what my mind already knew. This was my father, the man who sacrificed himself for me, the man who was the Angel of Death. He was reduced to a growing essence planted in the Garden of the Damned, his life force growing like an apple tree, ripening to harvest.

My entire being flooded with the need to save him. I pulled energy and power from the ground like I used to do in Orenda, but this energy was darker, angrier. It fell perfectly in line with the darkness already roiling in the pit of my stomach. Anger and darkness fueled my passion for revenge. Rage flowed down my arm, into the plant. My father would know I was here to avenge him, here to destroy, here to steal him back. Nothing would stop me.

My father's leaves quivered in response, each leaf clapping against another in a rustling noise that sounded like whispers. Darkness consumed me. The plant's leaves shook violently, so violently that they shook themselves loose, raining tiny sickles at my feet.

My skin erupted. I evaporated into a dark mist fueled by nothing but pure, blinding rage. I'd never felt so powerful, so vengeful toward anything and anyone that would get in my way. My desire for revenge was like a seed sprouting plans for the annihilation of the demonic, even if it meant destroying myself in the process.

I would let Edmund go. I would become the only feared thing in Hell. I would claim this garden and all inhabitants for my own, using them to propel me to where I could control this world.

Using whatever means necessary, I would destroy every living creature on Earth and in Heaven if I had to. I would find the demon that used my father's power and use that same power against him. I would fight fire with fire. By the time the demons knew what hit them, their power would be mine.

I would take it.

I would take it all.

I would swallow it all into the darkness within, expanding that darkness until it consumed every demon, every soul, in this garden.

I felt so large. I could see over the entire landscape. I used the power of this place to fuel my expansion. Just like I had used nature to pulse my power outward to feel what was around me, I could use hate, anger, rage, and revenge to do so now. I could easily find the demons in the garden.

I could almost count all of them in the building.

They would cower before me.

I would show them what a demon could become, how dark and depraved.

I would be the thing they had nightmares about.

As I began slipping into blind, reckless abandon, a new energy reached inside of me and grabbed my breastbone. The energy was calming and cool, enduring and kind, full of love and concern; it felt as if a hand had reached in and clutched my chest, pulling me back down, back down to sanity, back down to myself.

It was not the energy of my father. I felt the shock of my connection to him, but this energy wasn't masculine. This was intuitive and gentler than my father had ever been. It was more caring and familiar. This was an energy I felt in every single one of my lives. It was an energy that was present in Orenda, and also on Earth.

Now it was here in Hell.

I didn't hear the words as much as I felt them. The opening phrase shook me to my core. I'd heard it before. The implications stunned me.

Hello, young one.

I spun at the familiarity of the voice, for the first time seeing the source of the flames.

Mother Tree was the source of light in this world. She was the wonderful, loving, intuitive creature that fed the perpetual flames leaping from her branches.

I fell to my knees. Her twisted limbs and branches

took shape at the center of the fire. The image brought back terrible memories of the day in Orenda when Joshua had sent back a sorcerer's fire that consumed her. In my mind, I could still hear the flames crackling along her branches and the popping percussion as she and her children exploded.

Here, her flames were eternal.

I could feel emotion pouring out of her, but she was unable to form coherent words. I crawled toward her, but couldn't hear her whispers above the roaring of the flames. Even the feelings were jumbled and misguided. In her agony, I never felt her ask for help. Instead, she did everything in her power to help me!

It took great effort for her to reach inside me, to save me from going down the path of darkness, to stop me from drawing on the power of the garden.

As I pulled myself near, flooded with emotions I didn't understand, I collapsed under the weight of everything she was trying to tell me. I couldn't receive clearly because of the flames. Thousands upon thousands of thoughts and voices cried out from the flames. Mother Tree wasn't alone here. She was set ablaze by the essence and voices of all of her children. The flames she perpetually supported were the voices and souls of her own offspring—the other trees.

This was what Joshua had done to stop the trees from talking. This was why all they could do was shout incoherently in Orenda.

This poor mother wouldn't give up on her children. She would let them consume her.

I didn't know if Mother Tree told me this, or if I was able to pick it up out of the flood of flame. Listening to them scream in unison was like trying to read a book backward. Occasionally I could hear a clear word. If I could string them all together, maybe I could form an idea or a sentence out of the thousands of misdirected and unintelligible thoughts.

I wanted to be angry at Joshua, but even with all of the agony, sadness, and deep desires the trees had, Mother Tree was a true mother at heart. She was willing to suffer for her children, relentless in her care for them, and unwilling to blame others for the support and sustenance she gave her offspring. She included me as if I were one of her own. The outpouring of love and support from her drained my anger and replaced it with joy.

This brought my thoughts to Xia and the joy I would feel watching her have children of her own. I wanted to experience this connection, this joy, this unrelenting protection and connection she would have with her children, even as the thought surfaced that those children couldn't and wouldn't be mine. It didn't matter—I wanted her to *feel* what Mother Tree was feeling. I wanted to understand that happiness, and agony, all wrapped up into one complicated emotion.

I wanted to watch Xia's face light up and her eyes grow tired as she sacrificed her own body and desires for her children's happiness. I wanted to watch her fall asleep from a long day of playing—exhausted, but content.

I wanted to watch her frustration as she sat in the bathroom, aching for a moment to herself while little fingers tried to pry the bathroom door open from underneath, begging to be let in, begging to play, begging to never be left alone, begging to be supported and loved every waking moment.

Motherhood was a blessing and a curse. The blessing was tied to the curse and the curse was tied to the blessing.

As above, so below.

I understood my own mother now. I understood her sacrifice and willingness to do anything to protect me. It wasn't easy for her. Helping me get here was part of the curse, no doubt. But the release, the reason, the knowledge that her sacrifice would mean something for me—her son, her child, her offspring—was also a blessing.

My mother knew the only way to protect me was to put me here, to make me face danger.

As above, so below.

That was why Mother Tree granted my request during our first meeting. The reason she let me use her roots to see. She knew it was what my mother would have done.

She gave her life for me just like my mother did.

I realized in this moment that this line of thinking was not just Mother Tree teaching me about herself, about my mother, or about motherhood in general. There was more than a lesson here. She was trying to help me.

I returned to my last thought, to the time when I met Mother Tree. With the help of the emotion pouring out of her, I recalled the words she'd spoken before:

Your heart is troubled and I sense you have come to make a request, the wind hissed between her branches.

This was still true. My heart was troubled, but what request did I come with?

My roots are deep.

I was plunged into the same fear I'd felt while on a mountain, surrounded by the fog. The emotion was unique because I was full of terror, but was also coming off a high of excitement and anticipation when I thought I'd seen Ralph's flaming red hair dancing in the black and white world created on the Carlsbad Mountains. I met Mother Tree there as well; she showed me what it was like for her to die, and how it felt to travel from one world to the next. It had felt like her soul retreated in on itself and sprouted from the same roots, except on the other side.

As above, so below.

My roots are deep.

Like a lightning bolt, I knew what request I had. I now knew what this wonderful, beautiful, incredible tree was trying to teach me.

It was how the demons crossed into other worlds.

It was how they got the nickname 'Level Walkers.'

It was the entire point of the garden.

The plants grew roots deep enough that they interconnected. They grew roots deep enough to spiritually touch roots from other worlds.

Mother Tree showed me that the secret to level walking was something I'd already learned as a child. I'd done it that day in Orenda when I skipped across the connected roots to the rose plant in the center of the town square.

I could use the roots to see. More, she was offering to allow me to use her roots, which ran deeper than any other plant, into all three of the levels I had experienced so far.

This was something she hadn't let another do. This was why Joshua had set her ablaze with the spirits and voices of her own children—because she wouldn't allow him to do the same.

TWENTY

Descending into the entanglement of roots had a sense of familiarity and a sense of esoteric existence that was unfamiliar to me. Each root was a silver strand of light slicing through the darkness. These were like the same silver streams of light that I followed inwardly to escape the demon that tried to kill me in my truck. They were also the same streams of light that once led me between the mountains in Orenda when I rescued Xia and Nicholas.

This whole time I'd been using the system without even knowing what it was—a system of energy and outreach between the living and the dead.

The entire grid pulsed in shimmering light, forming nets of color like a giant fiber-optic network. It reminded me of human technology networks, but in comparison the human networks were crude replications of something that nature and spirit had already built.

Instinctively, I knew I could go anywhere. There was

a pathway that could take me to where my mom had been reborn. The one over there could take me to the river in Orenda where Linda Rose was sunning herself on her favorite tree branch. Being plugged in was like being everywhere and nowhere at the same time.

I knew exactly where I wanted to go. No silver thread held more draw over me than the one that ran right through my heart. Xia was on the other end.

I had barely even thought to go when I found myself walking down a hallway in one of the University of California, San Diego dormitories. The space was brightly lit, and laughter came from one of the common areas. It must have been the weekend, because a lot of people were up and about. Seeing the full moon through a passing window confirmed the early hour.

Catching a glimpse of my yellow eyes in that same window, I decided it best to raise the cloak around me. I didn't want to startle Xia, especially since she had never seen me in this demonic form.

I was filled with anxiety. Maybe I shouldn't be here. What if she was scared of me? What if she never wanted to see me again after the terror of seeing me with yellow eyes?

How much had Linda Rose told her about the plan to return my scythe and ring, about her plan to help me descend into the underworld? Did Linda Rose know and tell Xia that my path would lead me to become the thing we feared? The thing had spent our last few days together fighting?

What if she had moved on? She was obviously attending school, which meant she was caught up in a life of classes, homework, and frat parties. She was surrounded by guys.

What if she wasn't alone? What if she was only in her room tonight because she had someone in there with her? Could I see her like that? Would I be able to understand if she were to seek the company of others? Could I blame her?

I froze outside her door. Of course I wouldn't blame her.

I would just kill him.

Yeah. That was a good compromise.

I ran my hands down my chest as if straightening my shirt, then swallowed and licked my lips. Why was I so nervous? Maybe I should have brought flowers. Where would I have gotten flowers? Black roses from the garden wouldn't have been appropriate. Technically that would've been no different than bringing her someone's finger or earlobe. No, she wouldn't have liked that.

Should I knock?

Here I was, standing outside the door of the girl I loved, letting the decision of whether to knock hold me back.

I almost turned around. Maybe *I* didn't want her to see me like this.

I had to decide. Stay, or go?

No reason to knock. I should just walk in as a scary

black figure with a giant, hooded cloak.

Maybe I should extend my angel wings so she would know I was a gentle, loving creature… with yellow eyes and a desire to tie her to the bed. Okay, so she'd see right past the 'innocent-demon-Angel-of-Death' ploy.

She would just have to freak out, and *then* be happy to see me.

I could deal with that.

That was it.

That was the plan.

I took one step forward but stopped instantly when I came face-to-face with a giant white dog. Its ice-blue eyes were so close to my own that I was sure its snout was inside the hood of my cloak. I watched as the dog's lips pulled back over razor-sharp fangs that were so close to my eyes that I couldn't focus on them.

Hecate. I felt elation and terror at the same time. Xia was still using Hecate to protect her. What an amazing woman she was! Smart and powerful.

But I was a bad guy, and the dog was snarling. I felt warning in Hecate's eyes. I had come far enough, but would not be allowed to enter the room.

I frantically flipped through everything I knew about this goddess, but couldn't come up with anything useful. All I knew was that she carried a bow and twin torches, could manifest as a woman or as a white dog, and was protective of women. Xia had a special bond with her.

Maybe I could use that?

The last time Hecate had been summoned I was possessed. She was able to attack the demonic spirit inside me without harming my physical body, which meant she knew a thing or two about demons.

She knew more about me than I knew about her; she probably knew more about me than I knew about myself.

I wasn't just a demon, though. I was also an angel and a human. Most importantly, the woman I loved was a few feet beyond that door. Xia was so close I could sense her breathing and hear her heartbeat. I knew she was asleep, because her breaths were slow and even.

The dog's face retreated slightly as I drew my scythe. I knew I couldn't win against a goddess as a demon, but maybe I could use my role as an angel to my advantage.

"I am not here to harm the woman," I spoke, slow and calm. "I am not here to lay claim on her life as the Angel of Death either, though if I were here in an official capacity you would be opposing the natural order by stopping me." I wanted to be firm and persuasive, yet not provoking.

Hecate's lip twitched over a sharp fang, but she retreated further.

"Take heed! Whether man, angel, or demon, if your intentions are impure, I will drive you from this place," the dog spoke. "This woman is under my protection."

She flashed me her icy look once more, but stepped to the side, allowing me passage.

I should have knocked. It would have been easier

than risking the wrath of a goddess.

I put away my scythe and stepped into the room. It smelled like incense and candle wax, and was much warmer than I'd expected.

Xia's desk was littered with books and papers, many of which were related to her schoolwork. Others were heavier, older, and emblazoned with golden triquetras that glowed in the flickering light of a white candle that burned on a nearby windowsill.

That same candlelight flickered across Xia's bare shoulder. Her head was turned away from me as she lay sleeping, sprawled on her stomach, her face toward the wall. Her dark hair spilled across the pillow with an unusual unkempt chaos I'd never seen from her before; her hair always flowed and curled with such precision and ease that I took for granted how much time she must have spent to make it look so perfect.

I hoped her life wasn't so frazzled, so chaotic.

I touched the skin at the nape of her neck, causing goose bumps to race over her exposed skin and plummet downward, disappearing under the covers.

She cooed and stirred, rolling over without opening her eyes. Her skin looked so rich and orange with the flickering candlelight that her lips took on the blush of a ripe peach instead of their usual rosy red.

I wanted to stand there and watch her sleep. I wanted to breathe in her scent and watch over her like the white dog that sat stiffly in the corner, not taking her eyes off me. I wanted to be Xia's protection so she could sleep safely and comfortably at night.

But I also thought that standing here, looking down at her, was creepy.

I bent over and whispered in her ear. "Hi Xia, don't be afraid. It's me, Edmund. I'm really here."

Xia stirred again but still didn't open her eyes. Her lips twitched into a sheepish grin as she sighed. "You'd better be naked."

I couldn't get the giddy grin off my face. "This isn't a dream. Come on, wake up. Open your eyes."

"No," she whispered. "If I wake up you'll go away. You're only ever here in my dreams."

The way the words tumbled out of her mouth was haunting and empty. They expressed hope, fear, and a wish all at the same time. I wondered if the dream version of me was better than the real one; how often is fantasy better than reality?

When I looked back down, her eyes were wide and her face was twisted into fear and confusion. I watched her eyes flicker to Hecate at the foot of her bed before returning to me, seeking some sort of recognition within the dark hood that shadowed my face.

"Who are you?" she asked, harshly, taking the opportunity to scoot further from me.

"It's me," I said, instinctively reaching out toward her.

"No. Stop using his voice. Hecate? Help me."

She was fumbling over herself now. I heard her heart rate increasing as adrenaline hit her system. She was preparing to run or fight.

Hecate crouched, ready to pounce.

"Wait. Just wait," I said, raising my hand to the dog in a defensive position in case she decided to pounce anyway. "It really is me. I'm here. It's weird. I'm scary. But I'm here. I worked so hard to get here. I've missed you so much. Please believe it's really me."

Xia's lip quivered, her back now pressed to the wall the bed was against. "That night," she sputtered, "what song did we dance to?"

I knew exactly what night she was talking about. It was the night in the hotel after meeting Linda Rose for the first time. The night we'd made love. But we hadn't danced. *She* had danced.

I lowered my hood so she could see my face. I kept my eyes closed at first so she wouldn't have to associate me with the demonic. So she could make out my features among the shadows without being tainted by my entire demonic presence. But I had to look at her when I answered. I had to know she could see me.

She gasped at the fire in my eyes, but I kept them soft and honest.

"Me? Dance?" I smiled, my eyes stinging. "You wouldn't dare let me dance. You made me get on the bed while you put your iPod on the dock and reenacted 'Toucha, Toucha, Toucha, Touch me,' from *Rocky Horror*.

It was the cheesiest, craziest, sexiest striptease I could have imagined. That was the best night of my life. Best night of any of my lives," I corrected.

In that moment, in the soft glow of the candlelight, I knew I couldn't hide. It was a mistake to come in wearing the cloak, trying to get Xia to trust me while hiding who I was. I needed her to see me. I needed her to accept me.

I pulled in the smoky cloak and stood in front of her. Just as me. Just as I was. Just as the only person I could be at the moment.

The fact that I wore nothing but iridescent bird feathers didn't help me feel less naked in front of her.

Her lip finally stopped quivering, but her eyes were still unsure. "You look evil."

"I know. Sorry I'm so black."

"That was racist."

"I know. I've been thinking of how I could phrase it better, but decided that sounding like I put too much thought into it would make me sound more racist."

"No problem. I've been with a black guy before."

"What's his name and address? I'll be sure to pay him a visit. Grim Reaper and all," I grinned.

So did she. Her grin lit up the room and lifted my heavy spirit.

She pushed off the blankets she had been clutching and stood. It was a good thing I was already dead, because she wasn't wearing a shirt. My heart would have stopped. She walked right up to me and held her hand up, palm out.

"Can we touch?" she asked.

I didn't go for her palm. I went right for her lips.

As it turned out, we couldn't touch, not physically anyway. But that didn't stop me. I felt the heat of her lips on my own. I felt the quiver as her lips parted. I knew she could feel something too, but it was different. It was like feeling emotion. It was satisfying in a different kind of way. I could feel our spiritual connection, even if I couldn't feel the physical one.

It left us both happy and sad at the same time. We wanted more.

"You're cold," she said, pulling back. "And you tickle, like smoke."

She put her hand on my chest, causing a flood of fire in my heart. She burned in life; I froze in death.

I put my hand on her cheek. Her pores reacted by puckering into goose bumps again. She shivered.

Still, she closed her eyes and her lips parted as a sigh escaped. She was willing to experience my touch, regardless of how different and uncomfortable it might be.

I ran my hand down her side, the goose bumps on her skin following the trail of my fingers. As I ran down the sensitive skin under her arm, I heard her catch her breath as her heart rate quickened.

"I wish we could…" I started, but couldn't finish.

"Just keep touching me," she begged, as I ran my fingers over her collarbone.

She wrapped her arms around me, and I was

surprised to feel the pressure of her body against my own. I knew that for her it would be like trying to hold onto smoke, but I felt her nonetheless. She exploded into shivers while I was about to burst into flame.

"Can you stay with me?" she asked, nodding toward the bed.

"All I'd do is keep you awake, keep you cold."

"I'm not going to sleep anyway. Not anymore tonight. I can warm up in the morning. I need to feel you lying next to me. I need you to hold me however you can. Please?"

I couldn't think of anything I would rather do than spend the night next to Xia. As torturous as it might be to feel the fire of her skin against my own, unable to experience the night together I knew we both wanted, knowing she was next to me was enough to make the pain worth it.

"Lie down," I prompted. "I'll stay with you.

We didn't sleep that night. As soon as the sun peeked through the windows, I kissed Xia's frigid cheek and told her to take a hot shower. I debated following her around, experiencing her day, and grabbing coffee together. But how weird would it be to have your dead half-angel, half-demon boyfriend take you out for breakfast and follow you to class? I doubted Denny's took souls as payment anyway.

"Hey, before I go," I said, as she wrapped her towel around her and slipped on a pair of shower shoes, "I was wondering if you could keep something safe for me?"

"Of course. This isn't going to be one of those awkward goodbyes where you spend the night and never call, even though you left your good jockstrap here and are too embarrassed to come back and get it, is it?"

I laughed. "If that happens, it isn't because the guy who is too embarrassed to come get it. It's more like he left a piece of him here for you as a parting gift so that he *wouldn't* have to call. Makes you even. You put out. He left his underwear."

Xia rolled her eyes, "Please tell me you're joking."

I laughed again. "Depends on if you believe any of Nicholas's explanations for why he left his underwear places."

Xia grinned. "Leaves. Not left. He's still leaving them… all around town, I hear."

I scratched my head. "Yeah, no doubt. Anyway, here. This is… uh… a book. It tells my story. It's been writing itself ever since I died and was born on Earth. It will help you keep tabs on me and learn everything I've learned. It'll also help you understand how much I think about you," I said, setting my father's book, *Crossing Death*, among the others piled on her desk. "Joshua was looking for it at one time, but he couldn't read it. He gave it back to me."

"You've seen him?" Xia exclaimed, almost dropping her towel.

"Not exactly. He left it for me in a place he knew only I would find it."

"Is it dangerous?"

"No, I don't think so."

"Damn," Xia winked, giving me a smug smile.

"Hey," I said, as her hand was just about to tug open the doorknob. "There's something I wanted to say," I paused. "Before I died. I wanted to tell you in person—"

"Stop," Xia commanded, her voice full of anguish. The one word dripped with too much meaning. 'Stop' had become one of *those* four-letter words, the ones that meant more than four-letters are meant to mean. "I want you to tell me. I want to tell you," she continued. "But not now. Not like this. Tell me after you've won, after we're together. You can hold me while you tell me. You can look into my eyes with *your* eyes."

I understood, but her words stung and my head dropped. These *were* my eyes now. This *was* me. My fear of not being accepted by her in this form wasn't unfounded.

When I looked back up, she had slipped out the door.

TWENTY-ONE

I woke in my room on the fifth floor with another pair of yellow eyes floating above the edge of my bed. I registered that the shadow staring back at me was Ruth, so I rolled over and pulled the blanket back over me.

"Well, it's about time you're awake," she said, her voice high with impatience. "Do you know how long I've been sitting here?"

"What happened to the days when you knocked? Doesn't anyone in this place knock?" I asked groggily. I was still exhausted. Waking up felt like stirring from a Sunday afternoon nap after sleeping too long. Everything was dream-like and my head hurt.

"Alex— Edmund. Please tell me you're not stealing souls."

My eyes snapped open. Even though she couldn't see my face because my back was to her, I couldn't control my grin. "I don't know what you're talking about," I said, without turning to look at her.

"You sound prideful," she said, surprising me. "I can *hear* you smiling. I don't believe you."

I turned over and sat up.

There was legitimate concern in her eyes, as well as anger. "You don't know what you're messing with here... *who* you're messing with. Taking someone's souls is reserved for those who deserve to be punished. It's a punishment enacted only by the *very* powerful. It's not something you do for fun. It's not something you get away with. It's not something I can help you out of. I need you to tell me how you're paying for this room. The story better be that you found a bunch of dead people hanging around who said, 'Hey Edmund, take us because we're wicked.' "

I paused. The longer I waited while constructing my response, the more she'd know I was lying. Should I tell her I didn't know what she was talking about? Should I tell her I stabbed a demon with my scythe after he threatened me in the hallway and leave it at that? Or should I tell her the whole truth?

"Well, at least you being here means you're not mad at me anymore," I said, derailing the subject.

She didn't let me get away with it that easily, "I'm furious with you! I can't even describe how angry I am with you, but I had to know if it was you that everyone's talking about. If it's you they will soon be *looking* for."

"The concern means you care about me."

"You know what? Forget it," she said, rising from her seated position.

"Do you remember when we used to play chess as kids?" I asked, keeping my voice steady.

She stopped with her hand on the doorknob, but didn't turn around. "Yes," she responded sharply.

"It took me a long time to remember. I don't think it was until after I died and went back to Orenda before I remembered anything about the twelve years I lived in the orphanage."

She flinched at the word 'Orenda.' I was glad I wouldn't have to explain it to her.

"What's your point?" she asked.

"Well, one of the first memories that came back to me was how I used to win our games. I was young and you were smart. My strategy was so stupidly simple that I'm surprised it worked. But it did, every time. Because you thought you were smarter than me."

Her yellow eyes flashed at me in the darkness. "Well, if it's any consolation, I still think that. If you're doing what I think you're doing, then I *know* I'm smarter than you."

"I would have never won against you had you thought otherwise," I continued. "I used to put out my weak players, the pawns. Even as a kid, I knew exactly what a pawn was and how to make it live up to its name. I would set one out in the open, strand him all alone, and when you struck, I would swoop in with something bigger and badder. You were always too focused on what the pawn was doing *way out there* to realize the moves I was making where it mattered."

"This isn't a game, Edmund. The souls aren't yours. They don't even belong to the person you're taking them from! Do you understand that? We're all on the same side. The system works. It's a good system and it's *so* much fun to be a demon! There is no enemy. You are not some knight who gets to swoop in and conquer."

"You're right," I said smugly. "I am no knight. I'm just the pawn."

That surprised her. For the first time, her mind twisted toward a different possibility. "Then tell me your endgame, Edmund. Who are the power players? Let me help you."

I didn't answer her question, deciding instead to get one of my own answered under the guise of it mattering. "What can you tell me about possession? I found out how to cross over to different levels, but I couldn't touch anything. We can sometimes manipulate the physical ourselves, right? But we need to possess someone to have full manifestation of our physical abilities?"

Ruth's hand fell from the doorknob and she sighed, returning to the bed. She huffed herself onto it like she was about to throw a tantrum. "You can manipulate things that aren't living, or that don't have a will of their own. So you can slam doors, rattle chains, even drive cars. Possession requires that you destroy the will of the person you're trying to possess first. Technically, they could kick you out anytime they wanted to if their will came back."

"But I've been possessed when I didn't want to be," I said. "So how would I do something like that?"

Ruth looked at me like she couldn't believe I was asking these questions. Eventually, the promise of the revelation of my 'master plan' won out. She continued. "Well, knowing you, you were more focused on saving someone than you were on your own will. One of the easiest ways to break down someone who cares about other people is to put a person they care about in danger. When a person puts his own survival aside for someone else, that is a setting aside of his will. It's sad that selflessness is our easiest way in. But when you're willing to die for someone else, you've already resigned yourself to that fate."

"So you take advantage of people who are focused on helping others? That's wicked."

"Something you'll learn as a demon: you always work on maintaining your own self-worth. *Numero uno* is the only person who matters in the end."

"Good to know."

"So what does this have to do with anything? Are you going to possess the humans one at a time and make them jump to their deaths or something? 'Cause that's been tried. It's easier to possess a preacher and try the whole suicide pact thing."

"Actually," I grinned, "I was trying to figure out how

to have sex with my girlfriend again."

Ruth laughed. Her eyes softened, the grin remaining on her face even after her body stopped rolling. "Haven't you ever seen *Ghost*? You need a willing surrogate."

"Nah," I said. "That scene with Whoopi Goldberg always gave me the heebie-jeebies. Besides, I want it to really *be* me. Not some other guy."

"Sorry," Ruth interrupted, shrugging. "There isn't another way. You've got to get over the hang-ups. You'll possess some other guy and be okay with the fact that it's his equipment. She'll get used to the fact you'll be doing it with someone else, too. She'll end up banging the guy who is your surrogate while you're not there. All the while you'll be banging some demon over here."

"That brings a whole new meaning to 'open relationship,' " I chuckled.

Ruth shrugged again. "It's how most people make it work if they have someone worth it on the other side. It's awkward when you've got someone possessed. Besides, it's so much more interesting in our *demonic* forms. No one blames anyone else for getting some. Possession just isn't worth the effort for boring human sex over there. Not when there are so many depraved and exciting options here."

"Yeah, we're demons. Evil, sex-crazed demons," I laughed.

Ruth did, too.

"So your big plan is all about getting some girl?"

"Isn't it always?" I grinned.

It was good to hear Ruth's tone so friendly and understanding, but in the back of my mind I still heard her say 'Numero Uno' in a tone that scared me away from trusting her—or anyone.

"That's sweet, but stupid," she grunted. "If that's all there is, let me see what I can clean up for you with the other demons. If you promise me you won't do whatever it was you were doing again, I'll go with you to Earth and help you pick out a candidate for possession."

"No way." I wasn't joking. The idea of having Ruth get access to Xia would not happen, but I made it sound like I was joking anyway. I wanted to keep Ruth close, even if I didn't trust her anymore. "You're like a jealous girlfriend," I said, forcing a laugh. "I'm not letting you near her."

She responded with the same flirtatious, joke-but-not-a-joke tone, "Come on, baby! The three of us could have fun and I promise not to kill her. Until after."

"Well, you'll have to compete with Lilith for that honor." I moved another chess piece into position. How many pawns could I put out there before she noticed? "She's *totally* into me."

"That bitch? Some people never learn. She died from an STD and is making up her time with all the boys since she can't catch one here."

"The bubonic plague wasn't an STD," I smirked.

"Oh, close enough. It doesn't change the fact that

she'll sleep with anything that's got a penis. Or parts as large as a penis. I would assume that includes Josephine. That lady has a clit the size of Texas."

"Oh, please stop. I don't need the visuals." I covered my mouth and pretended to vomit. "You can't be serious. I thought Josephine was with that guy. What's his name?"

"Minyak? No. They're friends, but not together like that. Minyak made a name for himself on Earth by breaking into people's houses smeared with black oil, in only his underwear. He thought the oil would make him harder to see in the dark. It worked for a while, until he decided to upgrade to rape and murder. He still likes to walk around the towns where he was from and terrorize women. Malaysia mostly, I think. Or Sri Lanka. They call him the Grease Devil," she said, biting her lip.

"You *like* him!" I exclaimed, reading her body language.

"I think it's sexy, that's all. A giant, greased-up man breaking into my house in the middle of the night and having his way with me, all slippery. Personally, I think he was doing those girls a favor. Not one of the stories about him claimed he was bad in bed."

"You have no humanity left in you, do you?"

Ruth laughed again, but I didn't think it was funny. "How many times do I have to remind you, Edmund? You're a demon. We get off on things that are taboo and blasphemous. I know you're feeling it: the anger, the inner charge, the darkness. You wouldn't be stealing spirits in some *forsaken* quest for power if you weren't already a *forsaken* demon."

She grinned and bit her lip again with a little hum. "It won't be long until you're screwing every girl in this joint. Then you'll possess humans to make them do each other in the most depraved ways you can conjure. I'd bet you'll be the guy to be nicknamed something worse than Grease Devil, won't you?"

She got a little too close for comfort, bearing in on my personal space. Alarm bells went off in my head, but I was too late. She bit my lip. I had to admit that I didn't hate it. I knew I should have. Xia would have wanted me to, but Ruth was right—I was a demon and the pain from her bite made me… *feel*.

I was already charged from my visit with Xia. This conversation wasn't helping matters. Maybe the anger I felt in the garden that fueled my thirst for power, that I thought made me reckless and stupid, was what I was supposed to feel. Maybe Mother Tree was wrong to pull me back. Maybe abandoning myself to my murderous nature was the only way to gain enough power to do what I needed, wanted, and came here to do.

If I picked up a few allies by sleeping with them, manipulating them, or using them, what did it matter? The end result was that I'd get what I wanted. I still wanted to free my family, save the angels, destroy Joshua, and live happily ever after with Xia. If I had to do some questionable things to get there, did it matter? Didn't the end justify the means? That part of Ruth's mind-set made sense.

Besides, Xia would read all of this in the book I left behind. She had access inside my head. She would understand.

I had to look out for *Numero Uno.*

TWENTY-TWO

I grinned as I crossed the lobby to where Lilith was sitting. Her feet were propped up on the counter and she was thumbing through her usual magazine. She didn't look up as I approached but I watched her treat others the same way. There was only a slight difference; when I walked by, she glanced up at me after she thought I was too far away to notice.

Today I didn't walk past the desk. I had business to attend to.

I didn't stop at the counter either, like I normally would. Instead, I walked straight *into* it, *through* it, which put me on top of Lilith. Now that I understood what it meant to be a spirit, walls or solid counters didn't bother me. I could manipulate myself through them. No wonder no one needed a key around here.

Lilith feigned disinterest as she thumbed over a page in her magazine, but I saw the corners of her mouth tug upward. "You're not supposed to be back here," she said flatly.

"Ah, come on," I grinned. "You didn't like my new trick? I can walk through walls... whoooo!"

"Of course you can walk through walls. You're dead."

"Then how come we don't fall through the floor?" I asked, my grin widening.

She still didn't look up at me, but sighed and grumbled, "You could if you wanted to."

Not the best explanation, but I guessed since I was being facetious, so was she.

I placed a strawberry tart on the counter, sliding it back and forth to make sure it caught Lilith's attention.

It worked. She looked at it and smirked. "Bribery only goes so far. You're still not supposed to be back here. So walk yourself out of here, through any wall you desire, before you get me into trouble."

"What do you have back here that's so important, anyway?" I asked with an innocent tone.

Her eyes flickered toward the room ledger. That was what I had already guessed.

"Nothing of importance. I'm not supposed to *fraternize* while I'm working."

"Well, when can you *fraternize*?" I leaned in closer.

My invasion of her personal space had the desired effect. She pulled too hard on the corner of the page she was turning and the magazine tumbled to the floor.

"Seriously. You can't be back here," she said, her eyes

meeting mine. The look in them tried to hold her conviction, but her gaze slipped down to my lips.

I let her stare for just a moment longer before I leaned back and said, "All right, then." I grabbed the tart and pushed my way back through the counter.

"Leave the tart."

I grinned, turning back around. "I'm glad you like them. Josephine is swindling me over these things."

"Please tell me you've figured out that Ruth and Josephine work together to swindle you every time you come down here. Most people pay one soul for a week's worth of food, not one soul per cup of coffee. They're splitting the profits."

I knew Josephine was charging me extra, but I hadn't realized that Ruth was getting a kickback. I felt a twinge of anger. Now that I stood on the right side of the desk, I leaned on it and smiled, hoping the flash of anger didn't show on my face.

"I know. Everyone takes advantage of the new guy."

Lilith stood, leaning on her side of the counter as casually as possible while getting as close to me as she could. "Not everyone," she said. "Besides, you're not the new guy anymore. We had some new recruits come in. They're sleeping away their loans as we speak."

"So what happens if they can't pay?"

"Well, they either sell themselves into slavery as familiars to someone else—that happens often—or they have to leave."

"Where do they go?"

"Usually they wander for a little while out there," she said, flicking her hand around to represent 'out there.' I didn't understand the motion. "Then they'll either come back and sell themselves or get picked up by one of the barges. If they're unlucky, someone will send them there right away."

"What's so unlucky about the barges?"

"The barges are no cakewalk. If you're interested in having one of the newbies work for you, I can show you how to put together the contract," she said, changing the subject.

I let her, but only because this subject was more interesting anyway. "Sure, that would be great."

Lilith pulled the ledger from beneath the desk. I was surprised that she whipped it out so willingly. My anxiety rose at the thought of her knowing what I was doing.

She turned a couple of pages, pointed, and tapped her finger on three names listed one after the other. "Here they are. You can see their thirty-day loans here. If you want to employ them—"

"You can say 'enslave.' I think I'm past the point of balking at that word."

Lilith smiled, meeting my eyes before she let her gaze slide back to the page again. "You're a quick learner. Before long you might be running this place. Anyway, if you have them sign one of these…" she pulled a page from the front of the ledger that looked like a standard legal contract, except the paper was yellowed and burned at the edges.

I smirked at her.

"What? The visuals make for good theatrics. You can appear in smoke and wear little devil horns and talk about giving away your soul if you want. Actually, don't wear devil horns," she leaned in, finishing with a whisper. "Devils don't like it when we make fun of them."

I chuckled. "Get them to sign a contract. That's it?"

"Well, yes. Except you need to pay off their debts, always. If they buy a strawberry tart from Josephine," she snuck a glance into my eyes again, "and happen to overpay, you still have to settle the debt. So the overpaying part would be between you and Josephine. You can't take it out on them, technically. But their souls belong to you, so you can give them extra allowances as a reward or none as punishment. You work out the salary ratio with them before they sign."

"That's a lot of responsibility. What if I want out?"

"As long as their balance is zero, you can exile them. Then they can find another master, if anyone else will have them. Picking up someone's old slaves is like sloppy seconds, bottom-of-the-barrel type stuff. If they couldn't pull their weight with one demon, chances are they won't with another." She paused. "In the end, if they *really* pissed you off, you can pay a barge captain to take them."

"Wait," I said, my eyes widening in surprise, "I would have to *pay* someone to take them?"

"Well, yeah. That's how it works. They'll usually take someone for, say, ten souls. Then they'll pay you back as the person works off the debt. It takes a long time though, so it isn't a good investment. It's our form of punishment. No one goes to the barges willingly. The captains aren't nice to newbies."

Now there were two subjects I was interested in: the barges and what they did, and the ledger. I couldn't think of a way to incorporate both into the conversation, so I let it take its current course. "What do the slaves on the barges do?"

"Dunno," Lilith chimed, giggling in her high-pitched laugh, "I never thought to ask." She walked around to my side of the counter and stood next to me while showing me the ledger. "Anyway, if you want to approach these new guys, you should pay for their room before someone else does. Since they'll only owe thirty for the month, that's all you'll have to pay for now. Thirty is a good price to buy in."

I made a face like I was considering, but I was really forming a way to approach a dangerous subject. I needed to know how much she knew about me, about where my soul count was coming from. "Who paid for my room?"

Her finger was poised above one of the three names. She let it hang there awkwardly as she answered, "I don't know. I assumed it was Ruth."

"So if I wanted to pay for this guy's," I said, touching the page, "who would know it was me?"

"No one but you and me," she answered.

"Yeah, but you said you didn't know who paid for my room," I pushed.

She shrugged, "Maybe it wasn't me who updated it."

I was about to ask who else had access to the ledger when I became aware of the feeling of eyes on the back of my neck. I knew someone was standing nearby watching us, but the feeling was so faint and passing that I thought I was sensing someone walk by.

Lilith pushed the ledger a few more inches toward me and positioned herself so that her arm was resting against mine.

I turned to find Ruth behind me, giving Lilith a hostile glare. I didn't have much time to judge her expression, because the second I turned to look at her Lilith grabbed my hand.

"See, you're right here." She directed my finger to a name on the page, letting her hand linger much longer than necessary.

I almost glossed over the name 'Alexander,' but I paused on the number next to the name. It was the largest number on the page: 65,238.

That was higher than I expected.

Lilith's eyes flicked again, this time behind me. She wove her fingers into mine. Her hand was cool and calm, not sweaty or shaking like mine was. I realized I was not only in the middle of a fight between these two women, but the cause of it.

I felt validated. Every man only wants one thing, and that's to be wanted. I found it flattering, and couldn't help but puff out my chest as I filled with such a sense of... alpha-ness.

I tightened my grip on Lilith's hand; I realized I needed her, but that wasn't the only reason. It was nice to share a connection with someone. It was nice to feel someone physically. Ruth felt like she was using me, and I was using her. With Lilith, it felt more natural and genuine.

Lilith's eyes sparkled. If her cheeks weren't so black, they would've blushed.

"So, it's ten thousand souls for a level, right?"

"Yeah," she said, although the word caught in her throat.

Had I made her speechless? Maybe I had thrown her off. Maybe this was part of her plan and *I* was being played. Maybe it didn't matter.

"Can I give the new guys 9,999 each? No strings attached. Keep them on the same floor, but give them savings?"

"I'm sure your boss wouldn't like that," Lilith said. "You should get a contract from them first."

"My boss and I have an understanding. What salary I get, I do with what I want. He's not going to ask questions."

"It sounds like you're the boss then," she said, meeting my eyes.

"Well, it's all an illusion anyway, right? I mean, Joshua

owns it all."

Lilith searched my eyes, although I wasn't sure what she was looking for. "You're either smart and have it all figured out, or stupid and won't have much for long," she said, her tone expressing both concern and confusion.

I felt a gamut of emotions radiating from her. There was desire and a thirst for power, the same as any other demon. But concern was not so common, and her desire was intoxicating. The fact that she wanted me was a power in itself, although it was mirrored by my desire for her. I tried to push it down as some emotion tied to my demonic self. It couldn't be part of my humanity. That part still wanted Xia.

"How long did you know your girlfriend?" Lilith asked, just as I thought Xia's name.

I couldn't hide the shock on my face.

"I can feel you fighting, even though you want to…" she stopped. "It's a connection I noticed from the beginning."

I glanced behind me to make sure that Ruth was gone. I wasn't sure how much of the conversation she had been listening to.

"She's not here. It's just us." Lilith read my thoughts. "So how long?"

"Honestly, not long. I met her a week before I died."

Lilith laughed. I expected her to be surprised. I expected her to be wide-eyed in shock. I didn't expect her to laugh. It hurt that she didn't take my relationship with

DEATH OF THE SPIRIT

Xia seriously. It woke me out of my infatuation.

"I'm sorry," she said. "Love is so weird. But sometimes, when you know, you know, right?"

"It happened fast, yes," I said. "We went through more ups and downs in one week than most couples experience in a lifetime. We never had time to be fake or lie to each other."

Lilith started running her fingers lightly up and down my arm. The sensation silenced me. After we looked at each other awkwardly (I was talking about my girlfriend, after all), she dropped her gaze and changed the subject. Maybe she didn't want to talk about Xia.

"Here," she said, picking up a pen. She adjusted the ledger. "Nine thousand, nine hundred, and ninety-nine each," she enunciated, crossing out the old values and writing in new ones.

The crossed-out ink faded as the new total became visible: 9,999 for each demon.

Magical books shouldn't surprise me. I'd given a book that wrote itself to Xia, after all.

"Do me a favor and keep that between us?"

"Sure," Lilith promised. "Does your girlfriend know about Ruth?" she met my eyes, her stare hard and victorious.

"She will. Like I said, I don't have time to lie to her."

"She's going to break up with you, you know."

"I know," I said, lying. I only used sex to manipulate Ruth. It didn't mean anything. I needed to keep her close.

I needed to keep Lilith close. Xia would understand that. Xia would read the story and know where my actions were coming from. "How did you know? About Ruth?"

"You are smugger than usual this morning. I can still smell her on you. Don't worry, though. Human girls might not understand. Here it's different."

Then she kissed me.

I didn't mind. She had hundreds of years of experience on me. If Ruth was right, plenty of practice, too. Lilith's experience was evident in the way she melded her mouth to my own. Her lips were warm, but didn't burn. I knew mine felt warm to her, not cold like they had with Xia.

Every time I thought her name, Lilith pulled me back to the moment by increasing her fervor. I didn't know if it was the demon or the man that flooded me with lust, but the thoughts that ran through my head begged me to betray Xia. They were wicked, more serious than they had been with Ruth. Ruth was a power play. With Lilith, there were feelings other than just entertainment.

Xia wouldn't like that.

Xia. There was her name again.

Lilith pulled my hips into hers and wrapped her arms tightly around me. Her tongue tasted my upper lip. I was kissing her back and I knew it. Why didn't this feel wrong?

My hands fell to the small of her back. I knew if I didn't stop I would lose myself soon. The fact that it was wrong and that I was in love with someone else didn't make it easier to pull away. In this case, the love was a curse. It made what I *could* do even more exciting, more forbidden, more desirable.

The lust and the darkness merged inside me. I pulled away from the kiss, only I didn't pull away to stop it. I pulled away to take it further. "My room?" I asked.

"Mmmhmm," she hummed.

I took her hand and started to pull her toward the hall. As I turned, I caught the burning eyes of a demon that had been standing right behind me, watching us.

"Well, at least now I know why I can never get any service down here," he said, crossing his arms and leering.

I had no idea how I had missed him standing there this whole time. His eyes were penetrating. I was sure he could see right through me if he wanted. His presence filled the vast lobby. He demanded recognition by the way he stood. He was defiant and self-important, amused by our display of affection.

He addressed Lilith, but gestured toward me. The motion made me feel like I should be grateful he even acknowledged me. "Who's the flavor of the week?"

"Stop," Lilith responded, but the word didn't come off as a command like it normally would have. It was softer than I had ever heard her speak. The fear on her face was evident. She was afraid of this demon. "I mean… I actually like this one."

His face flashed with surprise. If I didn't know any better, I would say he was surprised by her defiance. But the way she talked to him didn't sound defiant to me. It sounded submissive. I half-expected her to bow to him with the same little bow my mother had been taught—a bow that was twisted and forced, a bow that was meant to make the person look smaller in the presence of someone who compensated for the fact that they didn't look powerful on their own.

I hated it when people treated others with dismissal, like they were less because of their own perceived superiority. A superiority that had no substance. A position they held only because they were able to convince others they were somehow superior.

The demon squared his broad shoulders as he looked me over. "You've definitely done worse," he laughed. "Maybe I'll *invite* you both up to my room later."

I had a feeling his invitation wasn't optional.

"What's the highest floor you've seen?" he asked, not hiding the way his gaze burned over my body.

"Nothing too pretentious for me," I said, squaring my shoulders. It was difficult and took every ounce of self-control I had not to cower in his presence. "I prefer my women down-to-earth."

Lilith jabbed her elbow into my side, resulting in my squared shoulders falling.

The demon raised an eyebrow, which had a curious sensation. The look was like he was plugging into my emotions, feeling the lust I had been experiencing with Lilith, and kindling it into a roaring fire. His emotional manipulation was unlike anything I had felt before. When his eyes fell away from me so that he could address Lilith, I felt empty. I was nothing unless he was looking at me. I wanted him to look at me again.

What was wrong with me?

"He must not have met someone *important* before. How long has he been here?"

At least he was talking about me. That made me feel better. He crushed my soul inside and made me want to do anything to make him happy. I felt small when he wasn't looking at me. The feeling was sad and familiar. Had I been crushed like this before?

"He's still in his first month."

"Oh?" he asked, looking me over again. I felt good when his eyes were on me. "One month and already awake? Already winning over the help? Already given so much into the dark? Already filled with such desire?"

"He'll end up great," Lilith said. I knew it was a dig against him, but not because she wanted to make him angry. She craved his eyes on her and tried to direct his attention away from me so that he'd look at *her!*

What a bitch. I couldn't believe she was so selfish.

His eyes widened in surprise again, shifting back to me. I didn't want Lilith to be angry with me for stealing his gaze, so I told myself I would only keep his attention on me for a few minutes, then I'd let her have a turn. I was selfless like that. I just wanted a few minutes of him first.

"Great, indeed," he said, his eyes raking over my

body again. His gaze felt better than any touch I had ever felt. Maybe he was the ecstasy demon, because every inch of me tingled.

As his eyes raked over my body, his gaze fell on my father's ring. I inhaled as the ring pulsed with frigid intensity. The air was so cold it tasted sharp, like fire.

The demon didn't pause on the ring. He pretended like he didn't notice my reaction. His face was so controlled that he directed his gaze between my legs before sliding back up to my eyes—but something was wrong. The spell slipped just enough that I was able to return to my senses. I felt him scramble to get me back under his influence.

His reaction was perfect. Any scramble was in magic only. His body position, gaze, and facial features remained under precise control, but his spell connected us emotionally and I could feel him. I felt a boil of excitement rise in his chest.

"Well," he said, his voice silky and clean, "I'll leave you two kids to play. You can borrow my handcuffs if you wish." He grinned at Lilith. "I don't think I needed what I came to ask for, anyway. Next time I come to the front desk, Lilith, I'd better find I have your undivided attention."

He turned to leave. Lilith, frantic for one more second in his presence, started after him. "What did you come down for? What did you want?" she begged.

He turned back to her and gave her what she

craved—his look. He looked at her the way someone might look at a puppy. The look was dangerous. "Why, I came down to talk to you," he flattered her. I knew it was a lie. "I needed your help to get what I've always wanted, but I think I've found another way."

His eyes didn't return to me. He didn't even steal a glance, but something in my head sounded like an alarm bell. I knew he was talking about me.

"I want what I've always wanted," he continued as he walked away and disappeared into the hallway, "the blood of all living creatures, pet girl."

I knew that voice. I knew that phrase. I had heard it before. It filled me with such terror that I had no idea how I'd missed it before. This demon knew me, intimately. He had possessed me. He had caused my soul to crumble. The only way I'd escaped him before was with Xia's conjuring of Hecate.

This demon had possessed Nicholas and flooded the hallways of my school with blood. I registered his comment about the handcuffs. Could this demon also have been the cop who had pulled me over in the desert and tried to kill me?

The terror I felt with this recognition was superseded by a realization. He flinched when he saw the ring. It wasn't a physical flinch, but one of power and control.

He knew who I was.

My feet broke into a run after him. I was terrified of him, but I was more terrified of the information he had. I needed to claim his souls, drain his power, and bury the sharpest part of my blade into his neck before he told anyone.

It didn't matter that Lilith was on my heels, running after me as I chased him. She probably thought I craved him. She probably thought I wanted to serve him. It didn't matter. If she saw what I was going to have to do, I would have to dispose of her, too. Nothing was more important than containing my secret. I wasn't ready yet. My full plan wasn't in place.

This could ruin everything.

I bolted into the hallway where the demon had disappeared moments before. When I rounded the corner, the hallway was empty.

TWENTY-THREE

I went to see Xia that night. I had planned on it anyway, but leaving had the added bonus of taking me out of this demonic realm for a while. I wanted to leave because I was excited to see Xia again, but also because of my fear of being discovered.

The garden was busy tonight, but the crowd thinned as I made my way back toward Mother Tree. I ran into two demons on the narrow pathways, one tending to their souls, and another who stepped out from between the plants. The latter must have just been returning from his trip through the root network.

Neither one of them would be heard from again. Taking their souls felt good for many reasons, not the least of which was the control it gave me to know I could do whatever I wanted with their plants. I could use their roots for myself, or I could buy an extra tart or two. I could pay off other demons' debts if I wanted. Their power was mine.

Maybe I would give them to Ruth.

After I was sure there weren't any other demons lurking, I made my way to Mother Tree. She barely acknowledged me today. There was no talk, no memory-triggering emotions. The only thing I felt was her soul brightening as I approached.

I used her roots to get back to Earth again. I was glad to find that the silver strand connecting Xia and me was as strong as it was the last time. I didn't know why I was worried about that—my feelings for her hadn't changed, but the feelings I'd developed for Lilith had me confused.

Xia was expecting me, or at least it looked that way. Hecate lay comfortably at Xia's feet and didn't try to stop me from coming into the room. Xia was propped up in bed, her back supported by pillows as she read my father's book. Her eyes were swollen. She had been crying.

"You know," she said without looking up from the pages, "it's really weird to watch this thing write what I'm saying as I'm saying it."

I smiled at the sound of her voice, but felt a stab of guilt as I realized that she was already caught up. She had already read about Ruth, already read about Lilith… probably read it as it was happening.

Her expression darkened. "Guilt, huh? Well, I understand that." She put the book down. Her voice was too calm, too controlled. "I can't seem to leave your story alone. Will the lovers separated by space and time, who can't even touch each other, have a happy ending?"

I didn't know what to say. The question was rhetorical anyway.

I didn't like the way she stared at me. Her look wasn't warm or cold. It wasn't soft or hard. It was emotionless.

I sat on the bed and covered her hand with my own. I was prepared for the blistering heat, but feeling the fine hairs on her hands bristle at my touch felt unnatural.

Shoot. She would end up reading that.

I meant it felt great. Lovely. Because I loved her and I was with her and that was all that mattered.

Please don't doubt me.

Xia's chocolate gaze dropped, looking at my hand on hers, avoiding my face. "I don't know if I'm supposed to talk about this or not. I don't know if I should tell you what I think, or try to help you, or if you want help."

Her eyes misted, but she wasn't crying. Her face was too stern to cry. I couldn't decide if it was better for her to be angry and deal with that in her own way, or if I wanted her to share her emotions with me. I knew what I would have wanted had I still been alive. I would have wanted to hold her while she cried on my shoulder. I would let her rest against me and release her sadness for as long as it took for her to run out of things to cry about.

Of course, had I been alive, none of this would have happened.

I still didn't know what to say.

"Lilith is right," she said slowly, painfully. "We did

297

only know each other for a week. It's kind of stupid to think that we could know or understand each other completely in that time. I don't think we can expect to force this. It redefines 'long-distance relationship.' Do you think we should let each other move on? Would it be easier for you? Would it be fairer to me? I mean, you're dead, Edmund. You're dead!"

I wasn't sure if Xia was asking the questions to me, or to herself, but I answered anyway. "People die every day. I don't think the dead expect the living to wait around. I'm battling expectations too. All I know is that I don't want to lose you. Xia, I know this is complicated. Look at me! I'm a demon! Had I known that I was going to have to become *this*…"

I changed my mind mid-thought.

"No," I continued. "You know what? I wouldn't have changed a thing. Do you know why?"

"Why?"

"Because you make me a man. You keep me human."

I expected my words to make everything better. I expected they would have the same impact on her as the realization just had on me. I was a demon, but I was also human and I owed the largest part of my humanity to Xia.

She looked at me, but her beautiful, sparkling eyes contained doubt. "If you can't maintain your humanity on your own, if it isn't part of who *you* are, then you aren't the man I thought you were. That's my point. A week or so of running away from demons, you dying, none of that adds up to the best circumstances on which to build a relationship."

I wasn't sure how her words made me feel, other than awful. This emotion was new to me. I wasn't sad, angry, upset, or hurt. I was all of those things at the same time. I tried to swallow my emotions, because the last thing I wanted was to say something hurtful. They stuck in my throat.

"I'm sorry. I don't know if it's worth it," I admitted. "I don't know if *I'm* worth it."

"I don't know how to need you and not be able to have you. I've spent longer mourning you than I did knowing you! Is that how it's supposed to be? Then you show back up. I get to see you once. And I read about you sleeping with someone else? I don't know how to get close to you when you're so far away. I don't know how to live life together when you're dead. I understand there are things you need to do. Would they be easier without worrying about me? Would it be better if you could use *all* of you to do what you needed, without worrying about saving a piece of yourself for me? Wouldn't it be better for you if I let you go?" she asked.

"No." The word spilled out before she completed the sentence, as soon as I knew where her mind was going with the question. "If you need to move on from me, for you, that's one thing. That I understand. That I could live with. Do it for you, but don't end this because of what you think is best for *me*. You don't get to make that decision for *me*."

"I don't know what to do. I don't know if relationships are meant to survive death. Was I supposed to move on? Because I can't. You wrapped me up in your life. Now I'm wrapped up in your death. Did you move on? Is that what this is about?"

"Of course not. I don't want to move on. I don't want *you* to move on."

"Do you feel guilty?"

"Of course I feel guilty."

"Not for Lilith," Xia clarified. "I know you feel guilty for her because you have feelings for her. But what about Ruth?"

How had she already figured out so much? I knew she would read and understand. I knew she would be able to pick out my emotions. But why would she want me to feel guilty for Ruth?

I searched for that answer inside, finding it difficult to connect to the way a human would think about the situation. The truth was that I didn't feel guilty for Ruth, at least not before. I didn't sleep with Ruth thinking I wouldn't get caught. I had given Xia full access to all my thoughts and to every event in my life when I gave her *Crossing Death*. I slept with Ruth as a tactic. How could I have thought that just because it didn't mean anything to me, it wouldn't mean anything to Xia?

Now I felt guilty.

Now I felt human.

The mages talked about sacrifice for the greater good. The demons didn't believe in sacrifice at all, only selfishness. Had I sacrificed my humanity, and in turn my relationship, because I let the darkness win? How did I not see it?

One week. Maybe it was insane and stupid to think that one week was enough time to cement two people together. Maybe it was stupid to think that our love story could end in anything but tragedy. People who heard our story would no doubt judge us harshly. They would think we fell too fast. I would be judged for not understanding love, for wishful thinking.

But those judges weren't there when I first saw Xia's scorching orange aura. They wouldn't understand that love always comes before knowing you're in love.

That is what those days with Xia gave me. They gave me the ability to admit my feelings faster than I would have otherwise. I had no reason to be afraid of them, to push them away or tell myself it was too fast, because I didn't have the time to be indecisive.

Who does? For me, I wouldn't be ashamed of allowing myself to fall quickly. I would rather hurt, like now, than regret missing out on the emotion. If love were the most powerful human emotion, if love united the world, why would I waste time trying *not* to feel it? Why would I risk the regret of living a life without it?

"What are you thinking?" Xia asked me when I fell silent.

I picked up my father's book and pushed it under her hand. "Read it when you're ready."

I knew she needed time. She didn't have to ask for it. I had messed up. I put my quest before my relationship. I let death separate us. The words of the marriage ceremony echoed ominously in my head, "Until death do you part."

I wondered if this was the reason for that phrase. Could love transcend death?

I still hoped so.

"You could come with me," I said, hopeful. "I am the Angel of Death, you know. I could move you to the top of the list." I meant it to sound like a joke, but it came off more serious than I expected. If she wanted to come with me, I would bring her.

I couldn't decide whether that came from the demon, the human, or the angel.

"I will die for you," she said, as I tucked the corners of her bedspread around her. I couldn't think of any other way to show my affection than to tuck her in. "Will you live for me?" she asked. It was an odd, yet totally comprehensible, question.

"I can't wait for the time when the answer to that question becomes evident," I said, kissing her on her burning forehead.

She shivered at the cold.

"I'm so sorry for the mistakes I've made. I'm sorry I let the darkness win. I'll give you time. But I will do anything to prove myself to you. Will you let me show you? Will you let me put you first? Will you let me discover my humanity not because of you, but because of us?"

Her lips cracked into an exasperated smile. She didn't disagree, and I was glad.

I left her room, but stood outside her door. I cried when I heard her cry. I broke as I felt her break. I knew there was nothing I could do or say to fix things for now. I knew the best I could do was to prove to her that I wasn't a demon.

I just had to convince myself of that first.

I ached to hold her, even though I knew I was the one who caused her pain. But I knew that she needed emotional release and repair. In front of me, she would hold it in. She wouldn't show me how she truly felt. She would wait until I was outside her door.

I couldn't leave until her sobs ceased.

I never wanted Xia to cry herself to sleep over me. When she managed to do just that, I picked myself up and resolved to be a better man. I would be a better man than I was angel. I would be a better man than I was demon. I would be a better man no matter what came my way.

I didn't leave Earth. There was someone else I wanted to see.

Xia's silver chord wasn't the only one I had tied to my heart. Most of the relationships I had developed were represented. I followed the one that led to Nicholas.

I found him just down the hall, not in his room but in the men's restroom. I entered the cloudy bathroom with trepidation—after all, I had seen Nicholas in a dream not too long ago. That dream had taken place in a steamy room. The steam reminded me of the fog on the Carlsbad Mountains. I couldn't help but hear whispers of my name whenever my vision was cloudy, just like the echoes from that day.

Luckily, I was now so cold that the steam cleared around me. The warm droplets condensed and fell to the ground around my feet. I crept down a row of shower stalls until I reached the one I knew Nicholas was in. He liked his showers way too hot, and the majority of the steam was pouring from this stall.

All of the scary shower scenes in the movies we used to watch flooded back to me. How should I do this for the greatest comedic effect? I needed to laugh, but I couldn't do a proper *Psycho* without a large kitchen knife and a dress.

I settled on being original, pushing my head through the shower curtain with an evil grin, just like the velociraptor pushed his head through the jungle plants in *Jurassic Park*.

Nicholas wiped water out of his eyes after washing his face, then let out a blood-curdling scream as he jumped and flailed.

I couldn't help but laugh at his flurry of profanities. He collapsed against the corner of the shower with a look of terrified confusion as laughter gushed out of me.

He recognized the laugh and swore at me. "Edmund!

You do remember I was possessed by one of you damn blood-suckin' fiends, right? You bastard."

He came to his senses, because he covered himself with his hands and raised an eyebrow at me. "Seriously, bro?"

"Since when are you shy?" I laughed. "You do look bigger. Been working out more? Hairier, too. Not shaving your chest anymore?"

He threw a loofa. It passed right through me. "Get outta here and let me finish my shower. But don't disappear or whatever it is you do. I'm glad to see you... kinda." He forced a grin.

I took a step back to let Nicholas finish his shower.

"You're so black." I could hear the grin in his voice.

"Isn't that a little racist?"

"Isn't thinking I meant it as racist, racist?" he shouted back.

"That's what I thought!" I chuckled.

"I'm allowed to be racist since those white people gave my great grandparents scarlet fever," he said, turning the water off. "Would you hand me my towel?"

I did. "Pretty sure by that same logic I'm allowed to be racist because I'm black."

"Touché," he said, a smile in his voice again.

There was something about true friendship, something Nicholas and I shared. It was like we were able to pick right back up where we left off, with no time passing between us. No explanation needed.

Nicholas slid open the curtain and looked me up and down. "Hmmm. Feathers were last season. You can still get away with them at night, but only in the *really* gay clubs."

"Not much selection at Abercrombie and Demon," I admitted.

"You only have an American Eagle, huh?"

"Ooh, that was a good one," I said dryly.

Nicholas collected his shower caddy and feigned a hurt look. "Now in all seriousness," he said, changing his tone and the subject, "you're not here to possess me, right? I mean, I'm handling this demon thing pretty well considering, but that little stunt you pulled with the shower curtain was a low blow."

"You flipped out. Admit it. It was funny."

"Maybe for you. The last time I saw eyes like that, I *ate* people," he said louder than I expected. Nicholas processed the look on my face and responded with a smug smile. "Like anyone would believe it. Besides, I'm *known* for eating people," he winked.

I followed him back to his room, considering whether or not to tell him that I recently ran into the demon that had possessed him. I decided it was best not to bring it up. It was good that Nicholas was joking about the experience. It meant he was healing.

"So how long are you... in town for?" he asked, pulling on a pair of pajama bottoms and a white tank top that was tighter across his chest than Xia's baby doll tees.

"Oh, I can't stay long. It's hard to maintain myself here. Makes me tired fast."

Nicholas nodded, even though I knew he didn't understand.

I quickly scanned his room, which was minimalistic, but still managed to have a masculine feel. I was always impressed by his ability to carry himself with so much pride and comfort in his masculinity. I only noticed one thing missing—one thing that had also been missing in Xia's room—but I didn't give it much of a second thought until now: there was no second bed.

"No roommates?" I said, accidently making the word plural.

Nicholas understood, not missing a beat. "Xia and I decided it would be best if we had single rooms this year. It's hard enough to deal with everything, but how would I explain that my best friend is a yellow-eyed shadow dude to a roommate? Mom left me a trust fund and hefty insurance, so why not have some privacy, you know? I'd rather be known as that weird, single-room guy instead of that crazy, sees-dead-people guy."

I smiled. "Speaking of, your mom is good. Really good. Fits right in."

"I'm glad her plan worked," he said. His eyes told me he wasn't glad at all. "I do still need to find someone new to have a consistent Sunday brunch with though," he smiled, trying to cover up his hurt.

"I'm sorry." Those were the only words I could say,

even if it wasn't enough.

Nicholas propped himself onto his side, his head braced by his hand and a pillow bunched under his arm. "She knew she could do more for me from there. I'm glad you got her. She said that The Reaper hadn't been able to collect, so everyone's been going to Hell. I can't imagine that would be much fun," he said, quickly adding, "no offense."

"It's a big, big garden." I didn't know how to do it justice, but I held up my hands like a guy explaining how big a fish he caught.

"Well, thanks for finding her. Sorry you had to turn black. But you know what they say…" he grinned, his eyes sparkling.

"No," I said. "Don't say it."

"Once you go black…"

"Shut up," I laughed with him.

He sighed and twisted the cap to a bottle of water he had on his nightstand. He took a few swallows before letting his gaze fall to the bottle. I knew he was using it as an excuse not to look at me while he decided how to change the subject to something I wasn't going to like. "Why are you here instead of with Xia?" he asked.

He was right. I didn't like the subject. But it was part of the reason I came to see him. "We're not okay," I said.

Nicholas nodded like he already knew. "I keep a pint of Chunky Monkey in the freezer over there for her. You're welcome to it tonight if you want."

"You probably know her better than I do now."

"Gross, dude," he said, making a face. He tried to lighten the mood while knowing the joke would fall flat. "I know. It's not fair," he added seriously.

"I thought when I found a way back, even like this, it would get better. But I think it's even harder."

"She's had a hard time. We all have. It's hard to mourn when you know, *really* know, that because someone's dead doesn't mean they're gone," he said. I knew he wasn't just talking about me; he was also talking about Linda Rose. "It makes it less sad, I guess, but not any easier. Xia doesn't want to move on, because she knows you're still so close. She doesn't know what will happen when everything is all over for you. Even in the best-case scenario, she'll be alone during this life, right? A lifetime is a long time to spend alone."

"I know." I scratched the back of my head. The guilt flooded back into me. I hadn't even lasted a few months.

Nicholas's eyes sparkled, but his face scowled. "Uh oh. Who is she?"

"A mistake. Someone I thought I could get away with using," I said.

"No man. No way. I know that look. If it was just a mistake you would feel guilty, but it wouldn't make you question. *That* look means there's something more."

I sat down at the foot of Nicholas's bed while he rose up and crossed his legs underneath him. "Well. The *first* one was a mistake. The second…"

"Dude," Nicholas said, the look on his face somewhere between pride and concern. He connected with this part of me, but knew what it would mean for Xia.

"Nothing's happened yet. We kissed. She manages this ledger, and I have a plan. For it to work I need her to help me..."

"... cook the books," Nicholas finished for me. "You know if she finds out you're using her she'll be the first to throw you under the bus?"

"I was hoping to get out by that time. But it doesn't really matter now anyway."

"Because you've got feelings for her?"

There was no judgment in his tone, for which I was grateful. "I don't know. I mean she's pretty. She wants me to want her, and that's so damn sexy, you know? But it's not like Xia. My love for Xia came from such a light, happy, *human* place. This girl... it's darker. I feel like I'm the prey. She's an animal."

"I get that. Sometimes it's fun to be hunted. It's exciting after you get caught. Until you're filleted and served for dinner."

I laughed, sighed, and pouted a little. "Sometimes I think demons are just selfish humans. Already in Hell and I'm even more conflicted. Still trying to do what's right, but going about it all wrong."

"That was the point, wasn't it? I know you had to become a demon and all of that, but does becoming a demon require you to give in to the darkness?"

"I don't know," I shrugged. "Sometimes I feel that part of me pull so hard I can't resist. It's like fighting your nature, like—"

"—me trying to get excited for a date with a girl," he said without a smile on his face, perfectly serious. "All because you believe society or God or your family want you to."

I never understood the struggle Nicholas went through, being brought up Catholic. I hadn't known him during his teenage angst years, when he struggled to accept himself. He had to pretend to be someone other than who he was, to fight to find his true self. The internal conflict was an appropriate comparison.

"Are you telling me I should come out of the demonic closet?" I tried another joke.

Nicholas gave me a pitiful smile. It faded quickly from his lips. "No, not at all. I'm telling you that your true self always wins, and *should* always win. You can't be anyone other than who you are."

"I'm a demon," I said, not understanding where he was going.

"Nah, dude," he said, his tone carefully controlled, "I think you're more like an angel in demonic clothing. Don't get me wrong. The darkness isn't just in you. It *is* you. But we all have darkness inside us. This demon magnifying glass is there to help you come to terms with it and accept it. It isn't about control, or coming out, or which piece of you should win. It's about letting it all define you. It's about the yin and the yang, the light and the dark, all of which makes us human."

"I'm not human."

Nicholas laughed.

I didn't expect him to laugh.

"Maybe the human part was an accident, but I think it's the most appropriate description for you. What other creature has both angel and demon, potential for both good and evil? You're human, dude. That's all you have to remember."

The demon and the angel in me wanted to disagree. My dark demonic side didn't want to admit he was right. My light angelic side didn't want to admit he was right, either.

"It's all about balance," he said.

"How Zen of you."

"Well, you taught me a thing or two." He winked at me.

I hoped, deep down, that he was right. I didn't want to be evil. I didn't want to be good, either. Maybe it made more sense to be flawed, to be both, to be human.

TWENTY-FOUR

After my visit with Nicholas I felt much better. I knew I had a lot of work to do, a lot to prove, and a lot to be for Xia. I wanted to think of her more, like I did in the beginning. I wanted to be the man she wanted me to be—flaws and all.

Most of all, I felt vindicated and less anxious about the battle waging within me. I didn't need to be perfect, but I didn't need to lose myself because of my circumstances either.

For a moment, I let myself breathe.

Until I saw Lilith give me a mischievous grin from behind the front desk as I crossed the lobby. All the anxiety, the excitement, the desire, came flooding back.

I could allow myself to want her, to like her, to appreciate her and her attention without betraying Xia. I didn't have to sleep with her. That's how I would have to approach it.

At the last minute, I diverted from my plan to go straight up to bed, and stopped at the front desk.

"Hey," I said casually. "I'm beat. I'm going to go lie down. Don't let me sleep my whole life away, okay?"

She grinned a radiant smile. "Sure thing. You want any company?"

I sighed. "I'm sure taking you up on that offer would be nothing short of amazing…"

"Uh oh," she said, her voice cheery but her gaze falling in disappointment, "an empty compliment. Guys are so predictable. I sense a *but* coming."

I paused. "…*however*," I stressed, "I think I need to figure some things out."

"Went to see the girlfriend, huh?"

Sometimes I was sure Lilith could read my thoughts. "Yeah," I admitted.

"You tell her about me?"

"Definitely." I thought that sounded like a compliment.

"Did you tell her about Ruth?"

"Yup."

"Okay. Remember *I'm* not the jealous one. *I* don't care if you keep seeing her. I'm not asking for something exclusive, just offering to help you…" she paused, glancing at me seductively, "…work out your *anxiety*."

'Anxiety' had never sounded so erotic or exciting. I shivered as the word rolled off her tongue and down my spine. "I'm not saying no… exactly." I stopped. I hadn't been back for more than a few minutes, and already this place was getting to me. It was like the dark pit in my stomach had expanded and grown deep enough to stretch down to my groin.

"I know," she said, waving me away. "I'm in no rush. When I get in a rush I'll pounce on you in the hall or something," she said in a tone that could have been serious. She reached for her magazine and propped her feet up on the counter. "Sleep well."

I wasn't sure if I had accomplished what I set out to accomplish here. Did I buy myself time while reassuring her I wasn't completely going away or disinterested? Did I let her down easy, or give her a reason to pursue me harder? No way to tell, but by her now-disinterested face, I knew the time for conversation was over. I would only know by letting it go and finding out when she was ready to let me find out.

I didn't get nervous until I got into the long hallways that stretched out in front and behind me. There were no demons I could see, but I couldn't shake the feeling I was being watched. I tried to remember whether I always felt like this in the hallways, but exhaustion crept into my mind. I couldn't remember what it felt like here normally.

Maybe it was always like this and I was tired. Maybe I was used to Earth since I had just come from there. I glanced over my shoulder to make sure I wasn't being followed anyway.

The feeling didn't stop when I got to my room and

settled into bed. I pulled the sheet up to my throat and looked around the room, expecting to see another pair of yellow eyes.

Part of my fear was what the demon knew about me. I knew part of it was that I was concerned about whom he could tell or what he could do, but I had woken up with demons in my room almost every time I fell asleep. What did it matter if he decided to come here? What did it matter if he was watching me right now? What could he do? It was a consensus here that demons couldn't die; the worst punishment was that someone more powerful could take souls and banish you from the garden. I already knew that because I was someone who *could* do it.

Even if he came, couldn't that fit into my plan? Couldn't I take his souls? Even if he won and I had to start from zero, would it be that hard to find other demons with souls I could steal?

I felt the scythe as easily as I felt my leg. I knew it was an integral part of me that I could wield as quickly and efficiently as someone could throw a punch.

There was no reason for me to be scared. Eventually, I believed myself and talked myself out of fear enough to sleep.

* * *

I didn't dream. I began to wonder if I had any dreams left. Maybe that was why sleep was like experiencing temporary oblivion. When waking, I couldn't tell how long I had been asleep in this world—it could have been hours, days, or weeks. If Lilith could be believed, it could be months.

I used the yellow eyes that haunted my room as a substitute for my mother's greeting to confirm that I was awake. When I woke up to an empty room, it took a long time for me to release the grogginess and believe that my eyes were open.

Someone had been here. My floor to ceiling curtains had been pulled back, exposing the garden below. Mother Tree's flickering light cast shadows of strangely shaped leaves from the garden—leaves that the light picked up and deposited on my walls the same way the wind used to pick up words and deposit them in my mind.

If only I could string the leaves together into something that made sense. If only I could use them to learn the secrets of the souls buried deep within. The dancing shadows mesmerized me and made me think that the souls were trying to communicate, trying to tell me something important.

Rising from bed, I stretched and took one last glance around the room to make sure I was alone. Walking over to the windows overlooking the garden, I scanned the plants.

The entire garden was deathly still. Normally, while I could only see the demons against the oily plants by searching for their eyes, their presence made the garden quiver with shadow. If the garden was quiet today, maybe it would be a good day to go hunting.

I could make out the top branches of Mother Tree deep within the orange glow of the flame. I was glad I hadn't noticed that the big burning ball was actually a tree when I'd arrived. If I would've suspected I'd find Mother Tree consumed by flame, I couldn't have handled it.

When she saved me she grounded me here. It was easier to play my part after she helped me understand sacrifice. I knew why she was doing what she was doing and I had time to save her. I wouldn't let her burden last forever. She would be one of the first I saved when I gained enough power.

Everything I needed to do relied on power.

I studied my own eyes in the mirror, using the moment to give myself an emotional checkup, to see myself and evaluate the demon staring back at me in the mirror. I was anxious and fidgety, but well rested.

Although I felt happy, there was also pain touching my heart. I knew that was for Xia. I would see her again tonight, whether she wanted to see me or not. I couldn't let her go. I would fight for her.

Closing the door behind me, I started down to the lobby. The long hallways remained cold and ominous. This time, instead of the sense of being watched, I sensed the vast feeling of being alone, a feeling that the world was both too big and too small all at the same time. All I could ask for was another person to appear in the void, to remind me that the world wasn't too big to conquer together.

The lobby was empty. My gaze darted to the front desk, where Lilith always sat, sometimes with sharp eyes staring back at me, sometimes with her face buried in a magazine. I checked to be sure she hadn't ducked behind the counter.

"Lilith?" I asked, scanning the room.

Nothing but silence replied.

I craned my neck and looked over at the café where sometimes I could see Josephine bussing a table or other demons enjoying food they didn't need. I held my gaze there, waiting to see a shadow flicker across the doorway.

When I was convinced no one was there, I reached under the counter where Lilith kept the ledger. My hand landed on the spine of the heavy bound book.

I pulled it out, sat it on the counter, and flipped through it, pausing on the names that had large totals next to them.

Minyak was one of the first names I recognized, with over a million souls. What was he doing hanging out with Josephine and peddling for mine? He moved quickly to the top of my to-kill list. Taking his souls would cause enough of a stir to get the demons talking.

I laughed out loud at some of the other names: Lucifer only had 347, Beelzebub had 250,000—a respectable number.

Lilith had 16 million. The number jarred me out of

the book. I looked around the room again in confusion. Lilith? There had to be more than one. I wondered if the Lilith I knew would have a nickname on the pages, like "Front Desk Lilith" or something. There weren't any last names on any of the pages.

I paused on a familiar page where the names of the new demons were written. Their balances showed 9,996. Since I had spent a day with Xia and Nicholas, that meant I'd only been asleep for two days.

Flipping a few pages back, I scanned the book as I'd seen Lilith do when she looked for my name. I should have been here somewhere.

I scanned the pages for 'Alexander,' but couldn't find my name. I knew I had spent 29,997 souls on the new guys, but wanted to see how much Josephine decided to charge me for the strawberry tarts.

My name had to be here somewhere.

It was the number on the page that caught my attention first: 25,241. It was lower than I had anticipated, but was somewhere around the ballpark. It was the only number on the last five or six pages that stuck out to me. It was the only number big enough, yet small enough, to be mine.

But the name next to it wasn't Alexander.

It was Edmund.

Lilith knew.

I shut the ledger and shoved it back under the desk. I half-expected to see her, or the demon that was the only one who could have told her, standing behind me when I turned around. But the room was still empty. I was alone.

My head spun an excuse, something I could tell Lilith about why I lied about my name that wouldn't require me to tell her the whole truth. How much did she already know? If she already knew the whole truth, would I get the chance to explain?

She must have gone upstairs with the demon. She must have slept with him. I imagined her in the throes of passion, him whispering into her ear about the guy she really liked who lied to her. Then again, why would he talk about me while in bed with her?

Where the hell was she, anyway? Would her boss be happy knowing she left her post? Maybe her boss *was* that demon. I needed to move him to the top of my list, not Minyak.

I would ask for Lilith in the courtyard, where the demons gathered in the center of the garden. Someone there would know where she was. I would tell her the truth... sort of. My given name in the orphanage was Alexander, but I always liked Edmund better. If the demon told her I was from Orenda, that I was an angel, it wouldn't matter. I should have forgotten in my fall to Earth anyway. She didn't need to know that I had any memory of my life before Earth. There was no reason to believe I remembered. Remembering was impossible. That's not how it worked. Any questions beyond that could simply be answered with "I don't know," because I wasn't supposed to know.

Anxiety prickled at the back of my neck. I balled my hands into fists as I made my way into the garden. I kept my eyes out for someone on the trails, but didn't expect to see anyone until I arrived in the courtyard.

As I walked, I realized that I should have known something was wrong when I woke up and there was no one in my room. I should have known something was wrong when the curtains in my room were drawn and I didn't see movement in the garden. I should have known something was wrong when I got to the front desk and Lilith wasn't there and the lobby and café were also empty.

I knew something was wrong when I got to the courtyard and the only sound came from the bubbling blood in the fountain. There was no one sitting on the benches, or bathing, or chatting.

I didn't see anyone on the way here and no one was loitering in the courtyard. There were *always* demons in the courtyard.

I still had a heart because I heard it beating in my head. That only happened when it was completely silent around me and I felt isolated. The last time I felt this isolated, the same chilly fear crept into my body when I was on a mountain in Carlsbad. The insidious fog made me feel cut off from the world.

Now I was cut off from the shadows.

I spun around, half-expecting to see Sister Mary Elizabeth's sunken, white eyes. Maybe in this world they would be yellow. I knew she was here. Ruth called her out by name as the demon that employed her.

The courtyard was empty… too empty.

But I knew I wasn't lucky enough to be alone.

"I know you're here," my voice sounding more confident than I believed. "You can hide…" I continued, walking down a row toward Mother Tree. If I got there, I had an escape route. It seemed only fitting. "…but you can't change the way you *feel*. Only you can make me feel like this. So isolated. So alone. Is it because you feel so alone yourself?" I taunted, hoping it would cause her to reveal herself, cause a flicker of shadow in the corner of my eye… anything. "Maybe I need to start talking about the scriptures? Prophets? The Bible? Last time I compared myself to Jesus Christ you didn't like it so much. Will you slap me again?"

Still no response.

"What was with the Carlsbad Mountains, anyway? Was your whole purpose to give me the amount of information I needed to point me toward my death? Betcha never expected me to end up here, did you? Demon and all? *Still* more powerful than you? Bet you wanted to plant me yourself? Use my soul to travel to other worlds?"

Turning another corner, I prepared to come face-to-face with the nun, but this row looked empty, too. Most rows back here were long and narrow, but this one was short and wide. It seemed odd and out of place. Since that was how I felt, I knew I was on the right path.

"What are you gaining from these games? How did you get everyone to go along with you anyway? I don't have enough souls to make it worth your while… and certainly *mine* isn't worth much now that I'm a demon myself."

Still no answer.

Even I started to doubt myself. Maybe what I thought I was feeling wasn't what I was feeling. Maybe someone knew who I was and was using the way Mary Elizabeth made me feel for his or her own purposes.

Or maybe I was alone and didn't want to admit that I was scared. Maybe that feeling was what I associated with the nun.

"Is Sister Chantale here with you this time? How did you convince her to come with you before? I'm sure she isn't a demon herself. She had a heart. You? You I can understand. How many people did you kill, exactly?"

I got to the end of the short walkway, which joined another path. I had a feeling of certainty that this was where I was being guided, but the pathways in all directions were empty.

I chose the way that inched me closer to Mother Tree. If anything, I wasn't alone if I still had her. If I ran, I could make it to her.

That last thought was odd. It confirmed that I was in danger. If I weren't, why would I feel the need to run?

The plants in this part of the garden were shorter,

which made me feel more exposed. I knew my shadow body blended in with the black plants, so I stuck close to them in case I needed to hide.

I couldn't see this second courtyard from my view on the fifth floor. Then again, I supposed I wasn't high enough to see over all of the plants. The courtyard was small enough that it could easily remain hidden unless you knew where it was.

Shaped in a perfect square, it had brick-lined walkways all around. In the center were hundreds of plants, all of them a variety I'd never seen before. They were short, stubby shrubs. Each had a single bright red flower. The flower glistened in the orange light from Mother Tree, and twinkled like stars. I felt drawn to them, not only because the color of the red flowers matched the ruby in my ring, but also because my ring hummed and pulsed warm on my hand. I couldn't remember another time when it had done that.

The entire scene should have been simple—just me in the middle of the garden, surrounded by a bunch of plants grown from the souls of stolen lives. But the air was heavy, and fear-filled curiosity oppressed me. Whatever I was experiencing right now wasn't good, but I couldn't look away. It was like knowing a plane was going to crash and being unable to do anything but watch, dumbstruck.

As I inched closer to the square, the flowers on the plants became clearer, the glimmering resemblance to my ring becoming evident.

The flowers were rings. These plants were growing death rings.

I reached for one before realizing that I'd mindlessly walked toward it. I was overcome with a sense of failure—I had fought so hard to protect my ring. Xia and Nicholas had sacrificed so much to get my ring back to me. Linda Rose! Linda Rose had allowed herself to be killed in order to carry the ring back to Orenda at a cost that I didn't fully understand; it was a cost I hadn't allowed myself to think about for fear it would turn out to be meaningless.

Now it was. Now, it was evident Joshua could have a ring of his own... *anyone* could have a ring of their own.

I had failed.

Even worse, these plants were my family line. What other family, besides the genetic line of reapers, would be able to produce the item that defined our job?

As my hand reached for one of the blooming rings, I was stunned and relieved to find that I wasn't able to close my hand around it. The ring looked real, but my hand passed through as if it were nothing more than a ghostly hologram.

When I had been driving back to California from visiting my sister in Prescott after my adopted parents had died, the demon cop had been interested in my ring. He had said it existed in his world but was unattainable.

This must have been what he'd meant.

The amount of relief I felt brought tears to my eyes. I

was so proud of my family. These souls who were planted and growing these rings, they must have known. They must have prepared for this. They must have built in a fail-safe so that the rings they grew wouldn't be able to be used.

"Beautiful, aren't they?"

The voice caused me to stiffen, but it wasn't surprising. Even in death, Mary Elizabeth had a presence that was felt long before she was seen. As I turned, all the hair on my body bristled.

She was behind me, standing in the middle of the pathway that bordered one side of the square. She must have followed me, because she'd come from the same path I just had. If she hadn't been behind me, I would have seen her sooner.

She was dressed in a nun's habit, or the demonic version of it, made entirely of iridescent black feathers that cast a purple glow when they caught the light from Mother Tree. The habit wrapped around her head and neck and spilled around her feet in a pile. When she stepped forward, the whole pile seemed to come alive, float into the air, and resettle around her.

Her yellow eyes were the color of yellow lightning instead of a burning flame. "We've been trying to produce a useable specimen for... well... much longer than I've been here. Joshua recently gave me the task of cultivating these plants, which has been exceedingly rewarding, but frustratingly unsuccessful."

I glared at her, her black skin and bright eyes. How long had she been a demon? Was Mary Chantale one as well? How did she trick me? How did she appear to look so human? So alive? Was she even alive in the orphanage?

Those were only my questions about her. I had more about the plants, about my family, and about Joshua. I couldn't organize my thoughts in order to ask them, because anger muddled my mind and the pool of darkness swelled within me.

"I've tried mating aspects of certain essences," she said, lacing her long fingers together to illustrate her point, "and cutting away whatever I could manage. But I've never been able to examine an actual, working ring. That, of course, is the key. I can unlock all of the secrets of your family, Edmund, with that ring on your finger."

She paused, waiting for a reaction. I wanted to tell her how wrong she was, how I wouldn't let her. But all that sounded childish compared to the satisfaction I would feel when I buried my scythe into her skull.

When I didn't respond, she continued, "Joshua had the ring, of course, but he couldn't possess Henric forever. By the time he made his way back, that idiot man had already lost it again, thanks to your friends." She grinned an ugly, knowing grin. There was something she wasn't telling me. "But do you see them here?" she laughed, looking around. "Do you see any friends here to help you now?"

I could see her entire plan. She'd set it into motion on

the Carlsbad Mountains, manipulating Linda Rose with an acorn she knew would get back to me. There, she gave me just enough information to drive me to my own death, let me discover her grave, made it look like she was helping Linda Rose help me. In reality, she was manipulating Linda Rose the entire time.

I doubted the manipulation stopped there.

"Whose idea was it for Linda Rose to bring the ring back to me by sacrificing herself?" I asked, already sure of the answer.

"We had to get it here somehow. Do you know of any other way?" she responded, confirming what I'd already figured out.

"So it was all to get the ring here, in the Level of the Spirit. All so that you could grow more? But why?"

"Joshua needs one… just one. But he isn't so keen on taking it from you anymore. He likes you, Edmund. You've surprised him. I always told him there was darkness inside you. I saw it when you were a child and hated you for it. I still do. But that darkness might save you. Just look at what you've become." She held out her hand. "I will save you and all of those you love, *if* you give me the ring and help me create one for *him*."

I clenched my hands into a fist. If I could die, they would have to pry the ring off my cold, dead finger. Just like last time. That would be the only way they'd get it.

I hoped I couldn't die. Then they'd never get it.

"Well, no one expected you to hand it over," she

shrugged, dropping her clenched hands and leaning forward a bit. The position was corrective, making her look like a teacher addressing an insubordinate child. "We know your weakness, Edmund. Look around you," she grinned, motioning. "Where do you think everyone is?"

The question caught me off guard. I had no idea.

"I think you'll be more cooperative when you learn that Joshua has commanded every demon to hunt down those you love most. You had a sister, right? Jane? And poor Nicholas and Xia are probably already dead by now. Lilith has a bit of a thing for you, I believe. She was more than happy to lead the charge against your girlfriend."

I took an angry step forward, but stopped instantly when Mary Elizabeth raised a hand and repeated the spell I'd learned as a young mage—the exorcism spell. It didn't work so well when a demon was not in possession of a body, but it did have a side effect I didn't know until now. Even out of a body, the spell effectively held me in place as the world around me grew blindingly white.

"Joshua gives you a choice. Give me the ring, and he will show you how to get back to Orenda and reunite your flesh body with your demon spirit. He will allow you to take Nicholas and Xia there with you. Deny him, and he will claim their souls and plant them here where you will be forced to watch them rise up and produce power that fuels his purposes."

I didn't doubt I could find my own way back to Orenda. Mother Tree's roots were deeper than any plant in the garden. If any of them could get to Orenda, Mother Tree could get me there, and further.

As the blinding white spell ended, Mary Elizabeth summoned her hellhounds. They emerged from the forest of plants with snarling teeth. Their numbers were so vast that I knew I couldn't fight them all. I was surrounded.

Raising my cloak, I drew my scythe. All of my emotion, including the icy fear that caused the surges of adrenaline that kicked my flight or fight response into overdrive, pushed out through the cloak. Dark smoke billowed angrily. I could tell it had an effect, since a twitch of fear flashed across Mary Elizabeth's face.

"Don't be stupid, Edmund!" she snarled. Her mutts did the same. "We will take the ring one way or the other. Save your friends. You cannot fight me, the hounds, and every demon in Hell."

She had to include every demon in Hell. Doing so betrayed her because now I knew she believed the dogs weren't enough.

That gave me an idea. If I could get to Xia and Nicholas first...

I knew Xia and Nicholas had prepared for something like this. They had prepared for this since I dragged them into this mess. Even if they couldn't stop a demonic siege, I knew they'd have a plan. They already knew they could become targets. If only I had figured it out sooner and Xia could have read it in the book...

If you are reading this, run! I'm coming, I thought, just in case I wasn't being clear.

I wouldn't have to take on every dog, only the few that were in my direct path.

"Fine," I said, "I don't understand…"

I cut my sentence short, purposely attempting to disorient Mary Elizabeth as I turned and bolted toward Mother Tree.

The dogs moved just as I expected them to. The two between Mother Tree and me charged, fangs bared, muscles rock-hard and sinewy.

I hit the first one with my shoulder as he lunged toward me. While he was midair, I pushed my feet into the fastest sprint I could muster. With my added forward movement, the dog misjudged and lunged too far.

My shoulder connected with his chest as my blade sliced a second hound in half. All three of us yelped.

A third hound was on my heels, but was caught up in Mary Elizabeth's exorcism spell.

She only had one shot and we both knew it. I was too close now. I would make the tree before she could cast again.

I lunged, hoping Mother Tree was prepared. I didn't have time to ask, didn't have time to generate the emotional connection I normally had with her. I felt nothing from her—no support, no love, no salvation. If she had to allow me to use her roots, if there was some sort of permission either of us needed, I would simply crash into her trunk. I didn't want to think about what would happen if she didn't let me enter. I would either be devoured by savage dogs—a prospect that sounded even worse if I couldn't actually die again—or be consumed by the hot flames that fed off Mother Tree.

I hung in the air so long that I thought Mary Elizabeth had managed enough time to cast the exorcism spell again. The bright, piercing white was missing, so I still hurled toward the tree. My vision filled with orange flame. The fire tossed my smoky body upward. The heat caused me to rise.

Something was wrong. I should have been going down, toward the roots, not up toward the heaving sky.

I spread my wings in an attempt to prevent my body from rolling. If I could do that, maybe I could redirect myself down through the branches. The heat from the rolling flame tossed me around like a rag doll. My head filled with the screams of the souls of the trees. I gladly added my own cry for help. I couldn't fail now. Not now. Not when Xia needed me most.

Fear, confusion, anger, worry, anxiety. I knew I was good at feeling emotion. The world spoke to me with emotion.

I was capable of feeling love, kindness, gentleness, and care while also feeling fear, confusion, anger, worry and anxiety. When Mother Tree reached out and grabbed that place in my breastbone, the shock of being filled with her positivity pushed out the entire set of negative emotion and flooded me with her spirit.

I didn't fall into her roots. She rose up and swallowed me.

My vision snapped from tumbling orange and yellow to the rainbow netting of the root network. I oriented myself using the strong silver cord that ran through my heart to Xia.

As I followed it to her, I knew how urgent it was for me to find her alive. If she were dead, Joshua would be holding her spirit somehow. Otherwise he couldn't guarantee I would be allowed to take her soul to Orenda. Assuming Mary Elizabeth wasn't lying about his plan to trade her for the ring.

If that were the case, she could be reunited with Linda Rose. She could live in heaven while I finished my work down here. Then I could return to her. How bad would that be?

Was it presumptuous to believe life wasn't as valuable as humanity thought? We all knew it was part of the cycle, but was that only because it had always been that way? Who was to say those cycles couldn't end, that death couldn't cease?

No. I couldn't be that presumptuous. I was the Angel of Death. I understood the importance of the role, and the importance of life.

People assigned too much value to death. Death was the transition. Death was the thing they couldn't escape. Death was the end of one cycle and the beginning of another.

I knew better.

It wasn't life that didn't have value.

It was death.

Death couldn't exist without life. Life was what couldn't be escaped. I was the proof of this, alive even now, even though I had died.

I didn't fear death anymore. Why would I?

What would stop someone who didn't fear death from killing himself or herself? If they understood the importance of the experience they were having, the game they were playing, the character they had chosen to be, the lessons they were learning, they would understand life.

Experience would never leave us.

Xia deserved to finish hers.

The silver root that tied me to her took a direction I was unfamiliar with. Xia wasn't at the university; she wasn't even in the state of California anymore.

I found myself standing in a familiar room. The air smelled like sugar, so sickeningly sweet that I wondered how I ever stayed here as a kid. I was in the small square house I'd grown up in after I was adopted. The silver strand of light led into my old bedroom.

How did Xia end up here? The thought crossed my mind that it might be a trap.

Nothing had changed in the house, not even since the last time I was here. It looked like Jane had never returned and hadn't sold the property. The shelves were still packed with dust-covered religious trinkets, but most of them were knocked over because the windows were all broken out. I hoped the inverted cross on the wall was because of the weather coming in, and not a sign of something evil.

I doubted it. It was too quiet. Something sinister was going on.

For the first time since being a demon, I was glad I was the same color as the shadows. I was able to slip around the beams of moonlight by hugging the corners of the walls. I was almost undetectable, except for the yellow eyes I knew would stand out against the darkness.

I held my breath. I knew a demon didn't need to breathe to stay alive, but I was so caught up in the habit that I'd never noticed just how unnecessary it was. I was grateful for this discovery now. I couldn't be any stealthier.

The light in my old room was off, but pale blue moonlight spilled around the loose door jam. The hall window was shattered. It looked like blood had dripped down the sill. The source of the blood was unknown.

Putting my hands onto the bedroom door, I prepared to push it open. Instead, I hesitated at the warmth of the wood. There was power and life behind this door, but I couldn't tell if it was from Xia, another source, or both. The magic was familiar, but frightening at the same time. There was another emotion behind the door, a loathing I didn't recognize and couldn't recall feeling before.

I pushed the door open slowly, and someone screamed.

TWENTY-FIVE

Jane, Nicholas, and Xia huddled in the middle of my old bedroom. They sat on a symbol I had drawn on the floor under my bed. It was written in Orendan script and contained the words of an entire book-length spell in one double helix wrapped circle. The power of the words glowed in the moonlight.

Jane screamed when she saw me. At first I didn't understand, then I remembered I was a demon with haunting yellow eyes. The same demon cop that stalked me had also stalked her. He had abused her and killed my adopted parents.

In the presence of the symbol, my demon side became inflamed. The thought of what this demon did to Jane and my parents, and subsequently me, made me envious.

I tried to step into the room, but the symbol flared and propelled me backward. I was nauseated and dizzy.

The loathing I felt prior to entering the room was for angels and their tricks. The familiar power mixing with it was my own old magic. But it felt distant, like a memory created from a dream.

"Edmund!" Xia exclaimed, running toward me.

She hit me at a full run, tears welling in her eyes. Her hot human body burned as she wrapped me in an embrace that was painful, but worth it. If she chose to stay this close to me until her fire consumed me, I would let her.

"I'm so sorry. I'm so sorry," she whispered in my ear. She was frantic, though I wasn't sure what she was apologizing for. "They came for us. Hecate brought us here, but I haven't been able to conjure her since. I'm not strong enough."

Nicholas tried to calm Jane, but settled for covering her mouth with his large hand while pinning her to his body.

Jane stared at me, wide-eyed in disbelief. I softened my gaze as recognition crossed her face. She said my name, but it was muffled against Nicholas's hand.

"*I'm* sorry. I'm sorry for everything," I said. "I didn't know they were coming for you. It's all my fault."

"I'm still mad at you," she said, pushing herself onto her toes and pressing her lips to mine. The kiss was unsatisfying and left me wanting more. I wanted to devour her like I used to. I wanted to be her fortress of stability. I wanted to give her the kiss that she would dream about. I would have to settle for that now—dreaming about the kisses I had once been able to give her. I played them over in my mind while I kissed her now.

I closed my eyes, remembering the taste of her lips. With the heat on my mouth, I imagined the pressure, the softness, the mix of cherry and mint. Her skin was the consistency of a pink cherry blossom petal.

That color reminded me of another part of her body. For a brief moment, I was back with her in the hotel room, the night before my death.

She exhaled a moment too soon, just as I was getting lost in the memory.

As she pulled away, her breath was icy. "You built us a safe place here. If it weren't for you we'd already be dead." She took a step back to hide her shivering.

"So good it's keeping me out now," I grinned, knowing I couldn't follow her into the room.

I noticed the bedroom window was broken as well. Like the hallway window, the edges dripped with blood.

"What's going on with the windows?"

"Oh, you know," Nicholas started, lightening a serious situation, "demons keep dropping gutted bodies on the roof."

The laugh caught in my throat, my lips curling into a grin. I had to give them credit. That's one way to wear someone down.

"They're trying to break your will, scare you to the point of possession." I addressed Jane, because I could see nothing but fear behind her eyes. She was the most vulnerable. "The less fear you can manage, the less power they'll have over you."

"Easy for you to say," Jane grunted, her tone filled with fire.

"Hi, Jane. Not my best look, I know."

"Mom and Dad were right. You're one of *them*."

I couldn't pretend not to be offended. "It's a long story, okay?"

"You should read the book," Xia said, laughing at how normal it sounded.

Jane stared at her like she was stupid.

"How did you find her?" I asked Xia.

"We didn't know she was your sister at first—"

"They *kidnapped* me," Jane cut her off.

"We *saved* you," Nicholas corrected, mimicking Jane's tone in a way that suggested he'd repeated it a few dozen times.

Before the argument escalated, the air temperature dropped. There was a thud as a body hit the broken window, spraying tiny droplets of blood into the room.

Jane screamed again, while Xia wiped the blood off her face. Nicholas pinned Jane against him again to keep her from fleeing the circle's safety.

"Dude, I'm almost ready to stop saving her," Nicholas said to no one in particular.

"Send her out!" a voice said, followed by a deep, throaty laugh.

"Go to Hell!" Nicholas shouted back. He turned to

me and added, "I seem to be saying this a lot, but no offense."

These three people were really all I had left alive. I had to admit, they were all amazing. Nicholas maintained his sense of humor, even though I knew he wanted to deny the supernatural happenings in his life. He managed to put his own doubts behind him and embrace a life that was not only dangerous, but also hard for him to acknowledge.

Xia had been strong through it all. It was, no doubt, thanks to her and her conjuring of Hecate that they were all still alive. I couldn't even imagine the conviction she'd had all this time. She got my ring back. She crossed into Orenda and helped Linda Rose get the scythe. She was involved in the planning and spell work. She risked herself for me in ways I didn't know about yet. Even now, with blood smeared across her face, she looked fierce and beautiful. How did I ever doubt I wanted to be with anyone but her?

Jane may not have been much, but she was the last piece of my family. She believed me when no one else did, which made my childhood bearable. I wished her a normal, happy life. I wanted to see her get married, have children, own a dog.

There was another thud against the side of the house, this one missing the window.

"Can Nikki come out and play?" a woman's voice rang with a giggle that was childish and familiar.

Nicholas's eyes grew wide. "Is that Ruth?"

I nodded slowly.

"I hate it when you call me that!" he yelled through a clenched jaw.

"Ah come on, you cocksucker. Come out here and tell me that to my face."

Nicholas raised an eyebrow. "She does know who she's talking to, right?"

Everyone laughed, which was good for our emotional well-being, but it made everyone outside angry.

"How about you send out my cousin?" a voice said in a thick Japanese accent. This voice was so haunting that it stopped everyone and caused chills to run over our skin.

Xia shot me a venomous look.

"I didn't know," I said. "You know I didn't know."

"Quon?" Xia whispered, moving toward the window.

Quon was Xia's cousin. He had shared a dorm with Nicholas and me. After Nicholas had been possessed, we hadn't been able to find him. We didn't know whether he'd escaped, or whether he'd been killed.

Now we knew. "No! Stop!" I shouted, stepping into the room and becoming overwhelmed by the symbol on the floor.

Xia froze as Quon's face appeared at the window. He wasn't a shadow figure with yellow eyes. Instead, he looked like he did when he was alive, except he had sunken, foggy eyes and wrinkled skin.

"Xia," I said calmly, although I didn't know if I was

trying to calm her or myself. "Sometimes I think demons can appear in that form, as someone who died but who wasn't a demon themselves. We can actually bring someone's spirit back like this, but that isn't Quon. The same thing happened to me on the mountains with Mary Elizabeth and Mary Chantale. The nuns were dead. Mary Elizabeth is a demon."

Nicholas was stunned. Jane simply rolled her eyes. "Seems like everyone's a demon," she said, unsure if she was pouting or making a joke.

Joking was good. Joking showed she had some inner fire left. I hoped she was joking.

Xia was still staring at Quon's face at the window. "Come out here and I'll show you that I'm fine," he said.

"My cousin wouldn't ask me to put myself in danger like that. If you really were Quon, we'd have nothing to fear from you. How about *you* come in *here*?" She crossed her arms in defiance.

That's my girl. Smart as ever. I was relieved to see that she wouldn't be so easily tricked.

Jane's shoulders relaxed and her face slackened as she looked at me. I wasn't sure how to read into the expression. "Oh good, the police are here." I realized she wasn't looking at me, but behind me.

Spinning around, I came face-to-face with a familiar figure. It was the same twisted face that peered at me through a truck window as he steered an oil tanker toward me. The same shotgun was pointed at my head.

This time, he didn't wait. I heard a click and the gun went off.

I expected an explosion of pain, but all that followed was a ringing in my ears and screaming from Xia, Nicholas, and Jane.

The cop threw back his head and laughed, his eyes yellow and vacant. His muscles flexed as powerfully as the darkness inside. This demon was powerful enough, but to be in possession of such a strong body... I knew from my teachings as a mage and as a human that an energumen's power was greatest while in possession of a body.

"We've been waiting for you, Edmund. Come outside and answer to us, or the next shot won't be aimed at *your* head," he gestured the barrel of the gun into the room. "I won't miss."

He reached out and rested his hand on my head. His hand felt hot and sharp, like when Xia touched me, but more condensed. The pain was so intense that I lost awareness of where I was. I slumped to the ground.

Somewhere in the back of my mind, I heard Xia gasp. By the time I processed what was happening around me, the cop was gone.

"Wow. Did anyone else notice that his shirt was two sizes too small? Before you kill him, can you find out what he does at the gym to get his chest so big?"

I couldn't tell if Nicholas was serious or joking, but either way it helped me shake off the lingering disorientation.

"What is wrong with you people?" Jane yelped. She was losing it. "How can you be calm? How can you make jokes?"

"We've been through this a time or two," Xia answered, returning to the safety of the circle and glancing at me as she did. "Fear is their biggest weapon. You have to learn to brush it off. If you let them get under your skin, they'll get under your skin."

"Y'all are crazy."

While they bickered, I assessed the situation. I wasn't powerful enough alone. I doubted we'd be powerful enough together. I wasn't sure how many demons were out there, but if the Level of the Spirit was empty, that meant there was an army. Worse, I didn't know how many of them possessed bodies.

Together we were stronger, but not strong enough.

"I need a body," I said, quietly. My voice was so low that I barely heard myself speak. But it was loud enough that they heard.

A stunned silence fell over them.

"What's missing is my connection to the world," I explained, unsure if I made sense.

When I still got no response I started over. "I need a body to have full access to all my abilities. Just like the cop. Out of the body he's nothing," I shuddered, knowing I was telling only a half-truth. "In a body, he's deadly. You saw how easily he overpowered me there. I need a body."

Xia stood up. "Well, I suppose I've let you inside me

before. Might as well again," she grinned. "It doesn't mean I'm not angry with you."

I looked at her blankly.

"It was supposed to sound sexy," she explained.

"No, that's not it," I grinned. "I need you to be… you. I need you to try to get Hecate back. You have access to feminine powers that won't accept requests from a man. You can use her to protect you and Jane."

Nicholas did the math. "Wait. Me? No. I've been there, done that."

"Nicholas. It's me. It's just me."

His gaze slid to Xia. "You're totally going to try to get with her in my body aren't you?"

I laughed, but he was completely serious. "Demons are gathering outside, Nicholas. I'm not thinking about sex—well, now I am—but the timing sucks."

"What if you come out gay?" Xia added with a smirk.

"I think if Nicholas was going to turn me, it would have happened by now," I mused.

"You don't have any better ideas?" Nicholas protested.

I didn't know how to respond. I wasn't even sure *this* idea was a good idea, but what I needed, our best chance, was power. That sounded familiar. How many times had I said that I needed power lately?

"I have a better idea," Xia said, her chocolate eyes looking dark in the dim light. She hardened them on purpose. "You can leave," she said, crossing her arms and looking tough. "Go, Edmund. Leave us to take care of ourselves. I'm sure most of them will follow you. We can handle the rest."

I didn't like this plan. I didn't like it at all. "They are trying to use you against me," I said. "They will kill you if I don't give them what they want. I'm not leaving."

"Then take us with you," Xia suggested. "We've talked about it before. You could—"

"If they kill us you'll have to save us on the other side anyway, right?" Nicholas interrupted. "If that's our only option, we might as well not give them the satisfaction."

"You don't know what you're asking me to do," I said, shocked. I had just given myself a pep talk on the virtues of life. I wasn't about to go back on my word, to consider their lives insignificant. "Life is worth fighting for," I said. "If this is your time, then this is your time. But *never* give up without a fight. Got it?"

"That's it? That's your speech?" Jane was irritated.

"I need you to stay strong, Jane," I said, as another body hit the window and sprayed blood into the room. "Don't break. Don't let them get in."

Then I addressed Nicholas with my plan. "If anything happens, if you want me to get out, I will. I promise I won't make you do anything you don't want to do. Just let me in so I can use the physical connection, and that's it. I'll teach Xia the exorcism spell, as a backup."

"Why can't you just use that on *him*?" Nicholas asked.

"I intend to, but I need to be in a body for it to work.

Otherwise, it only holds us in place."

"Fine." Nicholas finally gave in. "But if I say get out, get out. No matter what."

"No matter what," I promised.

TWENTY-SIX

I thought I still had a connection to my emotions as a demon, but being in a body again flooded me with such intensity that just *being* made me feel high. Nicholas was so strong. It made the memories of being in my own body pale in comparison. Every inch of him tingled; the cool air on his skin felt like magic. Even the fear he felt was more powerful than anything I'd experienced since my spirit had died and was reborn.

I flexed Nicholas's muscles and cracked his neck. I couldn't help but exhale as the feeling of stretching muscles raced over his body.

Inhaling was a bit more difficult. His chest felt tight.

You've been smoking again, I accused.

You know how I am when I get stressed. Running from demons is stressful, his voice echoed in my head... his head.

I have to do just one thing before we go out there, I thought. *Just in case.*

I swept Xia into my arms. At first, she tensed in fear. Being grabbed in the middle of this scene probably wasn't my smoothest move, but I couldn't help it.

I pressed my lips to hers. She recoiled at first, but her warm body melted as soon as she realized what was happening.

Ew, Nicholas kept repeating, but he didn't fight me. He could hear my thoughts and read my mind. I knew that he knew how important it was for me to feel her again. This may not have been his favorite moment, but he was willing to let me have it even though he'd protested earlier.

Xia's body responded to my kiss. She pressed herself into me—the pressure causing intense waves of pleasure to roll through my borrowed body. Her lips were hot, just like they had been when I was a demon. This time, my temperature matched hers.

Nicholas drummed his fingers in boredom and frustration, a gesture that mirrored in his hand at the small of Xia's back.

Xia pulled away, "Sorry, Nicholas." She smiled, pursing her lips and wrinkling her nose in a way that made my heart melt. "I had no idea you could kiss a girl like that."

Nicholas balked. He would have punched my shoulder had it not been painful for him. His frustration with me rose, even if he did understand. He swore at me and her, but I translated, "That was all me."

Xia rose up on her toes so she could give me a quick

peck, and then kissed Nicholas's cheek. "Thank you, Nicholas. Now let's go kick some ass."

I instructed Xia to stay within the protection of the circle. The symbols would protect her from demonic activity, but shouldn't stop her from doing magic of her own. "They'll still be able to throw things at you. Anything physical can still hurt you, so be careful and don't leave the circle if you can help it." I squeezed her shoulders before turning to Jane. "Keep it together, Jane. Don't get possessed. I don't want to deal with that, please."

She didn't answer as she slid down the wall and crumpled into a heap on the floor.

Taking a deep breath, I tested my connection to the world. It felt good to be back in the Level of the Body. I felt like I belonged. I drained Nicholas's negative emotions into the planet, allowing its power and energy to wash over us. Determination, love, and joy replaced the negative emotions.

I pulsed the determination outward, lighting up the demons in my mind like beacons.

They filled the pasture, hundreds of dark clouds descending on the little house. Nicholas flinched as he realized their numbers. I didn't know if it was him or me who pushed the fear down and out with a swallow. This was not the time for fear.

Now that I understood the root network and had control over my connection to this level, teleportation was easy. All I had to do was grab hold of one of the hundreds of silver strands that led outside and yank Nicholas's body along for the ride. I used this ability to walk through the wall into the back pasture.

The scene was chaotic, like a huge black storm swirling around the fields. Lightning struck as yellow-eyed figures took shape momentarily before vanishing into a massive, living cloud that billowed with demonic life.

The cop stood in the middle of the field, his hands on his hips. The look on his face was bloodthirsty.

"You brought the boy?" he sounded surprised.

"What can I say? He likes a man in uniform," I responded, half of the thoughts mine, and half of them Nicholas's.

"He's full of lust. It's a weakness. I wonder if he would expel you from his body in exchange for an eternity surrounded by beautiful men, all willing to cater to his every whim?"

"Tempting, but he's sure he's capable of finding his own beautiful men."

"Cocky, too. Another weakness."

"You have no idea." The denotation came from me; the double entendre came from Nicholas.

The demon tested our resolve as his eyes burned into ours. His attempt to make himself appealing, just like he had done with Lilith and me in the lobby, was feeble and transparent in this world. Nicholas found his physical body impressive, but the spirit magic he worked didn't hold my attention.

In response, I flexed my wings. They expanded magnificently on Nicholas's body. The scythe appeared in his warm hand, the metal cold and biting. It made me feel so alive. I understood now why demons spent so much time in the pursuit of possession.

Nicholas questioned whether it was something I would have thought before.

It didn't matter. I didn't have time to console him. The cop changed tactics and turned deadly in an instant. Instead of trying to lure Nicholas into submission, he would kill us.

He drew his gun, firing three shots in the time it took me to mentally respond to his aggression. I was ready to defend. I had already surveyed my surroundings. Pulling cold air and water together, I condensed the air in front of me into a solid mass. The bullets buried themselves into a block of ice that dropped and shattered at my feet.

Frustration showed on the cop's face. He clenched his sharp cheekbones. The dark cloud descended around us, cutting off our ability to see each other. When it lifted, a lone dark figure stood between us.

"Stop this! Now!" the voice said, frantic and concerned. "I won't let you kill each other. We're on the same side."

"Are we?" the cop asked. "Whom do you serve, Lilith? Joshua or Edmund?"

"I didn't realize they were competing for my affections," Lilith answered, walking toward me. Her hair tossed around her face like it was being blown by a tornado. Power and determination were evident in her eyes.

"Edmund," her voice softened, her stance remaining dangerous. "You're one of *us*. You possessed your friend for power, regardless of your intentions. You slept with Ruth to manipulate her. These are things demons do. Come back with me. I'll help you protect your friends. I'll help you accept who you are. I'll make sure you get the power you crave." She held her hand out.

All I had to do was take it.

"Just give me the ring and all of this will go—"

She fell silent as I buried my scythe up under her chin, the blade extended through the top of her head.

Xia was smiling. I could feel it. Her pride was so obvious and strong that it wafted toward me from the small house, from the window where she stood, watching, waiting for her moment to shine. I knew killing Lilith wouldn't solve our problems, but it was a start. I put Xia first.

Sixteen million souls. As a demon, the only way I knew my count was to guess based on the floor I was upgraded to. Or I could look in the ledger. While in possession of a human body, I could feel them.

It was like I had an enormous army. The power from millions of soldiers who were converging against me now turned in matching unison, saluting me as their officer-in-chief.

I felt parts of the root network that I now had control over. I had access to hellhounds—I felt them rush forward, almost to the field. Instead of feeling fear at their approach, they inspired hope. They responded to *my* command.

We might actually win, I heard Nicholas think. *This is incredible.*

But the demonic world watched what I had done. If there was any doubt in who, or what, I was before today, they all knew now. There were more than 16 million souls out there to be had. If we counted totals on each team, my power was still a drop in the bucket.

The black cloud descended as demons took shape around me. They moved in one fluid motion, advancing for the attack. I raised my scythe and let it flash in the moonlight, ready to strike. I knew the more I hit, the more powerful I would become.

I wished they would line up one-by-one for me. Their sheer numbers overwhelmed me.

As if on cue, Hecate emerged from the trees, followed by an army of hounds. The plan of the hounds became evident as Hecate led the pack, creating a line between them and me. She would stagger them; allow them through, one-by-one like I had just wished for.

They charged, coming much too fast and much too densely for them to realize that they were being staggered so that only one could strike at a time.

One-by-one coming up! Nicholas laughed as my scythe

devoured the demons.

I spun my scythe into one dark shadow after another, feeling my power grow each time.

"Enough!" The cop barked. He was in front of Hecate, his yellow eyes filled with hate while trained on me.

Hecate growled and snapped, lunging toward him.

He caught the dog midair by the throat, holding her snout inches from his face so he could see into her eyes. "I answer to no god," he growled through clenched teeth.

The demons coming after me changed direction, returning to their mist form. They surrounded the cop and Hecate, lifting the dog high into the air, striking her with lightning and trapping her in a web of darkness.

Xia screamed. It was guttural and angry. It was a sound I never wanted to hear from her again.

The cop, now with a clear path to us, had murder in his eyes. "Joshua promised you to *me*."

"Then come get me!"

This was it. This was the moment. Either I would survive or I wouldn't. I knew this demon didn't need a magic scythe to take my power or my souls. I knew he didn't need any help. This was no mere demon I was up against. He was a devil.

I closed my eyes, whispering to the wind in a way I could only do with a body of flesh and bone. A human body, or an Orendan body. "Get ready, Xia. I'll see you soon."

Thanks, Nicholas. You ready?

Abso-fuckin'-lutely.

If I caught the demon off guard as the aggressor and the one to charge first, his reaction showed no surprise. He lunged into his attack with such a quick response that someone watching from the outside wouldn't have noticed who took the first step.

I'd been in a situation like this before, a moment when I ran for my life and felt the world rally around me. Before, I ran away from Joshua—away from fear and uncertainty, away from the fight. Now, I ran toward it, head first into the path of conflict.

I wasn't alone. Nicholas, Xia, Jane, and millions of trapped spirits united around me. I felt the demons that were here, power hungry and prideful. Even worldly elements that had switched sides united around my enemy. Trees I had known in this field as a boy chose to support him. I imagined their branches reaching toward me, wanting to harm me, trying to get into my head and make me feel alone.

But I remembered how the trees had rallied behind me Orenda as I'd fled from Joshua. They'd completely uprooted. They'd made incredible sacrifices for me that these trees weren't willing to make for the devil.

I remembered the bush at the entrance of my father's office. That bush faced destruction by fire and by cutting. It had been forced to struggle through marble and stone, but under impossible odds refused to back down, refused to give up, refused to stop protecting me.

Then there was Mother Tree, who had given her life for me, supported me, and now was doing the same for all her offspring. She was the only reason the inner voices of the trees were sustained. She never gave up, and neither would I.

It was like we were playing a game of chicken. I barreled Nicholas's body forward with as much speed as I could muster. I knew he was helping me, willing his legs to move faster, to be stronger, to constrict the muscles tighter. He worked out every day for moments like these where he could play the hero.

The cop ran with such ferocity that he tore up the ground, splitting open the earth. He didn't slow down, not even as I felt his breath on my face and saw nothing but the yellow of his eyes. We collided with force both physical and spiritual, both natural and supernatural. As our bodies hit, the blow was in slow motion, with no sound except the rushing air in Nicholas's lungs as it pressed out of his chest. The sound was loud, like a whirlwind.

I wrapped my arms around the cop's waist as his fists rained down on Nicholas's back. I couldn't describe the pain as anything other than perfectly human. Nicholas would feel it in the morning, but I hoped he'd be grateful for it. It was his humanity that allowed him to feel like this. To me, the pain was a basic and necessary feeling that I found cathartic. It soothed my numb soul and pounded life into it like someone giving CPR to a dying body. The spiritual fight, the physical punches, beat back my darkness.

Xia's timing couldn't have been better. The cop and I hit the ground and rolled together a few times before the air around me turned white. I gripped the cop tighter, afraid to lose my grip as the exorcism spell threw both of us out of our human hosts. The experience was unpleasant, like the feeling from the symbol drawn to repel demons in my old bedroom. It made me sick.

Nicholas heaved and vomited me out, except that I experienced every gut-wrench myself. It took all of my mental faculties to keep my arms wrapped around the demon that was expelled from the cop's body as we were pushed back into the root network.

I spun out of control, losing the ability to stop myself from tumbling. I knew the exorcism spell could cast a demon back to Hell, but I didn't know how disorienting the experience would be. No wonder demons hated this. No wonder it made them so angry.

We tumbled through the space between spaces longer than it would normally have taken me to get back to the hotel lobby. Longer than it would take me to locate and follow the roots to Xia. Worst of all, longer than I knew it should have taken to return to where we'd come from. We stopped abruptly after colliding with a row of demons that had interlocked their arms in what looked like a giant game of Red Rover. Only we didn't break the line. The line broke us.

I landed on a piece of solid rock that floated in the middle of space, surrounded by dark shadows. The devil landed on top of me. His nose was resting on mine, but his eyes were wide and alert.

He laughed.

He laughed for a long time.

He laughed until I became uncomfortable and squirmed beneath him. I wondered if his plan was to lie on top of me, trapping me forever.

Finally he pushed himself up, pretending to dust himself off.

Then he did something I didn't expect—he held his hand out to me as an offer to help me up.

I didn't take it, but stood of my own volition.

"Well, what can I say? The man is always right!"

"What are you talking about?" I asked, taking a step toward the center of the rock we stood on. I was too close to the edge for comfort.

The demon blocked my move, stepping closer to me. "Joshua," he said. "He knew you'd use the girl to perform the exorcism. I told him he was crazy, that you wouldn't have the balls to actually attack first."

He took another step forward and pushed me backward.

"Let's see. He knew if he used the soul of that nun friend of yours, Chantale, that he would get you worked into such a frenzy you wouldn't notice that he'd possessed your friend Henric until it was too late. Then he knew you would save that disaster of a woman, Linda Rose. Did you know we were acquainted?"

I froze.

"Yeah. I helped you get your ring back. Mary Elizabeth did most of the work but she couldn't have pulled off something of this magnitude alone. You didn't know? Well, I'd bet you also didn't know that Joshua figured you'd find your way down here to save dear old dad," he laughed, stoking my anger.

I was still disoriented from the exorcism spell and a range of muted emotions; everything felt like I was under water. Even my anger was impotent. I tried to lock my knees into place, but stumbled as I tried to maintain balance.

The demon laughed at that. "He even knew you'd get distracted by that tree. All we had to do was keep an eye on that girlfriend of yours. You led us right to her!"

Now all of the demons were laughing. I was so exhausted I could barely stand. Now was not the time to get fatigued. Damn this existence and the seesaw between absolute power and absolute exhaustion.

"The soul-stealing was a nice touch, though. That was quite a trick for a brand new pony. No problem, though." He stepped forward with such aggression that he slid into me with perfect control and precision. "You won't need them where you're going."

He put his hands on my shoulders. I felt what he was going to do before he did it, but was unable to stop him.

My locked knees and vertigo were no match for a simple, easy push.

I fell over the edge with barely a fight, tumbling into the darkness.

TWENTY-SEVEN

I felt like I was drowning as I battled my way to the surface. I knew I didn't have to breathe to stay alive, but the water soaking through my body was as painful as if I were inhaling it. My lungs weren't the only things that burned, begging for air. That feeling expanded throughout my entire body.

I felt like a balloon that had taken on as much water as it was capable of taking on, moments before it popped. I worried that if I exploded I would be swept away in the currents—inky black smoke swallowed up by the ocean.

When I finally broke the surface of the water, I gulped for air. Breathing pushed water out of my body, but every exhale caused it to rush back in. The transition of the water in and out of my body felt like razor blades.

The ocean heaved in violent swells that were at least thirty feet high. Above me, in the sky, was a burning ball of fire. Mother Tree. From this perspective, she was the same size as the moon and gave off as much light.

At first I was disoriented, but figured out quickly that I was in the oceans that made up the sky in the Level of the Spirit. I rose with the swells, fighting to keep myself together as waves crashed down on me, pushing me under the water. Kicking my feet and flailing my arms didn't do as much to propel me toward the surface. Instead, every time I surfaced, it was like the sea had given me a gift—one more moment to live.

Maybe it wasn't a gift at all, because it meant that the pain and terror would continue for that much longer.

The Catholic nuns taught me that Hell was a lake of fire and brimstone—a never-ending torture of fire. Instead, I found myself surrounded by water and swimming through shards of glass. The sensation was the same either way, I supposed. My body was experiencing a lake of fire. The Catholics weren't so wrong after all.

I didn't see the ship until it was on top of me. It was hidden behind one of the swells until it rose up, gliding down the waves, headed right toward me.

Since I didn't have time to get out of its way, I braced for the impact of the giant wooden bow. It passed so close that I could make out the grain in the watertight planks. The ship didn't hit me as I paddled away. Instead, I was caught in its wake and drawn closer as it skimmed the water.

The ship dropped anchor and halted abruptly, the side of the vessel inches from my nose.

A competing swell rose up behind me, threatening to slam me into the side of the ship. Depending on how high it rose, I worried it would be big enough to capsize the boat.

The water pulled away, pulling me along with it as the swell stole the undulation it needed to birth a wave. The ship pitched toward me, so far that I caught a glimpse of the formidable masts and large, shadowed deck that was covered with hundreds of flickering yellow eyes.

The swell changed direction with the surging currents and rushed toward the ship as I had imagined it would. I braced again, this time for the feeling of my body smashing into the side of the wood, driven to death by the monstrous power of the water behind me. The wave was so large that I knew it was going to consume the ship, flood its deck, and roll it far enough to sink it.

I was thrown out of the water and into the air as the wave began to break, the white water following close behind. I landed on the deck of the ship with a thud, but knew the worst of the pain would come in just moments, when the water from the swell would bury us all.

The water fell like a thousand knives burying into my back with the force of a million pounds. The other unlucky demons screamed as the water hit them as well. Why had the ship stopped here? Why did it stop where it would be forced to take on the crushing blow of the water?

Opening my eyes, I discovered the entire boat underwater. Mother Tree's burning flames cast eerie aurora-like light deep into the shimmering sea. All of the demons on the deck of the ship stood perfectly still, glaring at me with resentful intensity.

The crashing wave had stirred up the water near the surface. Above us, a froth of air bubbles raced toward us. I knew it didn't make sense for the air bubbles to race downward. As I watched a bubble sink in front of my face, I realized they weren't moving down; we were moving up.

The ship burst out into the cold night air. Every demon took a collective breath, which painfully ejected water from our bodies.

Exhaustion overcame me as I collapsed on the ship's deck.

"Someone paid a hefty price for you," a voice boomed above me. I was too tired to care, respond, or open my eyes. "No sleeping. No resting. Not until you work off the debt."

Pulled to my feet by a pair of strong hands, I tried to force my eyes open.

"You make a much better worker when you're broken—more compliant."

A slap stung my cheek. It was painful enough to open my eyes.

"Ah, so you're one who responds to pain," the demon in front of me spoke. He was muscular and dark. There were no iridescent feathers covering any part of his body. "I'll remember that," he continued, still holding me upright. He slapped me again for no reason. "Tie down that sail over there while I announce you to the captain. If you don't know how to tie the knot, trade your shorts and someone will show you. You'll find items like that are a luxury you won't be able to afford as a Mammon worker."

I didn't like that word. The hostility I felt toward it helped me wake up a bit more, which, thankfully, prevented me from falling on my face when the man shoved me in the direction of a loose rope.

Forcing my feet to move forward and focusing my mind, I grabbed the rope and attempted to follow the knot from one that was already tied. It was a knot I didn't recognize, but that looked easy enough. Until I tried tying it.

"Here. Let me teach you," a voice behind me offered to help on my third failed attempt. I wasn't sure if it was the sound of the voice or the pitch of the ship, but I almost lost my balance.

"Henric?" I turned around to peer into another set of yellow eyes.

"I wish you would have missed our drinks," he said. While his tone was soft, the words were still sharp.

"Please tell me you weren't sent here because you killed me," I said, knowing he was under Joshua's control at the time.

"Nah," he responded, taking the rope from my hand and changing the subject. "Look, the knot is called a bowline. Do you know what a sheet bend is? It's kind of like that."

I shook my head.

"It's tied like this, but you have to be careful. Make sure it's lined up on the block. It slips if it's pulled sideways. Here, you try."

I repeated the steps he showed me. My knot wasn't as clean as the one he'd tied, but it looked right, more or less.

"Thanks, Henric. The big guy told me I'd have to trade my shorts for that. You want them?"

"That's Bosun, the boatswain. He runs the crew right, but in this case keep your pants for something more important. I came over to help because I know it's my fault you're here, and I owe you." His voice was layered with guilt, the same guilt I felt over him being here. It surprised me that he felt he owed *me*. "Make no mistake, though," he said, eyes burning, "I have enough debts to pay. I'll help you when I can, but don't overestimate my remorse."

"You don't owe me anything, Henric."

He grunted. I wasn't sure if it was in agreement or not. "You'd better tie that again. It won't be good enough for Bosun."

I made the knot cleaner. When done, I turned for Henric's approval but he'd vanished among the shadows.

They all moved like robots. The majority had vacant eyes. I wondered if that was what happened to a demon if they weren't allowed to rest or sleep. They were broken, stripped of their will. Demons possessed.

"Hey!" Bosun called from a distant stairway. None of

the other demons turned to acknowledge him. I must have been the one he was yelling at anyway, because his eyes were trained on me. "The captain will see you now."

I hadn't requested an audience with the captain, but made my way to where Bosun was standing anyway.

When I got to the bottom step, he motioned with his head behind him. "Up the stairs and through the doors."

I scaled the wooden staircase. The handrail was smooth and polished. It was made from a lighter wood that stood out against the teak deck. My anxiety grew with each step.

I knew where I was. I guessed the cop-demon had directed me here, likely paying for my passage on this ship as Lilith told me could happen. I still felt the amount of souls I had claim to. I could still sense and command my hellhounds. I thought being sent to the ships meant exile, meant losing the souls you had collected, meant losing everything to a life of forced slavery to the vessel's captain. Had I been wrong?

I saw defeat and worthlessness in the eyes of the demons on the deck. The way they moved, the way they looked, the way their shadows slithered across the ship without excitement or fear. They went about performing monotonous jobs waiting for their debts to be paid, spending an eternity with no will of their own. Like ghosts.

The thought made my smoky skin crawl.

The doors were French style, opening from the center, with glass panes that looked heavy and coke-bottle green. I couldn't tell if the glass was leaded, or if the green color came from the reflection of the water.

The glass wasn't a perfect pane like a modern window. Instead, it was dirty and flawed, skewing the light and blurring what was behind the doors. The only thing I could make out was orange candlelight flickering on a table deep within the room.

I pulled on the doors and let them swing open by their own weight. The pitch and yaw of the boat made their swing uneven. Behind the door, a wall of the same glass created a hallway. A room divider made up of large squares of heavy glass framed in thin boxes of warm-toned wood.

The air in the room matched the color of the wood; it was warm, unlike the cold air outside. As I closed the doors, I almost forgot how the ocean spray stung my skin on the deck. I almost forgot the pain of the icy water.

My eyelids drooped. In this warm hallway, mesmerized by the flickering candlelight behind the glass, I could have fallen asleep on the plush carpet.

Until I turned the corner and saw who was waiting for me.

Then I was wide-awake.

Candles and a low-burning fireplace lit the room. It was the kind of fire that burned long and slow, so hot that the red coals would burn themselves to nothing but sandy ash before they cooled. In the center of the room was a table stacked with a spread of food that would've put any

Thanksgiving table to shame. Tall candlesticks stood on the table, the candles reaching high in the air. I couldn't have reached the wick or the flame had I been seven feet tall.

The man sitting behind it all had just bitten off a chunk from one of the most emerald green apples I'd ever seen. That man was Joshua.

TWENTY-EIGHT

Joshua was dressed in his Elder's robes, their impeccable silver stitching glowing in the firelight. Flames danced in his icy blue eyes. I didn't know why I'd expected them to be demonic yellow. He looked exactly the same as he did the day he killed me, except he was rested. His grey hair was turning white at the temples, but his eyes were still quick, alive, and dangerous.

I froze, watching apple juice dribble down his chin. He glanced at me, an inner knowing curling his lips as he chewed. His posture was relaxed for someone whose enemy just waltzed in. Did he know how many ways I was thinking of to kill him?

There were no formal greetings, no exchange of pleasantries.

"Have a seat," he said, motioning to an empty chair near where I stood.

I had my scythe, my wings, and my cloak, but the

chair he gestured toward would put me out of striking distance. Sitting wasn't a good offensive or defensive posture.

Joshua propped his feet on the table, his right boot crossed over his left. He looked perfectly comfortable. Not ready for a fight.

Could I use that to my advantage? Could I kill him before he stood up?

I expected him to insist, or to read my thoughts, or to know what I was thinking without reading my thoughts. I expected him to say something like 'Don't bother trying to kill me, because I'm prepared,' or 'Sit down and let me kill you again,' but he didn't. He remained serene and patient, the only movement coming when he raised the apple to his mouth and took another bite.

The sound of the crunching was the only sound in the room.

I sat.

"You must be tired," Joshua said, his words laced with obscured meaning. Maybe this was his plan, to catch me at my weakest point, to take advantage of all I had been through tonight with Xia and Nicholas and the cop and the water, to take advantage of the exhaustion that was setting in. I was too weak to fight, and he knew it.

What he didn't know was that I would try anyway.

A demon appeared from behind me, making me jump. The vacant look on his face wasn't dangerous. He poured coffee into an empty cup.

"Cream and sugar?" Joshua asked.

"I'll take it black, thanks." Those weren't the first words I thought I'd say to Joshua after seeing him again. I'd planned all sorts of things—but never imagined I would be on a boat in the middle of Hell's oceanic sky having coffee with the man who murdered me… twice.

"The caffeine will help with the exhaustion," he said, plucking a few grapes from a nearby plate and popping one into his mouth. I jerked when his feet came off the table, but after he leaned forward for the grapes, he settled back and crossed his feet again. "There's some chocolate there, too. Have anything else you'd like," he smiled.

The smile seemed genuine. It didn't conceal any ulterior motives. It was friendly.

I stared into my cup, wondering if the wonderful aroma was worth the possibility that it was poisoned.

Joshua read my face, motioning for the demon to pour him a cup as well. He took a sip, setting the cup back down on a saucer. "Relax, Edmund. We aren't going to fight."

I wasn't sure if I should be relieved or call his bluff by starting the fight. I pressed the cup to my lips and let the coffee warm me from the inside.

"You've come far from that day," Joshua prodded. "Sixteen million souls you own in your first month. Thanks to the deal I have with the energumen, that makes you my top guy."

I set the cup down. He had to have known how I

came about such a staggering number. "They're stolen," I clarified.

Joshua laughed. It was a quiet laugh, subdued and controlled. "I'm going to do you a favor and let you in on a little secret," he said, putting his feet on the floor, folding his hands on the table and leaning in to look at me squarely. "The only thieves are the energumen. If you had taken zero souls from them, you'd still be my top guy. The spirits rightfully belong to you. All of them."

I remembered Ralph saying something similar to me in the cave before I killed my mother: only The Reaper had any claim to the spirits of the dead. Unfortunately, I still had no idea what that meant, other than I assumed it was why I was able to steal the spirits when I stabbed a demon with my scythe.

Joshua's face showed disappointment when his big reveal was met with confusion. He tried again, or changed the subject. I wasn't sure which. "You and I are equals now. Do you realize that?"

A minute ago he had called me his number one energumen. Now, I was his equal? I didn't voice the contradiction. Instead, I took another swallow of coffee. If it was poisoned, I would've been dead by now.

"We've both experienced two of the three deaths," Joshua said, catching my attention. "I've been through the Death of the Spirit and the Death of the Soul. You've been through the Death of the Body and the Death of the Spirit. Don't you see that together, we *control* death?"

"Is this the part where you ask if we can work together? Because that's a cliché straight out of a bad movie."

Joshua looked stunned and hurt. "Do you know which role you're playing, Edmund?" he asked with sincerity. "In any good story, won't the villain be the hero if the story were written from his point of view? Are you sure you're the hero here? Or are you just too wrapped up in your own story to see it from the outside?"

I had to give him credit here. Even my English classes I had taught me this principle. But this wasn't just a story. This was my life.

"Honestly, I thought you would have come to see that for yourself," Joshua continued. "I expected *you* to be the one to ask that we work together."

"I don't work with murderers."

Joshua leaned forward again, this time with crossed arms. "Have you looked in the mirror lately?"

My insecurities flared, resulting in anger squeezing my stomach. "That was different."

"How do you know? You made a sacrifice. I understand that. I did the same thing."

"You murdered thousands. Maybe even millions!" My voice rose in pitch.

Joshua's grin faded. He slouched back into his relaxed position. He took a few breaths and started over. "This was always the plan of the Council, Edmund. It was an idea your father first conceived. He knew, just like you know, that *death* is not a *permanent* condition."

"I know all about my father's participation," I spit out the last word.

"I don't think you do," Joshua said, not meeting my eyes for the first time since I walked into the room.

"He told me himself—"

"Yes. At the crossroads?" Joshua said, his gaze flickering over to mine. "That's what these boats are looking for, Edmund. Crossroads. We know there must be more, one that comes from this level and goes to the Level of the Body. So far we only know of two: the one Samuel uses that has a Going to the Level of the Body and a Going to here. The other is the one your father told us about, with the Coming from the Level of Body and the Going to here. But we need to find one that comes from here and goes to Earth."

I didn't say anything. Not only did I not want to help him, but I also didn't know of such a crossroads myself. He was lying. My father hadn't told him anything. Instead of responding, I snapped off a piece of chocolate and put it into my mouth.

"You already have a thirst for power, Edmund. I've seen it. I saw it when you almost lost control over that tree in the garden, and again when you fought for your friends. You even possessed one of them. Why? For power. Do you know what happened to him after you left? Were you watching out for his body *after* you were expelled?"

I felt sick. I hadn't been paying attention. I was too

busy keeping my grip on the demon. "What did you do to them?" I asked, deciding to place blame where it belonged—on Joshua.

"I didn't do anything, but Nicholas was hurt."

"What did they do to him? What about Xia?"

"*They* didn't do anything to any of them. Your sister and Xia are fine. Possession, Edmund, doesn't always end well. It can damage human tissue if you don't know what you're doing."

"Is he…"

"He's alive, but it proves my point; you're willing to harm the people you love for power."

"You're twisting everything I've done—"

"Are you sure you aren't doing the same thing to me?" Joshua interrupted, anger spilling across his face for the first time. His fist hit the table making me, and the food, jump.

"You threatened the people I love. I have never done that."

Joshua rubbed his forehead in frustration, breathing until he composed himself. "I only threatened them so that you would go back to Earth. They were never in any real danger. I needed you to go back to Earth so I could get the demons to block your way back from the root network. I needed you to meet me here on the boats so that I could tell you about what I'm doing. I knew you would go after Xia and Nicholas. I knew you would do what you had to do to win. That's where we are the same,

Edmund."

"You use demons to get what you want."

"So do you. The only difference is I don't flirt and manipulate my way… ahem," he laughed softly, "*into* them. I don't strike them down with Death's scythe when they get out of line. I use them openly and honestly. They are rewarded for their service to me. At least Ruth got the pleasure of your company. What did Lilith get?"

I stood, drawing my scythe. I wasn't going to listen to this from the betrayer of the mages. He wanted to talk? I didn't want to listen. I wasn't sure I was ready to fight, but it was better than sitting here letting him twist me into the bad guy.

"Yes! See? There it is." He stood, supporting his weight with the palms of his hands on the table. "This is exactly what I'm talking about. You lack control. You think that since you've become The Reaper, everyone should bow down and do whatever you say. You see enemies where there are none. I called you my *equal* and you raise your weapon to me? You are full of anger and lust for power. *That* is what makes a villain."

I stopped, relaxing my stance. He was right.

My eyes filled with tears. I didn't want to be the bad guy. I wanted to go home, to save my people, to make us what we once were. I had to restore everything Joshua had stolen from me.

Joshua sat, which made no sense to me. I had relaxed my position, but was still on the offensive. I could have struck then, but would striking make him right? Had I become an energumen?

"This was your father's plan," Joshua said, his tone soft. "He wanted to protect our people by making a deal with the energumen. He thought they would be satisfied with the souls of the humans. We were tired of planning their lives, watching over them on Earth, making sure they did good, taking care of them in Orenda, then sending them back in a never-ending cycle where they never learned and never became better people. Billions of souls to save a few thousand of our people. We thought it made a good deal.

"At first, the energumen agreed to leave our level alone, to possess only humans on Earth. Your father was so relieved that he finally decided to have a child of his own. The mages would be safe. *You* would be safe. The arrangement held for almost ten years. Your father occasionally brought someone across so the humans already in Orenda wouldn't become suspicious. We continued the Plannings and slowly sent the humans back. We thought we would continue this until only the mages were left in Orenda. We could finally live free lives of our choosing.

"Then the energumen got greedy. They came after the souls of the creatures in the levels above us. Since that level was part of our cycle, our population was put in danger as well. Mages began to fear death and the Council scrambled to put together a new plan. Your father was nominated as the man who would save us all. By going through all three deaths, he would use the power he would gain to seal the energumen in their level.

"The humans found out. The energumen told them. They started fearing the Angel of Death. Then, a human with the knowledge of our deal with the energumen made it to Orenda and warned the humans there. We still aren't sure how that happened. Maybe your father let someone through he shouldn't have."

"That's why the humans revolted? You're blaming my *father*."

"I don't blame your father. I don't blame anyone. But your father blamed himself. He wasn't strong enough to do what had to be done. When he learned what it took for the Death of the Soul, he hesitated.

"He taught the humans the spell to enslave the mages. He hoped that such knowledge would tempt them to save as many lives as possible. Many on the Council saw that as a betrayal. Most preferred death to slavery.

"My father understood the importance of life," I defended.

"He underestimated the value of death, Edmund. As do you. Death is knowledge, and knowledge is power. That's why no one is allowed to keep their memories through more than one incarnation. Doing so gives them too much power. I want to change that. I want to give everyone that power so that they can have the choice, so they can all be equal. Human, demon, mage, or angel, we all deserve to choose who we want to be, in service to none."

"So you enslave demons on this ship and hunt for souls to steal? Don't you get why I have a hard time believing you?"

"It's true that power will be required to change the system. It's also true that great power comes only with great sacrifice. Together, we may not have to *individually* experience all three deaths. Together, we can keep each other in check. Together, I will not have to face my greatest fear and you won't have to face yours. We can complement each other and do what needs to be done to build a new universe, with rules that allow us to all be powerful."

"What do you mean, my greatest fear?"

"I want to give you this ship and crew. I want to teach you how to find the crossroads and use the knowledge of the ones you already have." He continued laying out the plan and the offer he had for me, instead of answering my question. "By working together you can have the power you crave. You can use it to complete your father's work. We can do better than the Elders before. We can save the humans and the energumen, if they so wish. We can empower people to take claim over their own deaths, their own cycles. They can experience each one as you and I have, controlling their own fate."

I stopped listening. I ran through my fears—did I have any left? I wasn't too fond of the idea of drowning, but that had almost happened tonight.

I didn't want to have my memories taken away, but I didn't *fear* that happening either. If I forgot, at least I wouldn't be in the middle of this mess. Forgetting was what I thought Joshua had wanted from the beginning.

"I will give you the keys to the garden if you wish. You can do whatever you want with the spirits there. If you want to release them, I'll show you how. I'm serious, Edmund. The journey doesn't need to go any further than this table. Together, we already have all the pieces we need."

I found the idea intriguing, but wanted to test his convictions. "Release Mother Tree and her children."

"Done," Joshua said.

I watched the light outside the windows vanish. I imagined the trees finding their voices again, their fear and arguing having no reason to continue. I wanted nothing more in this moment than to curl up with Xia under the branches of a willow tree and listen to it softly sing her to sleep in my arms.

"How do I get my body back, like yours? You've died spiritually, but you look human."

Joshua chose his words carefully. I knew there was a reason behind that. A reason he hoped I would pick up on and ask about. "That isn't something you can do on your own, but it's something I can help you with. Your flesh body, the one you had in Orenda, is still there. Reuniting it requires knowledge accessible by the Death of the Soul."

I flinched. "How does one kill his soul?" If he gave me this piece of the puzzle, that would mean he was telling me the truth tonight. Essentially, he would be handing me the final death—the way to become more powerful than he was. If I was going to trust him *at all*, this was the required price. He had to hand his power over to me.

"Are you testing me, Edmund? I thought you already knew that," he responded, his word choice still deliberate and minimal. "Samuel told me you figured it out a long time ago. He sensed it in your thoughts; you repeated it in your mind once while you were with him."

"No games," I said. "Tell me exactly how you did it."

I saw pain in Joshua's eyes, but he brushed it aside. Watching him flip off his emotions and consider my demand from a logical perspective surprised and interested me.

"It was my first death, many years ago, just before you were born into your life in Orenda," he stopped. He bit his bottom lip, making him look younger and vulnerable.

"Go on," I demanded, feeling heartless as his eyes filled with tears.

"It was the price of breaking our cycle to the level above. The Council needed someone to harness the power of that death, in the hopes that we could stop the fear of death from spreading among our people."

I was impatient. Was he stalling?

"It had an unintended consequence that we didn't

understand at the time. It threw us into the human cycle. That was entirely by accident and required a sacrifice that defined me from that point forward. I want to save you from those consequences, Edmund. There is no coming back."

"I've already committed murder. If you want me to consider your proposal, I need to know I can do it myself. I don't trust you. Give me the secret so I can choose to do it myself or I'll figure it out on my own."

"I killed the woman you know as Linda Rose."

I shrugged. Joshua was still controlling his expression too well, but I could see emotion just under the surface. Emotion I didn't understand.

"Murder is the Death of the Spirit," I said. "I killed my mother."

Joshua buried his hands in his face to hide it from me. " 'I believed, or hoped perhaps, that love was the life force of the soul.' Does that sound familiar, Edmund?"

My mind performed its famous domino act. This time it was darker and scarier than any of the others. The connecting synapses that had helped me know Joshua was the betrayer of my kind also helped me connect that Linda Rose set up my mother to be the sacrifice that was required for my spiritual death. I realized that I already knew what would destroy the soul.

"Linda Rose was your wife," I whispered.

Joshua's tears spilled over. "Linda Rose was the love of my life."

The last domino fell into place. If Joshua was telling the truth, I only had two choices. I could accept his proposal to work together, or I would have to bleed myself of love, hemorrhaging until it was exhausted. I would be consumed by darkness, with no light to bring me back.

I was afraid.

I wasn't afraid of the darkness, or of being consumed by it.

I was afraid because I would have to extinguish the source of my light.

I would have to kill Xia.

DEATH OF THE SOUL

CROSSING DEATH:
BOOK THREE

COMING SOON

ABOUT THE AUTHOR

I've often been accused of having done more in my life than the average person my age, but if I were completely honest I'd have to tell you my secret: I'm really 392.

So after all this time, I'm a pretty crappy writer.

I'm the author of the *Crossing Death* series and *Facade of Shadows*, as well as 'Tailored for the King,' a short story found in *Twice Upon a Time*, and 'Obsession with the Bloodstained Door' in *nEvermore! Tales of Murder, Mystery and the Macabre*.

I've been favorably reviewed, featured on ReadFree.ly's Top 50 Best list of 2013, 2014, and 2015, and my how-to-write-horror articles have been quoted in scholarly (aka community college freshmen's) papers.

I enjoy the occasional Bloody Mary, although a Bloody Kathy or Susan will suffice.

Mostly, I just try to keep a low profile so people don't figure out who I REALLY am.

STALK RICK

ALSO AVAILABLE BY
RICK CHIANTARETTO

CROSSING DEATH
Death of the Body (Crossing Death #1)

TAILORED FOR THE KING
Twice Upon a Time: Fairytale, Folklore, & Myth.
Reimagined & Remastered

FACADE OF SHADOWS
Facade of Shadows

OBSESSION WITH THE BLOODSTAINED DOOR
nEvermore! Tales Of Murder, Mystery & The Macabre

SEE A MISTAKE?

As perfect as I want every book to be, something was missed. If you find an editing problem, please email me at rick@rickchiantaretto.com. I would love to reward you with some swag, free books, or maybe even eternal life (especially if your name is Mary. Did I mention how much I love a good Bloody Mary?).